'I'm really hungry.' – *New York survivor of the Red Death*

Cannibal – a person who eats human flesh. *Oxford English Dictionary*

To save a lot of time, right here at the start, let's be sure of our facts:

1. The world as we, you and I know it is over — wiped out by a plague. Those darned scientists!

2. But there are survivors. There are ALWAYS survivors. But you gotta watch 'em.

3. Jimmy and Claire were lucky enough to find themselves on the *Titanic* when the plague struck. Not often you get 'lucky' and '*Titanic*' in the same sentence.

4. You'd think they'd be miserable — but they're having the time of their lives.

5. Why does there have to be a five? Four is plenty.

6. But six is an even number. The new *Titanic* is fabulous — of COURSE everyone wants to steal it.

Prologue:
City of the Dead

She was running for her life. Twelve years old, and top of the menu.

Ronni came to New York from London for a vacation. She didn't particularly want to go, but her mother insisted – it would be educational, she said, think of the museums, think of the art galleries, think of that big statue thingy you see in the harbour. Her mother didn't have the slightest interest in education – what she meant was, I'll park you in a museum, then I'll go off shopping.

On the day it happened – *it* being the day everyone suddenly dropped down dead – Ronni was in the Museum of Natural History, a great, fantastic place, but after four hours she'd had enough, and after six hours, her mother being two hours late in coming to pick her up, she'd *really* had enough. So she decided, against strict orders, to make her own way back to the hotel. She'd already spent the meagre few dollars her mother had left her to buy lunch, so she had to walk – but almost as soon as she left the museum, people began to drop dead all around her. Well – perhaps it wasn't quiet as instantaneous as that, but it felt like it. What they actually did was start throwing up – here, there, *everywhere*. It was disgusting. Then they collapsed, too weak to move. Ronni just held her nose and kept walking. But even when she got to her hotel there was no let up. There were people throwing up in the lobby, in the elevator and along the corridor outside her room. She was incredibly relieved just to slam the door shut, lie down on her bed and flick the telly on – only to find that half the channels weren't working, and those that were were showing pictures of people throwing up.

Ronni wasn't stupid – over her few days in the Big Apple she had been vaguely aware of all the talk about this supposed 'Red Death' – some kind of a bug sweeping across America that lots of people were dying from – but New York didn't seem to be greatly affected, so she had supposed it was all being hugely exaggerated. There were a lot of things she wanted to see around the city, and some little outbreak of flu wasn't going to stop her enjoying herself, so she deliberately avoided watching the news after that and remained blissfully unaware that the situation was deteriorating across the whole world.

But now, as she lay back on her bed, she realised how much the day at the museum and the long walk home had taken out of her. Her legs ached and her head was sore. She'd drunk nearly a litre of water, but still felt really hot. Actually, now she felt a little . . .

Ronni dashed to the bathroom and threw up.

And then again.

She staggered back to bed and crawled under the covers. Damn – had she picked up the bug? Or maybe just a little bit of it? No wonder, with everyone being sick all around her. But she was young and strong and she'd soon shake it off. A bit of a sleep and she'd be fine.

In every corner of that magnificent city people were doing exactly the same as Ronni – climbing under blankets, lying down at work, stretching out on park benches and saying to themselves, 'A little rest, and I'll feel better soon.'

Think of it – by 2020 there were eighteen million people living in New York. And one day, they all just lay down for a little rest.

The Four Seasons Hotel was, without doubt, one of the finest hotels in New York, if not the world. *Was* is the important word here. It *was* a five-star hotel, luxurious beyond most people's wildest dreams. *Now*, if you had to decide how many stars it deserved, you would probably venture – oh, minus thirty?

That's minus ★★★★★★★★★★★★★★★★★★★★★★★★★★★★★★.

Six weeks after the Red Death struck it was dank, dirty and stinking. The toilets were blocked and overflowing, the stench from the kitchens was overwhelming and rats scampered along the corridors, gorged on decaying human flesh. Rotting corpses lay in the lobby or sat slumped over tables in the dining room. They were tucked in bed or curled up in the corridors. Some were even standing upright in the elevators, eternally waiting for a floor they would never arrive at.

And yet –

Ronni was sick for three days, too ill even to call room service, too fevered to wonder where her mother was or why no one had bothered to come and clean the room. But on the fourth morning she woke – and felt fine. She got up and had a shower and the most disturbing thing about it was that the water was cold. She tried calling her mother's room, even though it was only next door, but there was no response. She decided to let her mother sleep on – at least she could then slip down to breakfast without her mum's usual complaint about her choice of clothes. Ronni had slept for so long, and was now so hungry, that all memories of the Red Death and the collapsing population had been pushed to the very back of her mind. To her it was just another day of her vacation – until she stepped into the corridor and saw the first of the rotting corpses. She screamed and ran to her mother's room and banged on the door, but there was no answer. Perhaps she'd gone out already, and was unaware of what was surely a murder outside her room. Ronni edged past the corpse and rushed to the elevator – and screamed again; the door was wedged open by a woman's blue and bloated body. A double murder! But then as she took the stairs down to the lobby and saw the bodies there, and *there* and *there*, memories of reports of the Red Death came flooding back. But what if nobody knew that the hotel had been so badly affected by the plague? She had to summon help! Stop a policeman! She raced across the corpse-strewn lobby and emerged on to Fifth Avenue – and what had been a very noisy city, with bumper to bumper traffic and the sidewalks crammed with workers and tourists, was absolutely and completely quiet. Cars were crashed or abandoned; bodies lay everywhere.

It was horrible.

You might say Ronni was lucky to be alive – but it was 'luck' in the broadest possible sense, because if you woke up with millions of corpses for company, you probably wouldn't feel lucky at all. You'd feel terrified, and distressed, and confused, just like Ronni. But the fact is, she did wake up, she was alive, and now she had to figure out a way to survive.

There was no power in the city, which meant that the fresh food was already off, but there were still plenty of tins and bottles of water, both downstairs in the hotel kitchens, and in grocery stores in the immediate neighbourhood. Ronni learned to ignore the bodies lying everywhere, although she could never truly get used to the appalling stench. By day she explored the streets surrounding her hotel, spending hours in huge department stores like Macy's and Bloomingdale's, trying on clothes, painting her face with make-up, pretending she was a pop star, acting, playing, singing, doing everything she could to take her mind off the fact that the world had ended and she was utterly alone. At night she retreated to her room in the hotel. She cooked her tinned food on a small gas stove she had rescued from a camping store. She spent the hours of darkness staring out of her bedroom window. She slept only fitfully. For the first three or four weeks she actually supposed that she would be rescued, that a helicopter would land and take her away to safety. Yet she knew deep down that the catastrophe that had befallen her, the city, the country and the world was so indescribably huge that there was no possibility of it.

Ronni lost count of the number of times she stood outside her mother's door calling for her to come out, while resisting the temptation to try and break in. As long as she didn't truly know that her mother was dead, she could at least pretend that she was still alive in there and just refusing to talk. Perhaps her mum had been shocked into silence by what had happened or maybe she slipped in and out of her room when Ronni wasn't there, off on her own little shopping trips to the exclusive fashion stores up and down Fifth Avenue. Ronni had grown used to seeing the corpses in the hotel and on the streets outside, but she never wanted to see her mum like that. As long as she stayed on *this* side of the door she would remember her mother as she was – beautiful, elegant, and very, very bossy.

In what she guessed was her sixth week, Ronni woke hungry in the middle of the night and slipped down to the kitchens. Returning across the foyer with a tin of franks 'n' beans she found herself face to face with a wolf.

A wolf!

She was momentarily frozen to the spot. The creature looked vicious and savage, its teeth were bared and its snout was thick with the rotting innards of the corpse it had been tearing into on the hotel's marble floor.

Ronni and the wolf stared at each other for fully ten seconds, each of them frozen in the narrow band of moonlight streaming through the atrium glass.

Then the wolf snarled and charged.

Ronni hurled the tin at it and spun on her heel. The wolf staggered as the missile struck it on the top of the head. It let out an angry yelp – but it recovered quickly and immediately tore after her. Ronni reached the stairs and began to race up them three at a time, the wolf snapping at her heels. As she reached the fifth floor it finally hurled itself at her, but by luck she had just come to a set of double doors, and as they sprang back behind her they slammed into the creature, hurling it backwards. The respite was momentary. The wolf threw itself through the doors and hurtled down the corridor behind her. As the animal's dripping jaws snapped towards her Ronni finally reached her bedroom and threw herself inside; in the same movement she spun and slammed the door on the creature's jaw. It howled and fell back, leaving three teeth on the floor.

Ronni slid down the inside of the door and rested her head against it. She could hear the heavy panting and painful yelps of the wolf just a few centimetres away. But she was safe . . . for now.

A wolf in the Four Seasons – Mother would have had a fit.

But where had it come from? She knew there was a zoo in Central Park – perhaps from there? If *it* had been hungry enough and desperate enough to escape, then what if it wasn't alone? Not only might there be a pack of wolves out there, but also animals that were faster and stronger and even more cunning. Tigers and panthers and cheetahs and . . . Ronni shuddered. She spent the rest of the night slumped against the door, sweating through nightmare after nightmare about being torn to shreds by wild beasts.

By the morning, with the wolf gone and the bright sunshine lightening her mood, Ronni had come to a decision. She had spent the past few weeks in the immediate vicinity of the Four Seasons, never travelling further than a few blocks in any direction and never quite letting the hotel out of her sight. But because it was surrounded on all sides by tall buildings she hadn't been able to get a proper view of the rest of the city. What if there were other people out there using lights or flares to attract the attention of a rescue helicopter or a searching aeroplane? What if they were rescued and she got left behind? She had to find out if she really was alone. She thought her best bet might be the Empire State Building – from there she would be able to see every part of the city and far beyond as well. Whether she found other people or not, she knew she would not return to the hotel. It was no longer safe. She packed as many of the clothes she had 'borrowed' over the past few weeks as she could into her rucksack and left her room. She paused outside her mother's door. As she said her final goodbye, tears sprang from her eyes.

King Kong fell to his doom from the top of the Empire State Building. Ronni nearly died just getting there. The big gorilla had the advantage of being able to climb up the outside of the building. Ronni had the disadvantage of having to climb 1,860 steps to the viewing platform on the 102nd floor because the elevators no longer worked. It took her *ages* and by the time she got there her legs were like jelly and she could hardly breathe. She lay on the platform floor for another half an hour, quite lacking the strength to even drag herself up to look out over the city. At least part of her was thinking: *What's the point?* In the twenty-five minutes it had taken her to walk from the hotel to the Empire State, she had seen nothing but death and destruction. No hint of human life: plenty of rats, some wild dogs, even an ominous animal roar from somewhere in the far distance, but nothing to give her any hope at all.

Eventually she managed to pull herself up. She pressed her face against the wire fence surrounding the platform and looked out across the city. She knew from reading one of the tourist leaflets lying scattered about that on a clear day she might have been able to see nearly eighty miles in every direction – as far as the states of Pennsylvania, Connecticut and Massachusetts. But today was grey and overcast and she could barely see to the edges of the city. It all appeared so . . . *normal*. The landmark buildings were all there, and from such a height the cars on the broad avenues below appeared like toys and the people like ants – except it was more like a photograph than a moving picture: there was no motion, no life. By straining her eyes Ronni could just about make out the shape of the 'big statue thingy' her mum had talked about – the Statue of Liberty on its isolated little island. She knew that it had once welcomed immigrants to the Land of the Free. Now there was nobody left to welcome.

She felt suddenly hungry again. There was a restaurant half a dozen floors below which, thankfully, must have closed down before the worst of the Red Death, because it wasn't littered with bodies.

Unfortunately most of the food was off, but she was able to pick up cartons of fruit juice and bags of potato chips. She sat at a table and tried to think about her next move. So long as she wasn't eaten by wild creatures, there was enough tinned food in the city to keep her going for the rest of her life. But what was the point of living if there was nobody else left?

No!

There had *to be!*

She would search every corner of the city, and if she found no one, she would start looking beyond it. She wasn't alone, she *couldn't* be alone!

An hour later, with night fallen, Ronni returned to the observation platform. At first it looked as if someone had snatched the entire city away – where it would once have provided a dazzling, neon-lit vista, there was *nothing*. Then, as her eyes became accustomed to the blackness, she began to pick out the vague outlines of the skyscrapers surrounding the Empire State, but it was as if they had been snatched away, leaving only a shadowy memory behind.

Ronni froze.

There!

Lights!

Mere flickering pinpricks – but against a background of such total blackness that they shone out like beacons.

They had to be at least three or four miles away – but where, exactly? With her pulse racing Ronni

13

hurried along the platfrom until she came to a framed map, displayed for the benefit of tourists so that they would know which parts of the city they were looking at. It was difficult to read in the darkness, and she was half terrified that if she took her eyes off the lights they would be gone by the time she looked back. She finally stabbed her finger down on to the glass. There – Battery Park! That's where they were!

Survivors!

Ronni heard the music first, booming out of the darkness, rhythmic, almost hypnotic, and it filled her with elation.

She'd found a bicycle not far from the Empire State – somewhat squeamishly wresting it from a dead man's hands – and was now able to fly along at considerable speed. Luckily New York was designed in such a way that long avenues like Broadway could take her straight to a destination without her having to remember complex directions.

As she erupted from the avenue into Battery Park itself and got her first real taste of the sea air and spotted the flames flickering ahead of her, she couldn't help but let out a yelp of joy. Just ahead she could see the silhouettes of *hundreds* of people dancing to the music around half a dozen bonfires! Hundreds!

Ronni leaped from her bike, allowing it to crash away into bushes, and charged forward.

Spits had been erected over the flames and whole

14

animals were being roasted! Fresh food! Huge black pots bubbled away! Ronni's taste buds watered as they never had before. Civilisation!

Just as she reached the edge of the party the people all began to turn in one direction, cheering and clapping excitedly. Ronni wanted to be part of it, she wanted to dance and sing and hug everyone! She ducked down and began to wriggle her way through to the front of the crowd, her whole body tingling with excitement. Then she caught her first glimpse of . . .

. . . a woman, her hair dank and bedraggled, her clothes torn, being dragged out of a metal cage mounted on a trailer. She had what looked like a dog's collar around her neck, attached to a chain which was being pulled by a burly, heavily muscled man wearing . . . a wolf's head! He gave the chain a hard yank and the woman stumbled down a slanted wooden walkway on to the grass and fell to her knees. The wolf-headed man stood behind her and drew out a long, jagged knife from a sheath on his belt.

The crowd began to chant: 'Kill! Kill! Kill!'

Ronni knew she should have screamed at them to stop. But she couldn't do anything. As she looked around the faces of the people watching she saw a kind of madness in their eyes. They weren't happy survivors of a desperate plague – they were frightened people driven crazy by it. Ronni was suddenly more scared than she ever had been in her life. She began to back away through the crowd as the chanting continued to grow in intensity all around her.

'Kill! Kill! Kill! Kill!'

Ronni emerged by one of the bonfires, which was being tended by a solitary old man, slowly rotating a crackling animal on a spit. But then as the creature's head turned towards her she saw with total and absolute horror that it wasn't an animal at all.

It was a human being.

Ronni screamed. She couldn't help it. She screamed high and loud and piercing.

The chanting faded.

All eyes turned towards her.

She wasn't one of them.

Ronni ran for her life.

And then so did they.

The chase was on!

Pig

It all started with Babe the pig.

If Lucky Jimmy Armstrong and Claire Stanford hadn't been fighting over her, then they wouldn't have become separated, and if they hadn't become separated then the nightmare that followed – you know, with the **Cannibals**, the **President's Train**, the **Quest** and the **Murdering Minister** – well, it probably wouldn't have happened.

So, really, it was the pig's fault.

Pigs are like that. Always causing trouble.

Never trust a pig. Pigs have no sense of humour, and they can't juggle.

Yet the way Claire talked about Babe, you'd think Babe could tell a joke while keeping six balls in the air with her mucky little hooves.

Or trotters.

It started after they left Reunion Gap.

You won't find Reunion Gap on any map. Suffice to say it was one of hundreds of settlements that had sprung up along the eastern seaboard since the Red

Death had struck. It was little more than a gathering place for survivors, a crossroads where two RVs had stopped and set up camp one night, and by next morning there were half a dozen other vehicles parked right beside them. Then there were twenty, then eighty-six, then several hundreds of them, all shapes and sizes. Some had just a solitary driver; others were packed with family members or complete strangers, all intent on exchanging news, swapping or bartering food, drinking beer and wailing about the state of this new world. You've heard of that old saying – safety in numbers? This is what people thought: that if they all got together, they'd be OK. But it wasn't strictly true. People were frightened by what had happened, they were scared, horrified, panicky – so little communities like Reunion Gap were really quite dangerous places. People were short tempered, and although they craved other human company, they also armed themselves with whatever weapons they could lay their hands on in case they didn't like that company. In communities like Reunion Gap violence exploded quite regularly.

The *Titanic*'s Captain Smith, First Officer Jeffers, and the rest of the crew – and at least some of the passengers – were aware that they had a good, secure, modern home, and while there were occasional shortages of food, and lapses in power, and outbreaks of disease, and short rebellions and noisy protests, they had it better than most. Partly because of this, and partly because it was his duty, Captain Smith endeavoured to lend assistance to people in settlements like Reunion Gap. The ship would drop anchor up to a mile off shore and Dr Hill would land with a team of nurses to set up a clinic, treating those that he could there and then, and ferrying more serious cases back to the ship for surgery. First Officer Jeffers would escort ashore those who wished to leave the ship to search for relatives; and then he would vet those who sought to join the *Titanic* for transportation further up the coast (as most roads were still blocked, and those that were open were invariably dangerous). Chief Engineer Jonas Jones' task was to search for those with particular skills who might wish to join up as crewmen; the *Titanic* was a huge ship and had been left shorthanded both by the plague and the recent mutiny.[1] Jimmy and Claire usually went ashore as reporter and photographer, recording the (usually) sad stories of the survivors. There was also a pressing need for a regular supply of fresh food on board, which meant that often on their return journeys the speedboats and motor launches which served the ship were packed with livestock. The pig that would shortly become known as Babe came on board at Reunion Gap in the company of twelve other pigs, sixteen cows and perhaps a hundred chickens.

First Officer Jeffers, overseeing their importation – the mooing, grunting, snorting, stinking lot of them – sometimes couldn't quite believe what was

---

[1] As recounted in *Titanic 2020*.

happening to his beloved ship.

'I don't know if this is the bloody *Titanic* any more,' he wearily observed as he watched the latest arrivals trot nervously on board, 'or *Noah's* bloody *Ark*.'

It was, in fact, Lucky Jimmy Armstrong, standing right beside him, who first noticed the pig who would become known as Babe. She was smaller than the others, leaner. Where the others were content to play follow my leader, turning obediently off to the left as they came on board, this one defiantly turned right and charged forward, completely unconcerned that she was heading directly for a solid wall. She duly cracked off it, let out a high-pitched squeal, looked briefly in the direction of her brothers and sisters, then turned around and fired herself at the wall again. There was another squeal. One of Jeffers' team, who professed some knowledge of farmyard animals, attempted to steer her in the right direction and got butted and stamped on for his trouble. The pig made another attempt on the wall.

'That pig,' Jeffers pointed out needlessly, 'is stupid.'

As the squealing continued – in fact, grew louder – they were joined by Claire, hurrying up to show Jimmy the photos she'd taken at Reunion Gap. The latest edition of the *Titanic Times* was due to go to press later that evening, and they still had to select the front page photo. As Jimmy looked through the pictures, Claire studied the pig as she made her fourth attempt on the wall.

'Aw, isn't she cute?'

Without looking up Jimmy said: 'No, it's a pig.'

'She's lovely.' Claire raised the camera slung around her neck and fired off a series of shots. 'Aow!' The pig had bounced off the wall again. 'That had to hurt.'

Jeffers ordered a second crewman forward, and this time they were able to steer the witless creature in the right direction, although not before she had left them all a nice big present. Jimmy held his nose. Claire laughed.

'Jimmy, have you never been on a farm?'

'No, and I've no wish to.'

'It's the most natural smell in the world.'

'It reminds me of something . . .' Jimmy clicked his fingers several times as he made a show of struggling to remember. 'Oh yes – it's your perfume.'

Claire made a face. 'Very funny. As a matter of fact, I don't wear perfume.'

'Maybe you should.' Jimmy smiled triumphantly and turned away. As he did, he held up the photos. 'I'll see if I can rescue something from this lot.'

Claire stood fuming. She glanced up at First Officer Jeffers. 'What're you smiling at?' she snapped.

'*You.*' Jeffers ruffled her hair – like she was a *child* – then turned to follow the animals. He could no longer see them, but they had left an unmistakable trail for him to follow. 'Noah's bloody Ark,' he muttered as he stepped carefully along the deck.

Babe

Over the next few days, as the *Titanic* continued its slow progress up the eastern seaboard, Claire became increasingly obsessed with the pig. Jimmy thought she was off her rocker.

They had a hard enough job as it was producing a daily edition of the *Times*, without Claire slipping off every half an hour to coo over the dirty, foul smelling porker. As far as Jimmy could see it had no redeeming features at all. Even the cows were more interesting. And they were dead boring. Several times he had to leave the newspaper office in the capable hands of their chief reporter, Ty Warner, and the rest of their news team (which had grown over the past few months to five reporters, two photographers, an IT expert and an idiot who made the tea) to make the arduous trip to Deck 3 to drag her back up to work.

Deck 3 looked as much like a farmyard as any part of a ship *can* look like a farmyard. Petty Officer Benson had been put in charge as punishment for his latest breach of discipline, and he clearly wasn't enjoying himself at all. 'What do I know about chickens?' he complained when Jimmy arrived, looking for Claire. 'I grew up in London. Never been on a farm. Only been to a petting zoo once. I got bitten by a goat.' He sighed before pointing Jimmy in the right direction. 'She's still in there. I think she's in love.'

Jimmy rolled his eyes, then continued along the deck to where Benson had helped construct a sty for the pigs. Six of the filthy beasts had their noses buried in a trough, hungrily gorging themselves on waste food from the *Titanic* kitchens. Claire's pig was off to one side, having her snout stroked by the *Times*' chief photographer.

'Claire.'

'Shhhhh! She's almost asleep . . .'

'Claire, I don't *care*!' Jimmy clapped his hands together with a loud smack, but the pig paid no attention. Deaf *and* stupid, Jimmy decided. 'We've work to do, Claire. What is it with you and the pig anyway?'

'She's just . . . cute.'

Jimmy snorted.

'She *is*,' Claire insisted. 'The rest of them, they just want to eat all the time. Babe's more interested in being pampered and having a chat.'

Jimmy wasn't sure which of these ridiculous pieces of information to tackle first. 'Babe? You've given it a name?'

'Sure. Babe. You've heard of *Babe*, right? The book? The movie? *The sheep-pig?*' Jimmy shook his head. '*Jimmy*, it's really famous!'

'Not in my neck of the woods.'

'Well, take my word for it. Babe was a really clever talking pig who thought he was a sheepdog, and this Babe is just as smart. She's always getting into mischief, and anyone who gives Benson as hard a time as she does has to be doing something right.' Claire gave Babe's snout another delicate stroke. 'We have great little chats, don't we, Babe?'

Jimmy gave it a few moments, just in case by some miracle the pig suddenly winked at him and said, 'We certainly do, young man, now pass me a sandwich,' before asking Claire if she had mistakenly swallowed some mind-bending drugs.

Claire smiled. 'I know it's silly, but there's something about her. She's got such a nice personality.'

Jimmy shook his head. 'That's what they say about girls who aren't very pretty. *She's got a nice personality.*'

Claire tutted. 'And what would *you* know about girls, Jimmy Armstrong?'

Jimmy shrugged. 'I know about you.'

'And what is it you think you know about me?'

'I know you've got a nice personality.'

Claire bit her tongue. He was always trying to wind her up. She fought a constant battle not to respond in kind, or to punch him. She continued to pet Babe.

Jimmy looked at Claire with a very small measure of regret. 'Claire, look – I know you like it—'

'*Her.* She. *Babe.*'

'I know you like her-she-Babe – but maybe it's best not to get too close.'

'Why not? I get a better conversation out of her than I do with you.'

'Because, you know, in case something happens to her.'

Claire snorted. 'What's going to happen to her? She's perfectly safe here.'

Jimmy sighed. 'Claire.' He pointed along the deck to where the cows were lazily grazing from their own trough. 'Look, we have the cows on board for milk, right?'

'It doesn't take a rocket scientist to work that out, Jimmy.'

'OK, and those chickens running about all over the *bloody* place like . . . chickens. They're on board for . . .'

'Eggs, Jimmy. *Eggs.*'

'So, following that logic, the pigs are on board for . . . ?'

Claire was about to give another rapid-fire response – only she couldn't immediately think of one. She was thinking: cows – milk: chickens – eggs: pigs . . .; cows – milk: chickens – eggs: pigs . . . Her mouth dropped open a little. Her eyes met Jimmy's.

'*No . . . ?*'

Jimmy nodded. 'Unless you've worked out how to milk a pig. It's pork.'

'No!'

''Fraid so.'

'They *wouldn't*.'

'I think they would.'

'Not my Babe!'

Jimmy raised his eyebrows. Then a thought struck him. 'Unless . . .'

Claire looked suddenly hopeful. 'Unless *what*, Jimmy?'

'Unless . . .'

'Jimmy!'

'Unless she really *can* talk – then we could retrain her as a radio operator!'

Jimmy spun on his heel and strode away before Claire could attack him.

'I hate you, Jimmy Armstrong!' she yelled furiously after him. But as soon as he was gone she allowed the tears that had been welling up to spring from her eyes. She stroked Babe some more. *How could anyone . . . ?*

No!

It wasn't going to happen. Her dad *owned* the *Titanic*, he was the boss, even over Captain Smith, and she was her daddy's little girl. He would do whatever she demanded. Nobody was going to impose a death sentence on her friend Babe.

NOBODY!

The Speech

It's all very well, of course, stamping your feet and saying, '*NOBODY*!' when all you've got is pigs for company. They'd agree with anything as long as you kept their trough full of disgusting swill. It was quite different when it came to making the people in charge see sense. For a start, her father absolutely refused to intervene.

'I'm sorry Claire, but no. The pigs are on board for one reason and one reason alone. If we are going to get through this we need a good, healthy, balanced diet, and that means fresh meat whenever possible.'

'But she's my pet, she's my friend! Would you really eat one of my friends?'

'It's a pig, Claire.'

'Please, Daddy! My ponies were taken away from me, don't take Babe as well!'

'Claire, operational control of the *Titanic* rests with Captain Smith. I have promised not to intervene.'

'But what am I supposed to *do*?'

Her mother appeared in the bedroom doorway, swathed in a luxurious dressing gown and with her hair hidden beneath a towel. 'What about becoming a vegetarian?' she asked.

'HOW WOULD THAT HELP?' Claire yelled.

'Watch your tone, young lady!' her father immediately snapped out.

Claire stormed out of the suite. Her next stop was the bridge, where Captain Smith was seated before a computer screen, examining charts. She stood before him, breathing hard, and waited for him to notice her. And waited. And waited.

Eventually, without looking up, he asked her what she wanted.

Claire rubbed the back of her hand across her damp cheek. 'Have I ever asked you for anything before?'

'Yes, you have.'

'I mean, something really, really important?'

'What is it, Claire?' His eyes remained fixed on the screen.

'If you had the chance to save someone's life – someone who has never done anything wrong, who has never harmed anyone on purpose, who might get into trouble occasionally, but really has a heart of gold, and if I really, really begged you – would you do it, would you do it for me?'

Captain Smith typed something on his keyboard. Still without looking up he said: 'Claire, don't worry. We've already decided to keep Jimmy alive.'

'Not Jimmy!'

She could see now that his mouth was tightly shut

but turned up slightly at the sides, as if he was struggling to keep himself from laughing.

He already knows – and he's laughing at me!

'It's not funny! Babe is *my* pig! You're not having her!'

Captain Smith finally looked up. 'Claire, I understand that you've become attached to the creature, but I'm afraid that I agree with your father. We live in difficult times and discipline is important. The pigs were brought aboard for food. I'm sorry, but when the time comes, and I believe that will be within the next few days, the pigs will be slaughtered. All of them.'

'No!' Claire glared down at him. 'You are a cruel, horrible man and I will not allow you to do this!'

She stormed away from the bridge.

She was an expert at storming.

She'd had a lot of practice.

The deadline for the next edition of the *Titanic Times* was fast approaching and the newspaper office, deep in the bowels of the ship, was a hive of activity when Claire came – yes, storming – in.

Jimmy looked up from his desk, recognised the look on her face, and sighed wearily. 'What is it now?' he asked.

'They're going to murder Babe!'

All around the office, work stopped.

'Ladies and gentlemen,' Jimmy said quickly, 'relax.

Babe is a pig. Claire, you cannot murder a pig. Unless it's done by another pig. And even then I'm not—'

'Be quiet!' She looked deadly serious. Jimmy cleared his throat and signalled for her to continue. She looked around the room. 'I'm not stupid,' she said. 'I know the pigs were brought on board to provide us with fresh meat. That's fair enough. OK, so I've become attached to one of them. Babe's my friend. She's cute, she's lovely. But yes – she's still just a pig.' She nodded around the company. 'Captain Smith has said that all the pigs have to die. That no exceptions can be made – but what I'm asking is, why not?' Everyone, with the possible exception of Jimmy, was listening intently. 'Look,' she continued, 'our whole world has been turned upside down in the past few months. We've all lost relatives and friends. My father and Captain Smith are right when they say that to survive we must have order and discipline – but I know my history. When times are hard and people are weak, that's when dictators come along, like Hitler, like Stalin, and they take control and before you know it you have no freedom left at all, no right to make your own decisions, you're not individuals any more, you're numbers, you're slaves. Well I say – it stops *here*. We show them that we will not be ruled with an iron fist. We show them by refusing to allow Babe to be slaughtered. Babe must live!'

Ty hesitantly began to raise his hand. 'Surely—'

But Claire wasn't to be interrupted. 'You may ask

how are we going to achieve this? After
weak, and they are strong. But we have an ins
at our disposal with which to sway public op:.
The *Titanic Times*! We all believe in the freedom
the press, don't we?' The reporters nodded. 'Haven't
we protected that freedom in the past by defying
Captain Smith? And didn't he thank us for it in the
end? And didn't we defy the mutineer Pedroza by
continuing to publish the *Times* when everyone else
had given up?' There were murmurs of agreement
all round. 'Then we must do it again! This newspaper
must mount a campaign to spare Babe's life! We
must rally the people behind Babe! She represents
our freedom, our liberty, our future! Are you with me
on this?'

Jimmy had to admit that she was a fantastically
inspiring speaker. Their entire team of reporters and
photographers, even the delivery boys and girls
crowding in the doorway and the IT expert and the
idiot who made the tea, they were all fired up.

'Are you WITH ME?' Claire demanded again.

And this time they all rose to their feet, clapping and
punching the air and yelling: 'BABE! BABE! BABE!'

All except Jimmy, of course, who slumped down at
his desk and sighed.

The Campaign

So began the campaign by the *Titanic Times* to save the life of Babe the Pig. Before very long every passenger and crew member aboard the ship was aware of Babe's plight – the other pigs were conveniently forgotten – even if they didn't immediately have an opinion on whether or not she should be put to the knife. There were news stories with huge headlines and heart-rending photographs on the front page of Babe being playful and nuzzling up to children; if she looked suspiciously clean or there appeared to be an almost human glint in her eye, well, that was just the way she was, and no suspicion that her image had been polished up by a computer program was ever aired. Nor was the campaign confined to the pages of the *Times* – badges were made, posters were printed, *Save the Pig* fundraising concerts were held. They had all survived The End of Civilisation As We Know It, the planet was in tatters and everyone's future was uncertain, but for a brief period the fate of Babe the Pig seemed like it was the most important thing in the world. It became what would once have been known as a *cause célèbre*.

Jimmy, although he didn't really give a fiddler's elbow for what happened to the pig, was full of admiration for Claire and how she had mounted the campaign; he thought that Scoop, the decrepit old journalist who had attempted to teach them how to be good reporters – it seemed like an age ago – would have been surprised and delighted at Claire's progress. Yes, she was still sulky and spoiled, but when she got her teeth into a good story there was no stopping her. Stopping the captain getting *his* teeth into Babe was not, however, a foregone conclusion.

On the fourth day out of Reunion Gap, word filtered down to the newsroom that the decision had been made to slaughter the pigs at nine p.m. that night. A special edition of the *Times*, appealing to Captain Smith to spare Babe's life, was rushed out. A candlelit vigil was held on the top deck attended by two hundred and fifty passengers and crew. Babe remained on the makeshift farm below deck, guarded by Mr Benson. He had been personally warned by Captain Smith, by Mr Stanford and by First Officer Jeffers that if the pig happened to just disappear, then so would he. Overboard.

Claire, Jimmy, the rest of the reporting team and half a dozen of the passengers who had been most involved in the campaign gathered in the newspaper office at around six p.m. Their mood was sombre. They had done everything they could think of to convince the

33

captain to spare Babe's life, but he had yet to give any indication that he had any intention of changing his mind.

Claire dragged her eyes away from the clock on the wall. She slapped the top of her desk. 'We have to do something – something else!'

'We've done everything,' said Ty. 'Everything we can think of.'

'Well what *haven't* we thought of?'

'If we knew that,' Ty replied, 'then we would already have—'

'Quiet! I'm thinking.'

Ty sighed. He looked around the glum faces. 'When the time comes . . . how do you think they'll . . . you know . . . do it?'

Jimmy had an uncle who had once worked in an abattoir – or, he had *once* had an uncle who had once worked in an abattoir, because the chances were that the plague had killed him. Jimmy drummed his fingers on his desk to get attention. 'In a proper slaughter-house they'd use a gun,' he said, and all eyes turned towards him. He raised two fingers to the back of his head. 'It actually fires a bolt . . .'

'Is it painful?' one of the younger photographers, Alana, asked.

'Well I'm sure it's not very pleasant, but at least it's quick. Doesn't matter, though – because they're not going to have a bolt-gun down below.'

'So what will they do?'

Jimmy mimed slicing a knife across his throat, then waved his hands around to indicate blood spurting everywhere.

Everyone looked a little paler after that.

Claire stood abruptly. 'We can't allow this to happen. We have to seize control of the radio station.'

The *Titanic* had a small radio and television centre which, in the days when it was still operating as a cruise ship, had been used to broadcast news about events on the ship to the passengers' rooms. The television station had been lying dormant since the plague had struck, but the radio channel continued to be used by Captain Smith to talk directly to passengers and to monitor the airwaves for plague survivors.

'Why?' Ty asked.

'Because we've done our best with the newspaper – now we have to appeal directly to everyone on board and get them to go to Deck 3. If we get enough of them down there we can overpower the guards and get Babe out of there.'

Instinctively all eyes turned to Jimmy. Nobody had ever quite said it, but he was the boss. He was aware that they were looking expectantly at him. Over the past few months he had matured – he was more responsible, his head was screwed on a bit tighter. But he still liked causing a bit of trouble. He had allowed Claire to run the campaign to save Babe because he wasn't particularly bothered about the fate of the pig, but this kind of direct action appealed to him. He had never liked rules and regulations. He nodded slowly.

'OK,' he said finally, 'that sounds like a plan. We need to lure the radio operator out, then barricade ourselves inside. Anyone know how to operate the radio?'

One of the reporters, Christopher, thirteen years old but already wearing a half-grown moustache, cautiously raised his hand. 'My daddy owns – *owned* – a radio station. Been around it all my life, I reckon.'

'OK,' said Jimmy, 'no time to lose. Let's get going, we'll work out how to do it on the way…'

Claire was first to the door. She smiled hopefully back at Jimmy as she pulled at the handle – it seemed to be stuck – and then pulled again.

Jimmy rolled his eyes. 'Let me, earthling.' He pulled it hard. And again. But it wouldn't budge. 'It's locked – from the outside!'

Claire looked incredulous. 'But who . . . ?'

Jimmy shook his head. 'Who do you think?'

Realisation dawned on Claire. 'The captain? But why would . . . ?'

'Because he knows what we're like.'

The reporters and photographers and campaigners had crowded in behind Jimmy and Claire to follow them out. Now Claire pushed her way back through them to her desk and lifted her phone. She punched in the number for the bridge and tapped her foot impatiently while she waited for it to be answered.

'I want to speak to Captain Smith, *now*,' she demanded.

After another minute, the captain came on the line. 'Ah, Claire,' he said pleasantly. 'How are you?'

'I'm mad as hell!' Claire erupted.

'Yes, I imagine you are. However, locking you in seemed a prudent course of action. I really can't have you disrupting the ship, my dear, and although I haven't a clue what you were planning, I'm quite certain that you *were* planning something and therefore I decided to nip it in the bud. You will stay where you are until the . . . uhm, *deed* is done.'

'You can't do this!'

'Yes I can.'

'My daddy—'

'Your father has approved my action.'

A tear rolled down Claire's cheek. 'Please, Captain Smith, don't do this. Don't kill my Babe.'

'I'm sorry Claire, but it will be done. I understand your position, and you have mounted an admirable campaign to save the animal. But it is not a precedent I wish to set. I'm sorry.'

Claire felt a tap on her shoulder, and turned to find Jimmy standing beside her. He indicated that he wished to speak to the captain himself.

'It's no good, Jimmy,' said Claire, 'he won't change his mind.'

Jimmy nodded, but still held his hand out for the phone. Claire sighed and passed it across. She slumped down at her desk and buried her head in her hands. Jimmy raised the phone to his ear.

'Captain, it's Jimmy.' Captain Smith *mmm-hmm*ed. 'Is there nothing we can do?'

'No, son. Leave it now, all right?'

Jimmy took a deep breath. 'OK. That's your decision.' Claire looked up, fury freshly etched on her tear-stained face. 'But I have to ask your permission to allow a reporter to attend the execution. We've covered the story up until now and it's only right that we should be represented at the end.'

There was a moment's hesitation. Then Captain Smith said, 'Very well. You may send a representative. But I warn you – no funny business.'

'You have my word.'

Jimmy put the receiver down.

Claire looked at him in disbelief. 'You . . . just – gave in! You didn't put up any kind of a fight at all!'

'Claire, there's no point. He's made his mind up.'

Everyone was looking at him now.

Ty punched him lightly on the shoulder. 'You have a plan – don't you . . . ?'

Jimmy shook his head. 'No, Ty. No plan. Now who wants to go?'

There were no volunteers.

'OK then.' Jimmy lifted a camera and pushed his way back through to the door. He knocked on it, and a few moments later it was opened by First Officer Jeffers. He looked warily at the little group. Jimmy glanced back at Claire, gave a little shrug, and stepped into the gap.

The door was locked behind him. The imprisoned campaigners talked quietly or busied themselves with small tasks, trying to block out thoughts of what might be happening in the fake farmyard. But as the hands on the clock moved inexorably towards nine p.m. all work ceased.

Nine o'clock came.

Tears were shed.

Claire stared at her computer.

Nine-thirty arrived without any news. Nobody wanted to phone the bridge because nobody wanted to be the first to hear the bad news.

Finally, at a few minutes before ten a key was turned and the door opened. Jimmy stood there. Claire forced herself to look up from her screen. Jimmy's face was pale, the set of his mouth grim.

'Well?' Ty asked.

Jimmy took a deep breath. 'I have bad news, and I have good news.' He nodded around the news team. 'Which do you want to hear first?'

'The bad.' That was Claire. She was wringing her hands together.

'The bad news is that Babe was slaughtered at five past nine.' There was a communal groan. 'It was over quickly. She made no sound.'

'And the good news?' Claire falteringly asked.

Jimmy hesitated for a moment before producing a brown paper bag from behind his back.

'Fresh sausages!'

39

It was, he later acknowledged, a spectacular misjudgement. He had thought a joke might lighten the mood. There weren't *actually* sausages in the bag, he didn't *actually* walk in with bits of Babe minced up into pork bangers, but there might as well have been, given the instant, revolted reaction from his captive audience. If he hadn't had the presence of mind to realise the extent of his mistake and throw himself back out into the corridor and slam the door shut and lock it, they would have turned *him* into sausage meat.

Jimmy stood breathing heavily while the door was battered hard by the angry mob inside.

He rubbed at his brow, suddenly aware that his moment of stupidity had quite probably robbed him of all the respect he'd worked so hard to achieve.

Jimmy cautiously approached the door. 'Listen, folks, I'm really sorry – I was only trying to—'

'JIMMY ARMSTRONG.' It was Claire, her voice as cold and hard as he had ever heard it. 'I WILL NEVER SPEAK TO YOU AGAIN AS LONG AS I LIVE.'

The Old Man

Claire meant it. She *hated* Jimmy Armstrong. She would *never* speak to him again. He tried to apologise to her in half a dozen different ways, but she heard none of it – he might as well have been whispering in a force ten gale. She gave no indication that she was even aware of his existence.

Which made running the newspaper rather difficult.

In fact, *nobody* was speaking to him. Claire had a secret meeting with the news team early the next morning to decide what to do if he did turn up for work – he was, after all, still their boss. It was suggested that they quit their jobs, but they enjoyed working there too much to go along with that. If anyone was to quit it should be Jimmy – and if he wouldn't do it voluntarily they would force him out by sending him to Coventry. This was an old expression meaning to give someone the silent treatment.

If he was bold enough to come to work.

Nobody wanted to see him, but everyone was there to see if he turned up.

The working day usually started at nine a.m. Jimmy

41

was always late. At ten-past nine there was no sign of him. At half-past he had still not turned up. They were just beginning to relax by ten when the door opened and Jimmy sauntered in, cup of tea in hand and smiling widely.

'Morning all,' he said, crossing to his desk.

Silence.

'Beautiful out there – never seen the sea so calm.'

Silence.

'OK then, let's see what we have on today.' Jimmy took out the diary, a large red book which showed the various assignments he had to give to the reporters and photographers each day. Ninety-nine per cent of the time these were stories which needed to be covered on board ship, but occasionally, like today, there was something more exciting – overnight the *Titanic* had dropped anchor off another new settlement, this one called Tucker's Hole. They had requested medical assistance. Captain Smith was sending Dr Hill and a team of nurses ashore to help treat an outbreak of chicken pox – a disease that would once have been routinely dealt with, but since medicines were no longer readily available was now much more dangerous – in fact, potentially lethal. Places had been set aside on the speedboat for a reporter and photographer from the *Times*. Normally Jimmy's team would have been fighting to get ashore – but this morning when he asked for volunteers, not a single hand was raised.

Jimmy shrugged. 'OK then, I'll go myself.' Everyone kept their eyes down. 'But I still need a photographer.'

Still nobody volunteered.

'OK. Claire, as chief photographer, I'm selecting you to go ashore. See you up top in fifteen minutes. And seeing as how you've all lost the power of speech, I'll email you all your assignments before I go.'

Jimmy switched on his computer and set to work.

Tucker's Hole was set near the mouth of a small river and had been entirely constructed from panels of wood looted from a Home Depot about half a mile away. It was, essentially, a town constructed from garden sheds.

As the inflatable approached the shore, Dr Hill shouted out what had become a familiar list of orders. 'Don't get separated from the group! Stick together! Be pleasant, be respectful, but don't trust anyone! Do not wander off! If you see anything suspicious report it to me immediately! If you do get separated from the group and cannot make it back, the alternative pick-up point is two clicks to the east of the river – you've seen it on the map, so don't forget it!'

Jimmy always felt excited on these trips – because the unknown lay ahead. Everything had changed since the plague. They might be speeding towards a happy community full of jolly optimists – or into a violent ambush. The reality usually lay somewhere in the middle. The *Titanic* brought hope, and it also brought jealousy over the relatively good standard of living on board. It brought relief, but it also reinforced the knowledge that life could never be the same again. Usually he shared this excitement with Claire, but she sat stiff and remote. She would normally be snapping away by now, but the camera lay neglected in her lap. He smiled at her. She ignored him.

The clinic was set up in one of the larger huts and a queue of anxious mothers with their spotty children and pale-looking, blotchy orphans soon formed. Other women and children stood around watching from doorways or perched on teetering piles of wooden frames. The surrounding houses themselves stretched back for nearly two hundred metres, most of them running crookedly into each other. Some of their owners had added inadequate little chimneys which only seemed to disperse about half of the smoke from the small fires within, leaving the rest to blacken the faces and clog the lungs of their inhabitants. There was no system for getting rid of the sewage, and garbage lay everywhere. Rats wandered undisturbed. Jimmy had visited many settlements, but this was the worst yet. Winter had not yet arrived, but when it did he doubted if Tucker's Hole would survive for long.

Jimmy was pleased at least to see that the squalor had inspired Claire to wield her camera. Ordinarily he would have suggested ideas for photographs, or she would have sought his advice, but he decided it was better to keep his distance. Instead, after quickly checking that Dr Hill was too busy to keep a proper eye on him, Jimmy ducked into one of the narrow alleys that lay between the houses and began to make his way into the heart of Tucker's Hole. He was intrigued by the fact that there seemed to be no men around – yet he was sure he could *hear* them: raucous voices, snatches of songs. As he negotiated his way towards the enclosed centre of the settlement, scabby-faced children gawped at him as he passed. His first clue as to what awaited him came when he had to step over a man lying face down and snoring, clearly completely drunk. Then he found a pair of them, arms round each other as if they'd been singing together and then had collapsed into unconsciousness at the same time. There was a half spilled bottle beside them. Jimmy picked it up – there was a clear liquid within. He sniffed it cautiously – and his head shot back, his nostrils burning. This was what they called 'moonshine' in America, or 'poteen' back home in Ireland. Pure alcohol that was so strong it could turn you blind or kill you if it wasn't made in just the right way.

As Jimmy turned a corner the acoustics of the twisting alley became more concentrated and defined, leading him towards a much larger, windowless construction that was crammed with men drinking and partying. One was playing an accordion, another a tin whistle, both were banging their feet on the floor in time to their music. Onlookers clapped and sang along. Jimmy listened for a few minutes before pressing through the throng until he found himself in a short corridor which led to an even larger room beyond. This was just as crowded, but it was actually quieter – they were all listening intently to a grizzled looking old man perched on a bar stool on a slightly raised area in the centre of the room. His voice was raspy, his eyes red-rimmed from the wood smoke which hung around the ceiling, and he sat hunched over, as if he had the weight of the world on his bony shoulders. As Jimmy squirrelled his way forward the old man was shuffling crumpled sheets of paper.

'Here we are – here we are . . . This one's from Jacob's Hollow, 'bout fifty miles east of here. Says they have the malaria now – ain't been malaria in these parts for two hundred years, but they say they have it.'

Another man spoke up. 'My wife's right – we're all goin' to hell in a handcart.'

There was a murmur of agreement from the audience. The old man nodded grimly as he looked down at the sheet of paper. 'Have the names here of people who've showed up at Jacob's Hollow. Gonna read them out. You recognise any, you speak to me later, I'll see if I have any news of them. When I'm done up here, I'll take a list of your names with me to the next settlement along. Good to know if your loved ones are OK – but I tell you this, don't go trying to visit. Roads are impassable, bandits out there, shootin' and killin'. Not gonna harm an old fella like me, but you stay safe here in Tucker's Hole.'

When he'd finished reading the names from Jacob's Hollow, he pulled up another sheet, this time from a settlement called Miller's Crossing, and repeated the process. He read two more after that and was about to start on a third when he hesitated and glanced up at the audience. His mouth opened, then closed. He appeared to be debating with himself whether to say something.

'What is it?' someone shouted. 'We don't need any more bad news!'

'No – no, it's not – it's just . . .' He sighed. 'Well, don't see what harm it can do. Just – I heard this story. These days there's lots of stories, but the people I heard it from swore to God it was true.' An anxious hush fell on the audience. As Jimmy looked around he caught a glimpse of Claire on the far side of the room. The old man rubbed at his heavily stubbled jaw. 'Well, there were these couple of guys went hunting in the woods outside of Miller's Crossing, just ordinary folks like you and me. They were tracking this deer down through the trees, came out on the old railway track – ain't been a train through there since the early days of the plague – but this day, there was a train sitting about a hundred metres up from where they were, engine running and American flags flying front and back. Now our guys were a bit wary, you know how things are these days, deciding whether it was a good idea to approach – when these Marines jumped out of nowhere, surrounded them, took their guns off of

them, wanting to know what they were doing sneakin'
up on the President's train . . .'

At this an excited flurry of whispers swept through
the crowd.

'Yep – that's what they said. Anyways they were
marched to the train . . . and you know what? The
President himself got off and walked right up to them
and shook their hands and asked how they was doing!'

Another wave of excitement.

'Yep – it was the President all right, sure as I'm
sitting here. And that's not all. He asked them what
they did in their old life – one was a fireman, other in
computers. He said he was looking for good people.
He'd established his own settlement couple of hundred
miles north – had its own schools, electricity, good
food, television – said he was rebuilding civilisation.
President said he was looking for people to help and
did they want to come. Well of course, they both
wanted to go, and one of them climbed right on
board, was given a cold beer. The other, he said he had
a wife and family back in the settlement and could he
go fetch them, but the President said he couldn't wait,
there were bandits in the woods and all about and it
wasn't safe. But he said he'd be back, and that people
shouldn't give up hope, that the good times were
coming again, and to have faith in him, and have faith
in God.'

The old man nodded. 'Faith in him,' he repeated,
'faith in God.'

Questions were immediately shouted from the floor.

'When was this?'

'You sure it was him?'

'What they call this place?'

'They have *television*?'

'Were those guys drunk?'

There were a dozen more questions. Eventually the old man held his hand up. 'Told you all I know. This was about three weeks back, and I tell you, that guy's been down at those tracks with his family every day since. All I can say is, if I see that train, I'd be getting right on board too.'

He smiled then and there was scattered applause. He pushed himself wearily off his bar stool. At that exact moment a camera flash went off. The old man spun to one side with surprising speed and vigour as he sought out the culprit. Jimmy saw Claire pushing her way back through the crush of bodies. She had her photograph, and he had his story. They were a great team, even if they weren't speaking to each other.

Into the Woods

Jimmy was as excited as everyone else by the old man's account of the President's train. Partly because he was a newsman with a good scoop, but also because of the way it had affected the audience – for the first time on any of his settlement visits he had seen genuine hope in their eyes, the first inkling that there might be a real possibility of escape from their squalid existence. Electricity! Television! As he made his way back through the tangle of huts Jimmy could hear snatches of 'The Star Spangled Banner' being sung.

It was a pleasant relief to emerge back into the fresh air. Jimmy looked across to where Dr Hill was now getting towards the end of his line of patients. Three sorry-looking children lay on stretchers, ready for transportation back to the *Titanic*. Since he'd been gone a second boat had arrived from the ship. First Officer Jeffers and several crewmen had set up a folding table and chair and were now interviewing locals who wished to board the *Titanic*. There weren't very many of them; they stood lethargically and answered Jeffers' questions as if they

50

didn't care one way or another if they were successful.

As there was still clearly some time to kill, Jimmy decided to do a little more exploring. He began to circle around the outside of the settlement. Several dogs snapped at him. Soot-faced women stared at him as he passed their homes. He stepped over another drunk. When he had landed he had wanted to ask as many of these people as possible for their personal stories of what had happened to them during and since the plague, but since hearing about the Presidential train he could no longer summon the enthusiasm – he wanted to write something positive for a change, he'd had enough of death and disaster.

When he was about halfway around the settlement there was a scream from up ahead. His view was obscured by a jutting wall – yet he immediately knew who it was.

Claire!

Jimmy charged around the corner and saw her lying on the rubbish-strewn ground about a hundred metres ahead. A boy of roughly his own age was standing over her.

'*Hey!*' Jimmy yelled.

The boy looked startled, then reached down and grabbed Claire's camera. She held on to the strap and pulled back, but the boy punched at her face and she let out a cry of pain. The boy ripped the strap from her grasp and darted back into the maze of interconnected sheds that made up Tucker's Hole.

Claire pulled herself up to her knees just as Jimmy reached her. There was a thin trickle of blood coming from her nose.

'Are you all right?'

She gave him a look that said *Stupid question*.

'I'll get Dr Hill . . .' Jimmy started to turn, but she grabbed his arm and shook her head. 'Claire! This is stupid! Talk to me . . .'

But instead of talking, she jabbed her finger after the boy and grunted. The camera.

Jimmy took her hand and hauled her to her feet. She quickly disengaged her hand. He reached up to wipe the blood from her lip, but she turned her head away. Jimmy tutted and turned towards the gap in the jagged wall where the boy had disappeared.

'I'll get it back,' he said. But as he started to follow, Claire was right behind him. He stopped and shook his head. She nodded. He put his hand up to stop her. She put her hands on her hips and gave him a look. He sighed.

'Oh please your bloody self, you half-wit.'

He turned into the alley. Claire followed.

For the next forty-five minutes they played cat and mouse with the thief. Several times they caught glimpses of him, only for him to disappear again. And it wasn't as if they could report him to the police. There *were* no police. There were no laws or courts or punishments. If they wanted to get the camera back they had to get it themselves. They got lost, they were shouted at, they fell over drunks, they found themselves accidentally standing in people's bedrooms, more than once they disturbed someone having a pee – all without a word being spoken between them. They were tired, sweaty, determined, but eventually had to concede that they weren't going to get Claire's camera back. They agreed this just by looking at each other. Jimmy shrugged, Claire shrugged; he nodded towards what he thought was the twisting path back to where the other crewmen were; she nodded back.

When they stepped back out into the late afternoon sunlight they were immediately aware that something had changed – but for a moment couldn't quite put their fingers on it. The same sullen people were standing around, there was the same fetid stench, pockmarked children were still running back and forth playing soccer with a burst ball, presumably over the worst of the chicken—

'They're gone!' Jimmy exclaimed.

With a dreadful lurch in his stomach he'd realised that there was now no trace of Dr Hill, the nurses, the sick children, or indeed Jeffers and his crew.

'We spent so long chasing that camera that . . .'

Claire was giving him a look that said *So it's my fault?*

Jimmy rolled his eyes. He stopped the closest footballer. 'Hey – the doctor, the nurses, how long ago did they leave?'

The boy, who was only about seven, looked frightened. Another, older boy shouted across: 'About half an hour ago. Did they leave you behind? My parents did that a couple of weeks ago. You can play for my team if you want.'

'Thanks, but . . .' Jimmy was already looking around, trying to decide on the best course of action.

Claire pulled at his sleeve and pointed away from the settlement – not towards the beach where they'd landed a couple of hours before, but to the east. Jimmy remembered now – Dr Hill had told them where to meet in case they got split up.

Two clicks to the east of the river.

Whatever the hell a click was. Jimmy hadn't been paying much attention when this rendezvous point was discussed at the planning meeting on the *Titanic*. But it seemed that Claire had. She strode out in front of him, and then broke into a jog. Jimmy took a deep breath and followed.

They were running through dense woods, following an ancient path that twisted up, then down again towards the coast. The sunlight through the branches gave the kind of lovely rippling, flickering effect that might have caused epilepsy if you were prone to it. Claire loped confidently along.

'You know,' Jimmy said between breaths, his eyes glued to the ground so that he wouldn't trip over the tree roots poking out every few metres, 'you're going to have to talk to me eventually.'

54

Claire didn't respond.

'I know you're pig-headed, but you'll cave in, I know you will.'

Nothing.

'And when I say you're pig-headed, that wasn't a reference to Babe.'

Nothing.

'Even if you do look quite similar.'

Claire stopped. Jimmy smiled to himself. He'd gotten to her. Even if she hurled abuse at him, at least they'd be talking. But she didn't turn. He saw now that the path ahead of them was split – in *three* directions. Each path was still generally heading to the east – but which one to follow?

'Lost, are we?'

Claire's head snapped towards him – but then a sudden *crack* diverted their attention. They had both seen enough action in the past few months to recognise a gunshot when they heard one. And close at hand. There was a moment when their eyes met, before they threw themselves off the path. They lay with their faces pressed into the mossy forest floor, breathing hard, their eyes urgently scanning the trees.

'Wasn't aimed at us,' Jimmy whispered. Claire nodded. There was nothing moving ahead. 'Probably hunters.' Claire nodded again. 'The sensible thing to do . . . would be to keep going . . . we have a boat to catch. Investigating would be time-consuming, and possibly dangerous.'

Claire looked at him. He saw the merest sliver of a smile. Then she raised herself to her knees and crawled across the path and into the trees on the other side – i.e. in the vague direction of the shot.

Jimmy had expected nothing less. He followed a moment later.

They moved forward as quietly as they could – but in the almost absolute silence of the woods it was difficult not to make a noise. If there were birds in the trees they were watching, not singing. There was no breeze to produce the aching sound of swaying branches.

They had progressed about a hundred metres when they heard it: soft, yet unmistakable. Somebody was singing. A man's voice. Light, melodic. A hymn.

> *'Give me oil in my lamp, keep me burning.*
> *Give me oil in my lamp, I pray.*
> *Give me oil in my lamp, keep me burning.*
> *Keep me burning till the break of day . . .'*

It drifted eerily through the trees. It was so out of place. Jimmy and Claire exchanged glances before advancing again. Perhaps only ten or twelve metres further on they came to the edge of a clearing and stopped behind the cover of a small clutch of low ferns. Ahead of them they saw a man in a long black coat and black, wide-brimmed hat, with a rifle in his hand. He was crouching over something, and singing

to himself. Jimmy thought at first that it was indeed a
hunter, examining the animal he'd killed, and was on
the point of rising to ask for directions when the man
moved a little to the side, affording them their first
proper view of his kill.

Of the dead man.

Of wide, staring eyes.

Of a gaping, bloody hole in his chest.

Of the man in black searching his pockets.

And singing, singing that hymn.

The man in black moved around to the other side
of the corpse, and now they saw that he was wearing a
minister's collar around his neck. His face was pure
white and dominated by a long, thin nose. He
reminded Jimmy of the austere seventeenth century
Puritans he'd been forced to learn about in school.

Claire squeezed Jimmy's arm. She indicated with
her eyes that they should back away. Jimmy nodded.

But immediately his foot found a twig and it
snapped with surprising volume.

Instantaneously the minister's eyes shot up. Their
heads were already pressed hard into the mossy forest
floor as he scanned along the trees. He rose from his
crouching position and raised his rifle. He was about
twenty metres away from them. Slowly he moved the
rifle from left to right – one long, bony finger curled
around the trigger.

He began to move in their direction.

Claire's nails dug into Jimmy's arm.

He was coming, slowly, but coming.

Wait and hope he stopped, or make a run for it?

Jimmy wasn't going to lie there and wait for him. This minister had already killed one man – there was nothing to stop him shooting them either. He looked at Claire. She nodded.

He mouthed – '*One, two . . .*' They sprang up on three and sprinted back the way they'd come. At first there was only the soft pad of their feet on the forest floor . . . until the first shot shattered a branch centimetres from Claire's head. She let out a scream, but didn't miss a step.

A second and third shot rang out just as they came to the diverging paths. The third smashed into a tree to Jimmy's right and a wood splinter sliced along his cheek; Jimmy charged along the path that veered slightly to the left. A fourth shot cracked out further to the right and there was another scream from Claire – but further away.

She'd taken the other path!

But which one was the minister—?

A branch exploded to Jimmy's right. He tumbled to the ground, rolled, sprang back up and kept running. He had his answer.

But did that mean Claire was safe . . . or was she already dead?

Or lying wounded and the minister was going to kill Jimmy first before going back to finish her off?

Either way, there was nothing he could do!

Just keep running!

It was then that the minister's high pitched, whiny voice rang out. 'I see you, boy! I'm coming for you, boy!'

Wounded

It was the pain that woke her. Claire opened her eyes in the darkness and instinctively tried to rub some ease into her arm. She immediately let out a yelp. What had she done to it . . . ? Come to that, where was she? Why was she so cold and damp . . . ? Who switched off the lights? She felt around her with her good hand – soft . . . twigs . . . a reassuring smell of pine – the forest! She tried to tidy her jumbled thoughts together – *The last thing . . . the last thing I remember . . . oh, my God . . . the minister . . . !*

I'm shot, I've been shot!

Adrenaline coursed through her veins.

She desperately tried to catch her breath.

No . . . wait . . . wait . . . calm . . . don't panic . . . I'm alive . . . I'm still alive . . .

Claire carefully turned her injured arm so that she could see her watch, and pressed a button on the side to illuminate the face . . .

Six o'clock!

They'd been hurrying to meet the boat for four o'clock!

They were two hours late!

They . . .

Jimmy!

She remembered now! The gunshot, the incredible pain in her arm and then stumbling off the path and running as hard as she could. Then she'd fallen and didn't have the strength to get up again. She'd heard the minister calling out to Jimmy and then more gunshots.

A terrible feeling of dread swept over her.

Jimmy's dead!

Her best friend in the whole world – even though she'd hated him – was dead.

She immediately followed that with: *No, I don't know that! Not for sure. Jimmy's a survivor, he'll find a way to survive. He's probably back on the ship already, writing up the story for the paper.*

He probably hasn't given me a second thought.

Nobody has.

They think I'm dead! They've sailed on!

No! They're looking for me . . . they MUST be looking for me – but if Jimmy's dead . . . how will they know where to look?

Claire peered into the darkness – but there was nothing to see. If the minister was still out there then he could surely no more see her than she could see him.

She gingerly touched her arm again, and the pain of it caused her to momentarily black out. Her head fell back and cracked on the trunk of a tree. It was enough of a shock to jolt her back to consciousness.

This isn't good . . . this isn't good . . .

Oh my, oh my, oh my − I've been left behind! Jimmy's dead! I'm going to die! Small furry animals are going to find my body and eat me! Help! Help! Helllll—

No! Get a grip!

Calm down . . . calmer . . . think sensibly . . . If I was going to die, I wouldn't have woken up. I'm OK − for now . . . but if the minister doesn't find me, then I'll probably bleed to death. I have to get out of here . . .

She took several long, deep breaths to steady herself, but they just made her feel woozy. She rested her head more carefully back against the tree. Her eyes were drawn upwards − it was dark on the forest floor but there was still some light up there above the trees.

Which way to go?

Back to Tucker's Hole? They can radio the ship! But what if the ship is out of range already? Or the minister is there?

And I've no idea which direction the village is in. I must have lost a lot of blood − how long can I walk for? If I get lost in the woods . . .

She pulled and pulled at the arm of her shirt until finally the material ripped. She wrapped it around her wound and used her teeth to pull it as tight as the pain would allow.

East. I have to go east.

I have no idea where the rendezvous point is from here, but I know the coast is east. If I can strike the coast then there's some small chance someone might spot me.

62

And if they don't . . .

Claire forced herself up. She leaned against the tree, steadied herself, then cautiously let go. She was dizzy, her legs felt like lead and her arm – well . . . she'd been *shot*.

She had no choice but to start walking.

She had to . . . go . . . *now* . . .

The emergency rendezvous point was at a short stretch of beach a mile from the rivermouth where Tucker's Hole had been built. First Officer Jeffers stood on the sand, scanning a tree line that stretched as far as the settlement on his right, and then as far as the eye could see to his left. He glanced at his watch. It was now three and a half hours past pick-up time and it was almost completely dark. He was certain that something pretty terrible had happened to Claire and Jimmy.

His radio crackled.

'Mr Jeffers? Stanford here. Anything to report?'

Jeffers took a deep breath. Claire's father had been on the radio every ten minutes since she'd been reported missing. His desperate concern was understandable, and Jeffers was frustrated that he'd no positive news for him.

'Mr Stanford, sir, just waiting on the patrols returning. But it's almost pitch black in the forest now, sir.'

'I understand that. What about this settlement – Tucker's . . . ?'

'Tucker's Hole, sir. Sent two patrols in. Nothing there either.'

'Did you search thoroughly, Mr Jeffers?'

'We searched every building. As I told you earlier, sir, some kids thought they saw them going off into the forest and then . . .'

'Gunshots.'

'Yes, sir. It doesn't mean—'

'I know what it means, Mr Jeffers.' There were several long moments of radio static. 'I know you'll do your best, Mr Jeffers. She's a headstrong girl, but we do love . . .' His voice faltered, and what he had intended to say remained unspoken.

'We're doing everything we can, sir.'

There was another burst of static and then Captain Smith spoke, his voice calm and authoritative. 'Mr Jeffers, you may give it another ten minutes, then call off the search for the night. We will resume at first light.'

'Yes, Captain.'

Thirty minutes later, with the patrols returned and no sign of Claire or Jimmy, First Officer Jeffers reluctantly gave the order to reboard the inflatables and return to the ship. He knew that the more time passed the less likely it was that they'd be found alive. This new world was dangerous, and particularly dangerous for knuckle-headed, rebellious kids like Claire and Jimmy.

'All aboard, sir.'

Jeffers splashed through a metre or so of water and climbed into the hi-tech, high-speed boat. 'Very well – let's take her back to *Titan*—'

But he was suddenly interrupted by one of the crewmen crying out: 'Look, sir! There!'

All eyes turned to where the sailor was pointing – about half a mile away along the beach a small figure had emerged from the tree line and was hurrying towards them – albeit in an odd zigzag pattern. With an overcast sky and no moonlight it was impossible in the darkness to make out whether it was Claire or Jimmy or just one of the locals, running along the beach.

'Well spotted, Martin! Cut engines! Dalzell, bring the flashlight!'

Jeffers threw his legs over the side of the inflatable and waded back to shore, quickly followed by half a dozen others. He began to jog along the sand. Ahead of him the dark figure weaved off to one side before abruptly falling to the ground. Jeffers picked up his speed and seconds later slid to a halt beside . . .

'Flashlight!'

Dalzell appeared behind him, gasping for breath, and flicked on the torch.

It was a girl, for sure, but it was several moments before Jeffers realised it was Claire. Her face was a mass of cuts and scratches, as if she'd been dragged through bushes. Her hair was hanging dank across her face and her clothes were badly torn.

'Claire?'

Jeffers gently pushed the damp hair away from her eyes. He softly shook her arm – she winced in pain and let out a moan. He took the flashlight from Dalzell and shone it on her arm – then gasped as he saw the wound and the dirt surrounding it. He cursed himself for not insisting that Dr Hill remain ashore until the search was over. He began to check her pulse.

'Stretcher!' he snapped.

'Got it, sir!' Martin was already snapping open a foldable stretcher.

'Let's get her back to the ship! Dalzell! Call Dr Hill, have him standing by!'

'Sir!'

The stretcher was laid on the sand, and they were just preparing to lift Claire on to it when she opened her eyes. With her good arm she reached vaguely out in Jeffers' direction. 'Please . . . Jimmy . . . you have to find . . . Jimmy . . .' Her voice was barely audible. Her eyes rolled back in her head. 'Please . . . Jimmy . . . Babe . . . I'm not . . . talking . . . to . . . him . . .'

Jeffers took her hand. 'It's OK Claire, we're taking you home.'

He stood back then and gave his crew the signal to lift the stretcher. The *Titanic* was less than a mile off shore. He had absolutely no idea if she'd still be alive when they got there.

The Tree

It was a risk. A *huge* risk. But he couldn't run any further.

Jimmy considered himself to be relatively fit – but so was the minister. He just kept on coming. Not faster – but relentless. Every time Jimmy chanced a look back he was right there, running like a machine at exactly the same pace, his rifle carried in one hand at his side, his wide-brimmed hat shadowing his eyes. There were no more shots.

He's saving them.

Jimmy ducked in and out of the trees, crisscrossed animal paths, ran up hills and down; plunged through undergrowth and leaped across streams; but still the minister was right there. In the end he knew he had to try something radical or his legs would become so weak that he would stumble and twist an ankle and then the minister would be on him.

He had to go *up*.

Jimmy hurtled through the next thick bank of trees, laboured up a short incline and disappeared briefly over the brow.

Now!

He had perhaps fifteen seconds before the minister would appear. Jimmy threw himself at the closest trees – he was a veteran tree climber from his days in Belfast. These trees had slender trunks with few lower branches, but he was still able to wrap his aching legs around the rough bark. He was drenched in sweat and could hardly catch his breath, but he had no choice but to try and wring the last ounce of strength from his body to shimmy up the tree. He didn't even dare look back to see if the minister had come over the brow yet. He just pulled and pulled until at last his feet started to find proper, weight-bearing branches.

He was about halfway up the pine when he heard the dull thud of the minister's feet on the soft forest floor. Jimmy froze. The minister was coming straight towards the tree he was hiding in. Jimmy knew he wasn't far enough up it yet to be properly hidden. If the minister looked up now, he was a dead man.

The minister passed directly below him – and kept going.

As carefully as he possibly could Jimmy climbed further up the trunk.

The minister stopped twenty metres further on. The trees before him had thinned out, giving him a clear view of the forest ahead. And obviously he could no longer see his prey.

The minister turned and began to retrace his steps.

Jimmy stopped moving. He already knew the

danger that lay in the slightest noise in this forest.

The minister drew closer. He was walking slightly stooped with his eyes fixed to the ground. Jimmy tried desperately to slow his breathing as he approached.

Now he was directly below him.

All Jimmy could see was the top of his black hat and its wide brim. It was like looking down on a dead planet.

The minister moved left, right; then circled the tree.

A bead of sweat rolled off Jimmy's dank brow, down his nose, and sat precariously on its very tip. He felt so weak that his grip on the tree was now quite insecure and he didn't dare try to wipe it away; all he could do was *will* it to stay where it was.

But, of course, he was Lucky Jimmy Armstrong.

The drop *dropped*.

In a movie, to eke out the agony, it might have fallen in slow motion.

But this one just fell fast and pinged on to the crown of the minister's hat.

Immediately he looked up.

That's it. I'm dead.

He raised his rifle.

I am absolutely dead.

It didn't even cross his mind to beg for his life. He knew it would be useless. The minister was a cold-hearted killer.

Jimmy just stared down at him and waited.

The minister stared right back – but then he

blinked: once, twice, three times; he rubbed at his eyes, then held a hand up to shield them.

He's looking straight at me – but he can't see me because of the sun!

Jimmy turned his head very, very slowly upwards. The sun was low in the sky, but the position of his tree at the foot of the incline was just perfect for catching it. However, it was sinking rapidly and might only give him such blinding cover for a few more minutes.

The minister remained where he was, looking up, gun raised; but now he was ranging it along the tops of other trees which weren't in the full glare. He brought it right back round to Jimmy's tree, looked up again, squinting, then shut his eyes tight and turned away. He lowered the gun and rubbed the knuckles of his left hand into his straining eyes.

When he had recovered sufficiently, the minister again surveyed the surrounding trees. His voice, when it came, was shrill, and every bit as spine-chilling as the first time: 'You can't escape from me, boy!' he screamed. 'I will hunt you down!'

Another bead of sweat swept down Jimmy's nose; he watched it, cross-eyed, for an agonising moment until it shot off the end and continued down on the exact trajectory of its predecessor.

But this time it splashed harmlessly on to the spongy forest floor.

The minister was gone!

★ ★ ★

It is difficult to sleep in a tree. One moment you're drifting into peaceful slumber, the next you've fallen ten metres to the ground and you've broken your neck. He did nod off, three or four times. Once he actually let go of the branch and that awful dropping sensation was already ripping through his tummy when he frantically dug his fingernails into the bark and was just about able to hold on. He was desperately tired, but there was no way that he was going to venture down. It was pitch black, he was being devoured by ants: his cheek, where the sliver of wood had sliced into him, was sticky and sore, but he still wasn't going down there. The minister was waiting for him. He worked for God. He could probably see in the dark.

In those precious seconds where he did sleep, he endured odd, weird dreams which came and went in a flash – the minister bearing down on Claire and Jimmy saving her, swooping down out of the sky on angel wings.

For the most part, though, he stared into the darkness. He was hungry and his throat was parched, but he was neither hungry enough nor thirsty enough to take a chance on the minister being out there. He began to wonder what had driven the minister to such murderous acts, and who the man he'd shot was . . . but then he stopped himself. It didn't matter.

Claire's dead. That's all that matters. My friend Claire is dead.

He was certain of it.

Or almost certain of it.

The minister had pursued her, shot at her, then satisfied with his kill, turned his attention to him.

Or . . .

There was a very small chance that she was still alive. But was that necessarily better, if she was lying wounded somewhere, unable to move, dying a slow, agonising death? They had shared danger before and survived, but this was different. Before they had been able to support each other; each of them was ingenious and brave in their own way – they were a great team. Apart, somehow, they were diminished. And now they would never be together again. All because of a stupid pig. If he hadn't bloody tried to be so bloody smart then they would never have stopped talking, and if they had still been on good terms then that kid from Tucker's Hole would never have been able to rip off Claire's camera, and if . . .

If, if, if, if, if . . .

Ifs were no good to him now. He had to concentrate on one thing.

Surviving.

He slept.

He fell.

Jimmy was lucky that several branches on the way down broke his fall, and that the ground at the foot of the tree happened to be particularly soft. But he still landed with a tremendous *whumpf*. It was almost five minutes before he could bring himself to try moving. It was light now and a low mist hung upon the ground. Jimmy cautiously pushed himself up to his feet. Remarkably, although every single bone in his body ached, nothing appeared to be broken. He took several tentative steps forward. He didn't feel too bad at all, considering. And the fact that he hadn't yet been shot dead suggested that the minister was no longer a threat – or not at this moment, anyway.

Jimmy had absolutely no idea where he was. But he started walking anyway. He needed to get his bruised legs working so that they wouldn't stiffen up any further. And he couldn't just sit still. Nobody was going to come and rescue him. He was on his own. The best thing he could do, he thought, was to try and find his way back to the path. If he was lucky he'd make it to Tucker's Hole. They had a radio there, they could call the ship. He thought there was a strong possibility that the *Titanic* would still be there – not because they'd wait for *him*, but because they'd certainly wait for Claire.

But could he even face going back to the ship? He would have to tell the Stanfords and Captain Smith – and everyone else on board would soon find out – that he had run off and left Claire to her fate. He knew it wasn't as simple as that, but surely that's what people would think.

Perhaps it would be better if he didn't try to find the

ship at all, if instead he made a new life for himself in one of the settlements.

He was still thinking about this thirty minutes later while rather forlornly searching for the path, but wasn't paying sufficient attention to where he was walking. The ground suddenly dipped down a steep bank. Jimmy lost his footing and tumbled down, coming to a stop when the bank flattened out with the breath knocked out of him. It was all he needed, with his body already bruised and battered. Jimmy shook himself, got to his knees and looked around him. A broad swathe had clearly been cut through this part of the woods, and as he stood he understood why – just a few metres ahead of him there was a partially overgrown railway track.

Jimmy smiled – something good at last. It had to lead *somewhere*.

Turn left, turn right?

Jimmy turned to his left. He walked for five metres. Then he turned back and began to walk to his right. It felt better, somehow.

The track ahead curved around a bend . . .

That's where he found the President's train.

The Engine

She woke suddenly, like someone had just switched her back on. She knew immediately where she was because she'd spent so much time there during the plague. The *Titanic*'s hospital wing. In a nice clean bed. Her arm bandaged, but not sore. A pleasant buzz in her head. Drugs to kill the pain. An IV tube attached to her good arm. She had two thoughts:

I'm alive.

And then:

Jimmy!

There was a dull throb beneath her. That meant the *Titanic* was moving. Claire threw her covers back and swung her legs off the bed. She stood up, and immediately a wave of dizzy nausea hit her and she sat right back down again. A nurse appeared in the doorway and hurried across, waving a warning finger.

'No, no, no, young lady. I don't think so.'

The nurse reached down and lifted Claire's legs back up on to the bed.

She lay back on the pillow – then almost

immediately sat up again. 'My father, I need to speak to my—'

'All in good time.'

'I WANT TO SPEAK TO HIM NOW!'

Her legs might have been weak, but her voice was strong. The nurse quickly backed away. 'I'll get Dr Hill.'

'MY FATHER! I WANT . . .'

Dr Hill, alerted by the shouting, was already on his way in. 'Ah, Claire, how are you—'

'Where's Jimmy?'

'How's the arm?'

'Where's Jimmy?'

'You almost lost it, you know, it was a bad wound, and infected.'

'Tell me where Jimmy is!'

'We don't know,' Dr Hill said bluntly.

It hit her like a hammer blow.

'What do you mean you *don't know*?'

'We just don't know. We searched for him, Claire, but no trace.'

The door opened again and Claire's mother came rushing in, quickly followed by her father.

'Oh darling, darling! You're awake . . . my poor, poor sweet girl!'

Mrs Stanford bent down for a hug and kiss. Claire ignored her. Her eyes bore into her father.

'Dad. What about Jimmy?'

'I'm sorry, Claire.'

'That's not good enough!'

'We did our best! Now you have to tell us what happened.'

'Did that wretched boy try to kill you?' her mother asked.

'WHAT ARE YOU TALKING ABOUT?' Claire exploded. 'The preacher tried to kill both of us! The reverend! The minister! We had to run, we got separated. There was all this shooting . . . I fell, I fell and there was more shooting . . . Jimmy . . .' Claire abruptly burst into tears. Her mother moved in for another hug. Claire shrugged her off. 'No!' She dragged her arm across her face. 'You didn't look hard enough! We have to go back! Why are we even sailing, we need to know what . . . *aaaaow!*'

Dr Hill had snuck up on her other side and jabbed her good arm with a syringe. As he pushed the plunger in he said, 'I'm sorry Claire, but you need to rest. You've been through a major trauma and the surgery . . .'

But she was already asleep.

They stood around the bed, looking down at her. She was still deathly pale and the skin on her face was pulled tight by a dozen lacerations.

'You didn't think it wise to tell her?' her father asked.

Dr Hill shook his head. 'I don't think it would have helped.'

One of the patrols had found Jimmy's footprints and a spray of blood on a tree trunk with a bullet hole in it.

'She'll sleep until tomorrow,' said Dr Hill. 'I gave her enough sedative to knock out a horse.'

'She's not a horse,' observed Mr Stanford. 'Horses can be trained.'

It was after three a.m. and nearly all of the passengers and crew were asleep. Others passed the dark hours by watching a movie in the ship's cinema or ice skated. On the top deck an elderly man who had lost his wife to the plague was approaching the summit of the climbing wall. He climbed it every night. He had no idea why. Benson snored uneasily in the makeshift farmyard. In the engine room, having been summoned from his own slumbers, Jonas Jones cursed furiously before storming out. He made his way to the captain's quarters and hammered on his door. It was a full minute before a rather dishevelled-looking Captain Smith opened up.

'Jonas? What is it?'

'It's trouble, that's what it is.'

Without waiting to be invited the engineer stepped into the cabin. The captain, in dressing gown and pyjamas, watched his old friend stride across to a small table, pull a chair out and sit down heavily.

Forty minutes later they were still talking urgently when they became aware of a noise outside the cabin – light footsteps perhaps, but with an accompanying grating sound, like a prisoner dragging a ball and chain. They exchanged glances. Neither of them was superstitious, but it sounded like a ghost might sound – in a very bad movie.

Captain Smith moved to the door, hesitated for a moment, then flung it open.

Claire was standing there, her fist already raised to hammer on it. Her IV was still attached to her arm and to its stand. She had dragged it all the way from the hospital. Her hair lay dank upon her head and sweat was rolling down her brow. But her eyes burned with determination.

'You . . . will . . . turn this ship . . . around *now* . . .'

She staggered forward, and the IV tripod would have toppled behind her if the captain hadn't caught it. Jonas Jones jumped up, took hold of Claire and guided her across to his chair. As he lowered her into it he purred softly, 'Easy now, girl.'

'I'm OK . . . I'm all right . . . tired . . .' She took a deep breath. Sweat dripped on to the floor. 'Captain . . . Smith. We have to go back for Jimmy. We *have* to.'

Captain Smith reached across and patted her hand gently. 'Claire, we *can't*.'

'Of course you can! You just . . . turn her round and we go back and we search . . . until we find him. He's out there still . . . I know it. Captain Smith?' She slipped her hand free and instead took hold of his hand and squeezed it hard. 'Captain Smith – have you forgotten what Jimmy did for you, for us, for the *Titanic?* He *saved* us. You *owe* him. We *all* owe him.'

Captain Smith nodded slowly. 'I appreciate how much we owe him. Claire. We searched thoroughly. We did everything we could. But he's gone. These are dangerous times, Claire. He's gone. You're going to have to accept it.'

Tears rolled down her cheeks. 'But he *must* be alive. He's Lucky Jimmy Armstrong.'

'Nobody's that lucky, Claire.'

'*Please.*'

Jonas Jones patted her shoulder. 'Claire, the captain's right. We did our best. And we really *can't* go back. We have engine trouble.'

Claire blinked at him. She was still a *Times* reporter. 'What . . . are you talking about? What kind of engine trouble?'

'*Big* engine trouble. We're going to limp to the next port and try to make some temporary repairs. If we're lucky they might just be enough to get us to New York.'

'New York? Why . . . ?'

'Well, I've always wanted to go there.' He smiled. 'But mostly it's the only place this side of the Atlantic we might be able to get the part we need.'

'And what if you can't?'

'Well then, enjoy your time on board, because this is the last voyage of the *Titanic.*'

The President's Train

Lucky Jimmy Armstrong had vaguely heard of Air Force One, the President's private jet. He seemed to remember him flying around the world in it, solving problems or causing them. But he'd never heard of a Presidential *train*. Nevertheless, with a scar on his cheek and hurting from head to toe, Jimmy *ran* towards it as it sat idling on the tracks a hundred metres ahead of him as if he was finishing a race. He could now see an American eagle emblazoned on the rear of the last carriage, and the Stars and Stripes flying above it.

Finally my luck has changed!

I'm bound for the Promised Land – and if they don't let me on board, well, I'll stow away, I'm good at that!

The first shot stopped him dead. It pinged off the rusting track a little to his left. The second shot, this time to his right, made him raise his hands.

He immediately realised how stupid he'd been – *running* at the President's train! These were dangerous times, people had been driven to madness by the collapse of civilisation. The President's security guards would be nervous of someone just charging out of the woods – he might have a gun or bomb or anything.

Three men dressed in army fatigues climbed down from the rear carriage and advanced cautiously, rifles trained on him. As they drew closer Jimmy saw that they weren't actually that much older than him – surely no more than sixteen. Two had cropped hair. The third boy, who seemed to be in charge, had a Mohican.

'Who are you?' Mohican snapped. 'What do you want?'

'This is the President's train?' Jimmy asked.

'Sure.'

One of the crop-heads began to search him.

'I heard he was setting up some new settlement. Thought I might be able to help.'

'You? How?'

'I'll tell him that.'

Mohican snorted. He nodded to his comrades. 'Bring him.'

They took a rough hold of him and guided him to the back carriage. Mohican went aboard first. Inside Jimmy saw that about half of the seats were occupied by similarly dressed soldiers – and none of them appeared to be any older than the boys accompanying him. Some were considerably younger. But they were all carrying guns.

Jimmy was led through two similar carriages. As they entered the next one, the train began to move.

Mohican motioned to an empty seat.

'Wait here,' he snapped before continuing on. Jimmy sat. The two other guards remained by the door behind him. The seats in this carriage were also half occupied, again by boys of roughly his age — but none of them were wearing army fatigues, and they all looked every bit as nervous as he was.

Jimmy nodded at the boy on the other side of the aisle from him. The boy nodded back. There was something vaguely familiar about him.

'I know you,' said Jimmy.

'No talking,' said one of the guards.

The boy opposite shrugged. He looked out of the window. Even sitting down, Jimmy could see that he was quite small, but broad shouldered and tough looking. 'I *definitely* know you,' Jimmy persisted.

'Quiet,' said the guard.

Jimmy glanced back at him. 'Sorry,' he said.

'That means no talking!'

'OK,' said Jimmy. 'Get the message.'

The guard moved his rifle from one shoulder to the other.

Jimmy made a zipping motion across his mouth. 'Not a peep,' he said.

The guard took a step forward. His comrade put a restraining hand on his arm. The first guard glared across, then jabbed a warning finger at Jimmy. 'Later,' he said.

Jimmy shrugged. He knew he was being thick. But

he tended to say stupid things when he was nervous or confused. He didn't understand what was going on here. He was on the President's train. But it didn't feel right. He didn't like these boys with guns. He didn't like being manhandled. He didn't like being told to be quiet. And he didn't like the boy in the opposite seat. Their eyes met. The boy raised his hands and made a kind of rectangle shape, pointing at Jimmy. He raised one of his fingers, then moved it down quickly. As he did he made a clicking sound. And smirked.

Claire's camera! The *thief*!

Without even thinking about it, Jimmy threw himself across the aisle and upon the boy. He grabbed him by the throat and received a punch in the mouth for his trouble. They wrestled each other on to the carriage floor.

The guards thundered down the aisle screaming at them to stop just as Jimmy managed to get on top and smash his fist into the boy's nose. 'You stole her camera you little mugger!' Jimmy yelled. He aimed another punch. The boy rolled his head to one side, avoiding contact.

Jimmy was grabbed from behind and dragged off.

Blood rolled down the boy's face. 'It was only a camera!' he shouted. 'There's thousands of them lying around!'

'Because of you she's—'

He never finished saying it. Mohican had suddenly reappeared and grabbed him by the throat. He walked

Jimmy backwards until he was pressed hard against the divider between the seats.

'Cut it out – *now*!' Mohican snapped.

Despite the fact that he could hardly breathe, Jimmy strained against him. 'He stole . . .' he whispered, his eyes bulging. 'He . . .'

'NOW!'

Jimmy, lacking oxygen, finally nodded.

Mohican relaxed his grip. 'Right. Now follow me, you little creep. The President wants to see you.'

Mohican let go of him, turned and marched away along the aisle. Jimmy glared across at his enemy, sitting defenceless once again. Renew the attack or meet the President of the United States?

He had no choice, really.

The President Himself

Jimmy was led towards the front of the train. Although every carriage still had its share of armed men, a lot of space was also taken up with boxes of supplies. It reminded him of the *Titanic* – its corridors were often crammed with goods salvaged from abandoned warehouses or bartered at one of the settlements.

Mohican stopped before entering the next carriage and gave Jimmy a hard look. 'It's the President,' he snapped, 'tidy yourself up. Be respectful.'

Jimmy was on the verge of saying, 'He's not my President, I'm Irish,' but he thought better of it. If it meant getting into the Promised Land, then what harm could it do? He smoothed down his hair, straightened out his T-shirt, and rubbed as much of the grime and blood off his cheek as he could manage. When he'd finished Mohican gave him a quick check, shook his head, then turned and knocked lightly on the door. Unlike the other carriages, there were curtains hung behind the glass for privacy.

'Come,' said a voice from inside.

Mohican opened the door, and indicated for Jimmy to enter. Jimmy brushed through the curtains. Mohican stayed where he was, pulling the door closed after him. It was just Jimmy and . . .

Well, he wasn't quite sure at first. The carriage was gloomy, thanks to the curtains hanging on every window. Directly ahead of him was a desk, with a leather swivel chair facing away from him, so he couldn't see its occupant. A reading lamp threw a weak light on to the top of the desk, and he could see files of paper spread out and a man's hand busily writing.

Jimmy stood where he was, close to the door. He cleared his throat lightly.

If my mum could see this – just me and the President!

He suddenly felt quite emotional. He hadn't thought of his mum in such a long time. He had no idea if she was dead or alive.

'Name?'

The President still hadn't turned to face him.

'Jimmy. James. Jimmy Armstrong.'

He could hear a little quiver in his own voice.

'Jimmy Armstrong,' the President repeated. 'Where are you from, Jimmy?'

'Ahm . . . Ireland, I suppose.'

'You're a long way from home.'

'Yes, sir, Mr President.'

'How come?' The President continued to write.

'I . . . uhm . . . stowed away on a ship.'

'That was very . . . enterprising of you.'

'Not really, Mr . . . uhm, President. I, uh, did it by accident.'

A low chuckle came from the man in the chair, which now began to revolve towards him.

Jimmy gulped. *Just me and the . . .*

Jimmy had seen the President on TV. He was in his late forties, he was tall and thin. But *this* President was an old man. In fact, now that he looked at him properly, he was *the* old man, the old guy Jimmy had listened to on the makeshift stage in the bar back at Tucker's Hole. The old man who'd told a mesmerised audience *about* the President's train and how wonderful it was. Except, he didn't look so old any more – there was nothing decrepit or stooped about him. In fact, he positively glowed with health. But he was still definitely the old man from Tucker's Hole.

Jimmy just stared at him furiously. 'You are *not* the President.'

The old man clasped his hands in his lap. 'Yes, I am.'

'No you're not,' Jimmy snapped. 'I've seen him. He's twenty years younger than you. Thirty.'

'I'm not arguing with you, Jimmy.'

'Good. You'd lose.'

The old man laughed. 'You're not afraid of your own voice, are you Jimmy? Have you considered the fact that we are on a train full of soldiers, every one of them more than willing to put a bullet in your brain if I order them to?'

Jimmy bit his lip. He hadn't actually thought

about the consequences of opening his mouth. He rarely did.

'I thought not.' The old man nodded to himself. 'Well,' he continued, 'perhaps a little bit of anger is no bad thing. Shows you have spirit. Let me put it another way for you. I am not the President of the United States that you may remember. My name is Daniel Blackthorne, and before this great plague I was a senator representing the great state of Nebraska. I was in Washington when the plague came, and then the President disappeared – dead, as far as anyone knows – so power passed to the next in line, and then he died, and so it went, passing on down the line until it got to me. I am the last elected official in these United States. So yes, James Armstrong, as far as you are concerned, I *am* the President of the United States, and it's my job to rebuild them. That's what I'm doing.'

Jimmy had no reason to doubt what this Daniel Blackthorne was saying. But it didn't explain why he was riding around in a train with a bunch of kids with guns, or why he had appeared on that stage in the village pretending that he was a feeble old man.

So he asked him.

Blackthorne rose from his chair and came towards him. Jimmy fought the urge to take a step or twelve backwards. The President, now that he was right up close, towered over him. He looked down at Jimmy and clasped his shoulders. His gaze was intense.

'Jimmy, I go from settlement to settlement and I

pretend to be a passing traveller bringing news. But what I'm really trying to do is inspire people, get them thinking. America wasn't built by accountants and civil servants and people who run grooming parlours for dogs. It was built by heroes, it was built by adventurers who spat in the eyes of fear, who didn't know when to stop trying, who never considered giving up. And that's the problem, Jimmy, people have given up. They sit in these ramshackle villages moaning and whining and waiting to be rescued, and it's just not going to happen. I'm building something new, Jimmy, but I can't take everyone with me. I want people with imagination and ambition and vision, I want people prepared to take a chance. So I sow the seeds. I tell them about the President, I tell them about the train. And if they're brave enough and bright enough, they'll work out how to find me. People like you, son, kids like you who still have those kinds of guts.' He squeezed Jimmy's shoulders and smiled benevolently. 'So that's my pitch, son. I'm building these United States from the bottom up, and I need good men to help me. It'll be hard. It'll be dangerous. But by God, it'll be an adventure!'

It was an inspiring speech, delivered passionately.

It prompted a hundred jumbled thoughts.

But Jimmy didn't have time to think them all through.

All he was certain of was that he was being held prisoner on a train full of heavily-armed kids who were under the control of a nut who thought he was the President of the United States.

'So what do you say, Jimmy, are you with me?'

'Yes, sir, Mr President!'

Maggots

After a long, sleepless night – she would have tossed and turned, but her bandaged arm and IV drip prevented her from doing either – at the first hint of dawn light Claire finally rang the bell beside her bed and demanded of the bleary-eyed nurse who eventually arrived that Dr Hill come and release her from her purgatory. By the time he arrived, an hour later, Claire was *fuming*. She had already phoned her dad upstairs to find out *exactly why* she was being kept a virtual prisoner.

'Doesn't he know who I am?' she had demanded.

'I think he has a fair idea,' her father responded, and hung up.

She wasn't just fuming about being kept in the hospital wing when she was obviously completely fine. She was fuming because the *Titanic* had dropped anchor off its next port of call; passengers were shortly going to be dropped ashore, others picked up, and the usual medical and scavenging teams would do their jobs as well. She wanted to go with them. She wanted to search for Jimmy. Claire was *also* fuming because the nurse, in a misguided attempt to keep her nice and calm, had given her a copy of the *Titanic Times* to read. Ordinarily this might have worked – but the copy was two days old. Claire had immediately demanded that morning's edition – the *Times* was printed late at night, and delivered in the early hours so that passengers and crew could read it over breakfast – only to be told that there wasn't one. Claire had told her that there must be and had ordered her to go and get one. The nurse had given her a stern look and spun on her heel. She returned ten minutes later and announced with no little pleasure that there was no *Titanic Times* that morning, that it hadn't been printed and that no one had any idea when the next edition might appear.

At this point Dr Hill arrived. He endured a five-minute rant while examining Claire's charts. Then he endured another five minutes of it while he carefully unwrapped her bandages and examined her wound.

'This is ridiculous!' Claire complained. 'You can't keep me here.'

'Actually,' said Dr Hill, 'we have restraints and a nice straitjacket, so we can. We just choose not to. But I'd very much prefer it if you would stay in here – nice and quiet and stationary, so your arm has a chance to recover.'

Claire was having none of it. 'I'm fine. I need out of here. I need to go ashore.'

'No.'

'What do you mean *no*?'

'What I say.'

'But I'm better. Wasn't I able to walk all the way up to see Captain Smith last night?'

'Yes you were. But then you had to be brought back here on a stretcher.'

'Only because I'm all woozy because of the drugs *you* gave me!'

'No, Claire, you're all woozy because of the blood you've lost. You will stay here for another twenty-four hours, minimum. And then you'll only be allowed out if I see positive signs of improvement, the kind which only come with lying still and doing nothing and letting the maggots do their work.'

Claire's head jerked to one side. 'The *WHAT*?'

Dr Hill nodded down at the bandage, which he had now peeled away and set on a small stand beside her bed. It was alive with little, white, twisty-turny creatures about a centimetre long. Claire looked horrified.

'Oh, yes,' said Dr Hill, gloating at her discomfort. 'Maggots, of the green blowfly variety. We're a bit short of antibiotics Claire, and to tell you the truth these little beauties work one heck of a lot better. We breed them here on board. They eat all the dead tissue away – stops you getting infected.'

'But . . . but . . . but . . .'

'They're saving your life, Claire.'

'But – they're . . . *maggots* . . .'

'Yup – and now we need a fresh batch.' Dr Hill

turned and nodded at his nurse, who handed him the replacements already secured in a fresh bandage. He began to tape it into place. 'So Claire – rest, relax, and let them do their job.'

'But—'

'No buts.'

'Jimmy—'

'Rest.'

'I have to go ashore—'

'Relax.'

'I have to find out about the paper—'

'It can wait.'

'But what if the maggots get into my bloodstream, into my brain . . . ?'

'Claire, that hardly ever happens. It's been several days since anyone . . .'

Claire stared at him. Then she stared at the open bandage and the mass of maggots. Her eyes rolled back in her head, and then her head hit the pillow. She had fainted.

The nurse looked at Dr Hill. 'It . . . it doesn't *really* ever happen, does it . . . ?'

'No, of course not,' said Dr Hill. 'But she doesn't need to know that.'

He smiled briefly down at Claire before turning away. It was time to go ashore.

She slept for twelve hours. She didn't dream. There was no dramatic fever. When she opened her eyes and scanned the room her only hope was that Jimmy had somehow miraculously returned.

But there was only the sterile, empty room.

She did, at least, feel significantly better. The wooziness was gone. The IV had been removed while she slept and a small plaster covered where the needle had attached it to her good arm. Her wound boasted a new bandage, less bulky than the previous ones, which, she hoped, suggested that the maggots had satisfactorily completed their work. When the nurse came in with a cup of hot tea for her, Claire asked if she'd heard what had happened ashore, but she just shook her head. Twenty minutes later First Officer Jeffers appeared in the doorway. He smiled across and Claire allowed herself a brief moment of hope.

'Did you find . . . Jimmy?'

The smile faded. 'No, Claire, sorry. We searched, we talked to the locals, there was no sign of him. It was always a long shot.' He could see that Claire's lower lip was trembling. He sat on the edge of the bed. He thought for a moment about taking her hand, but decided against it. 'You didn't do anything wrong, Claire,' he said quietly. 'Remember that. And he's a survivor. He may not be with us, but he's probably still out there somewhere, causing trouble.'

That won half a smile from her.

'I know it's hard losing your boyfriend like that.'

Her eyes grew suddenly cool. 'He wasn't my boyfriend,' she snapped.

* ★ ★

Dr Hill finally gave her the all-clear to leave the hospital – but only on condition that it was under the supervision of her parents. When she called her father to tell him the good news he said they would be down in five minutes. Claire waited for them for the next hour. She phoned them three times, and on each occasion was told they'd be another five minutes. She held her temper in check. She knew what the problem was – her mother refused to go anywhere without her war paint on. Even Claire had rarely seen her natural face; it was almost always covered in thick make-up.

The nurse rolled a wheelchair in.

'I'm not getting into that,' said Claire.

'Yes you are.'

'Yes I am,' said Claire.

She wasn't going to do or say anything else that might jeopardise her freedom. She settled into the wheelchair.

Her mother finally swept into the hospital, followed by her exasperated-looking husband.

'Claire, darling! We came as quickly as we could! My sweet girl is coming home!'

Behind her, Mr Stanford rolled his eyes.

'Just . . . get . . . me . . . out of here!' Claire hissed through gritted teeth.

Dr Hill warned her for the third time that she would have to rest. Claire nodded.

'Claire, I know that nod.' He gave her a hard look. 'I mean it.'

'I know you mean it,' said Claire.

Mrs Stanford wiped at a tear. 'My little girl – in a wheelchair!'

'Mother,' said Claire, 'I'm *fine*.'

'I know dear, I know. You will walk again, I know it.'

Claire sighed and looked at her father. 'Please get me out of here!'

Mr Stanford waited for an approving nod from Dr Hill, then took hold of the handles and began to roll her forward. Mrs Stanford followed behind, dabbing her damp cheeks with a handkerchief.

Claire was pushed out of the hospital, along the corridor and into the elevator. As soon as the doors closed she pushed herself up and out of the chair.

'*Claire . . .*' her father began.

'She can walk!' her mother exclaimed.

'Dad, I'm *fine*.' Her father had pushed the button for their penthouse cabin on the sixteenth floor. Claire pressed the button for the sixth. The elevator stopped almost immediately and the doors opened.

'Claire – what on earth do you think you're doing?' her father asked.

Claire raised calming hands towards her parents. 'I'm going to *work*.' She stepped out into the corridor. As the doors began to close her mother clasped her hands in front of her. 'It's a miracle,' she whispered.

★ ★ ★

Ten minutes after discovering the offices of the *Titanic Times* both empty and locked, Claire tracked Ty down to the restaurant on the twelfth floor. He was happily working his way through a plate of doughnuts.

She stood behind him. 'Enjoying those…?'

Ty started to nod – but then he recognised the voice and his latest doughnut's happy trajectory towards his mouth stopped halfway there. He turned slowly. She looked furious.

'Ccc-ccclaire . . . how are you . . . ?' His lips were coated with sugar. 'I came – I came to see you . . . but you were . . . asleep . . .'

'Why has the *Titanic Times* not appeared?'

'We didn't—'

'Why is the office locked?'

'We thought—'

There was a terrible cold fury about her. 'FIND EVERYONE. GET THEM TO THE OFFICE IN THE NEXT TEN MINUTES OR TONIGHT YOU WILL SLEEP WITH THE FISHES.'

Ty's heart was beating wildly. He knew Claire had a temper. They all knew she had one. But he had never experienced it so intensely before. She glared at him for a very long five seconds – during which not a single word of explanation or apology managed to make its way from his brain to his mouth.

Then she pointed. 'GO!'

Ty looked at his doughnuts. He looked at Claire. He pushed the plate away, stood up and *ran*.

It was actually about thirty minutes before the editorial team, the IT guy, the delivery boys and girls and the idiot who just wandered around looking helpless were all assembled. They had entered the office in ones and twos, all of them looking sheepish. Nobody wanted to be first to speak. Claire sat staring at a switched off screen, acknowledging no one.

Eventually Ty plucked up the courage. 'Claire, I think we're all—'

'Quiet.'

Ty blew air out of his cheeks. Quietly.

Claire rose to her feet. She looked around the room. She made eye contact with every single one of them, and even those who had been staring at the ground somehow knew to raise their eyes when Claire's deadly gaze fell upon them.

'I am *shocked*,' said Claire.

It sat in the air.

'I am *horrified*.'

It sat in the air beside her shock.

'I await an explanation as to the non-appearance of the *Titanic Times*.'

'Well,' Ty began bravely, 'with Jimmy dead and you shot we thought . . .'

Ty stopped. He knew immediately that he had said something very, *very* wrong.

'Don't you *ever* say that again!' Claire towered over him as he sat at his own screen. 'Jimmy is *not* dead. He is alive. And he will find his way back to us. Do you understand?'

Ty nodded.

'Do all of you understand?'

Everyone nodded. Ty was still nodding.

Claire's icy gaze roved around the room like the searchlight at a prison camp from which nobody was brave enough to attempt an escape.

'Now I want you all to listen to me.'

As if they weren't. They were too scared not to.

'Jimmy made the *Times*. He turned it from a boring little news-sheet designed to keep lazy, fat passengers happy into what it is today – the paper of record. What we've been writing over these past few months – it's *history*. It's important. People need to know what's going on out there. How we set about surviving. They're scared. We've all lost friends and relatives. We give them hope. We show them that there is a way forward. It is our responsibility to make sure that the *Times* appears each and every day. It is a little bit of certainty in an uncertain world.' And then she surprised them by letting out a small chuckle. A *very* small chuckle – but it was something. 'I'm just thinking how Jimmy would've reacted to what I'm saying. He'd say, "Claire, get over yourself, it's only a bloody newspaper."' At least two of the other girls, and one of the boys, had tears in their eyes. 'He would say it, and he would mean it – but I'm telling you, if anyone messed with the paper he would fight tooth and nail to make sure it survived, and that's what we have to do. We don't give up the *Times* for any reason. If Jimmy's gone, it continues. If I'm gone, it continues. The *Times* is not Jimmy, it's not me, it's not even the *Titanic* – it's all of us. Do you understand?'

They all nodded.

Even those who hadn't a clue what she was talking about. Like the idiot who made the tea badly.

'OK, then let's not let it happen again. The *Times* appears every day without fail – starting tomorrow morning. That means getting to work *now*. OK?'

Claire had surprised herself with the passion of her speech, but it was working. They were smiling now, they were up for it. It was such a relief. She clapped her hands together. 'OK. Ty – you know the *Titanic's* lost half her power and we're heading for New York?'

'Uh, no . . .'

'Well neither does anyone else! Get on it!'

'Andy?' A skinny boy with freckles and glasses looked up eagerly. 'I want an article on Jimmy, his whole life story.'

'But I don't really know what—'

'Find out! That's your job!'

'Debs?' A pretty blond girl stood to attention. 'Talk to everyone who came aboard today, find out what happened in their settlement, how they ended up there, where they're going . . .'

It went on like that for another ten minutes – Claire firing out stories, giving photographers their assignments, discussing front-page designs, organising a schedule for printing the paper, making sure the delivery team knew their routes. She felt exhilarated to be back on the *Times*, but also, and suddenly, very, very tired. Her hands gripped the side of the desk where she was standing as her legs began to give way. She held herself up, aware of a sudden sweat breaking on her brow. She looked about her. Everyone was so busy, they hadn't noticed.

I *will not* faint. Not now.

She had just managed to re-enthuse them about the paper – if she fell on her face now they could just as easily give up again. She had to be strong. Claire took a deep breath, steadied herself, then told Ty she was going upstairs to talk to First Officer Jeffers. Ty was already on the phone talking to Jonas Jones about the problem with the engines, so he gave her the thumbs-up. She walked as steadily as she could to the office door and slipped out. She made it to the elevators, then up to the top deck and out into the fresh air before collapsing down on to one of the sun beds. She lay there, feeling impossibly weak, her arm aching. But at least it was cool up here, and after a few minutes she began to feel a little bit better. Dr Hill had ordered her to rest and now she would, for at least twenty minutes. Maybe thirty. But then she would get back to work. She had to. For the *Times*. For Jimmy. She closed her eyes. She was still thinking about the paper, not just tomorrow's, but the day after, and the day after that.

She was just beginning to pleasantly drift off into a light sleep when she heard footsteps coming along the deck. Lots of people took a stroll here in the evenings, it was usually so pleasant. But then she heard something vaguely familiar, a tune being hummed. In her dreamy state it took more than a few moments to pin it down.

But then she had it.

Her eyes flashed open.

The minister was coming straight towards her.

Fort Hope

Jimmy had visited many devastated areas on the *Titanic*'s journey up the eastern seaboard of the United States. He had witnessed horrific scenes, observed the pathetic state of the settlements forced to grow up away from the diseased cities, and had interviewed countless survivors. But it was perhaps only on the President's train, sitting with his nose pressed against the window as it travelled hundreds of miles across country, that he began to truly appreciate the massive scale of the disaster that had befallen mankind. For hours at a time nothing moved on the landscape. Civilisation was nothing more than an overgrown memory now – although if you believed President Blackthorne, it was still possible to rebuild it.

Only thing was, Jimmy wasn't quite sure if he was buying what the President was selling.

As he stared out at the passing countryside Jimmy tried to imagine what Claire would have made of Mr Blackthorne. She would probably have drawn up two lists – one of positive things in the President's favour; the other negative.

Jimmy tried it.

IN FAVOUR
1. At least he's trying to do something.
2. Maybe his story's true – if he was a senator, then power could well have passed to him.
3. He has already convinced lots of people.
4. He has his own train.

AGAINST
1. He's trying to do something – but is kind of reluctant to say exactly what.
2. No proof he was a senator. He could have been a plumber or a baker.
3. The only people he seems to have recruited are kids. And he's given them guns.
4. He might have been a train driver.

There were other points to be made, but Jimmy couldn't carry them all in his head the way Claire would. He thought that if there was a trial to decide whether he really was the President and only had the best interests of humanity at heart, then the jury would have been split down the middle. All Jimmy could really add to the argument was that he was usually pretty good at reading people, and meeting Blackthorne had left him feeling uneasy. But then again – you could be uneasy with some people, and it didn't mean they were necessarily bad. He'd felt a bit like that with his old headmaster, Mr McCartney – yet he'd undoubtedly run a pretty good school.

Jimmy was still gazing out of the window when the Camera Thief plopped down into the seat opposite. He was chomping on a thick sandwich. When he'd swallowed about half of what was in his mouth he waved it at Jimmy. 'You should get one of these,' he said, spraying crumbs across the way, 'they're great. Just down the corridor and ask—'

'I'm not hungry,' said Jimmy.

Actually, he was *starving*. But he was determined not to pay any attention to the Camera Thief.

The Camera Thief shrugged. He took another bite. 'So you've been to see President Whatisface? Whaddya reckon?'

Jimmy fixed him with his best steely look. 'I reckon you should keep your pie-hole closed and stop spitting bread at me.'

The Camera Thief nodded. He continued chewing, now with his mouth closed.

'Maybe we got off on the wrong foot,' he said.

'Maybe you killed my friend,' Jimmy shot back.

'I didn't kill anyone.'

'Right.'

The Camera Thief stood up. 'Please yourself.'

He walked off down the aisle. Jimmy returned his attention to the countryside.

The steady rhythm of the train induced sleep. He wasn't sure how long he was out for, but he woke to the sound of brakes that needed oiling and the train slowing to a halt. It was dark. Jimmy pressed his eyes to the glass, but could see nothing.

'Everyone off! Everyone off!'

The voice came from outside. Camera Thief, who had evidently been sleeping in the seat opposite, stretched before moving to the carriage door. Jimmy followed him. They stepped down on to a small wooden platform along with the soldiers and dozens of other rather dazed-looking kids.

He's been picking them up all along the line.

Mohican came marching down the platform, barking at them to form into lines three abreast. He said they had a long walk in front of them. Jimmy asked where they were going.

'Fort Hope!' Mohican snapped out. Then he paused, grabbed a handful of Jimmy's shirt and pulled him close. 'And don't speak until you're spoken to,' he snarled.

Jimmy just stared at him. Mohican's eyeballs bore into his for at least five seconds before he abruptly let him go. Jimmy fell back. Mohican turned and shouted down the line. 'All right! Let's move out!'

They all bustled forward, dragging Jimmy along with them. Mohican was at their head. He led them along the platform, down a flight of steps and out on to a road littered with abandoned vehicles, his armed 'soldiers' marching along on either side – either to guide them; or to prevent them from escaping.

The train station had evidently been a small country halt, because very soon the sidewalk on either side disappeared and the road narrowed significantly until they were marching along between dark hedgerows.

After about ten minutes they heard a car engine behind them. Mohican ordered them to the side of the road as a long, slick, black limousine sped past. Jimmy caught the briefest glimpse of President Blackthorne in the back. Mohican and the other soldiers stood to attention and saluted as he passed. Camera Thief, who had slotted into the small troop beside Jimmy, saluted as well, but out of the side of his mouth he whispered: 'Always the same – the rich travel in style and we're left out here, cold and hungry.'

'Shhhh,' said someone on his other side.

'At least it's not raining,' said Camera Thief.

Naturally enough and within five minutes, thunder rolled across the sky, and very soon after, torrential rain began to pound down.

'Nice work, Rain Man,' somebody spat angrily from behind.

It was a nickname that stuck.

Jimmy was well used to the rain at home in Ireland – it rained there virtually every day. And he'd thought he knew what a heavy downpour was, but this was something different. It was harder, thicker and, somehow, wetter. It came down like bullets. There was no question of taking shelter. Mohican led them on without slackening the pace. Within a couple of minutes they were all absolutely drenched, and shivering, and miserable.

This Promised Land had better be bloody good.

The bedraggled troop had been marching for nearly an hour when they first became aware of a growing brightness low down on the horizon ahead of them, and they were soon nudging each other and speculating on what it might represent.

'It's a city, I'll bet,' one of them said.

'You've got nothing to bet with,' another answered.

'Fort Hope, that's where he said we were going,' said one.

'Maybe Fort Hope's a city, but I never heard of it.'

'I've been watching the road signs,' said Rain Man, 'and none say there's a city near here.'

'Where are we then, Rain Man?' someone asked.

'East of somewhere,' said Rain Man, 'and north of nowhere.'

Muttered curses came in response. Jimmy just wanted to poke him in the eye. Rain Man thought he was a wise guy. He didn't like him *at all*. If Claire had been there, she might have said of Jimmy and Rain Man that they were like mirror images of each other. But she wasn't there, and the thought would never have struck Jimmy in a million years.

The rain finally began to ease off. Jimmy was exhausted and hungry. He marched with his eyes half closed, his feet moving automatically while his mind drifted. He allowed himself to fantasise pleasantly about what lay ahead, that this Fort Hope with its brightly lit streets would welcome him, give him a nice apartment with hot water, a fridge full of fresh food and hot, sweet food. It would have a big Plasma-screen television which played new shows, not like the television on the *Titanic* which only showed reruns. There might even be a phone. He could call home to Belfast and finally discover that the plague had bypassed Ireland completely, that his mum and dad and Granda and the rest of his extended family were all alive and well. They would tell him how much they missed him and he would do the same, he would tell them that the *Titanic* was bringing him home and to make sure his room was ready and his school uniform was pressed, because he was going right back there. This time he wouldn't play truant, he would do exactly what the headmaster, Mr McCartney, told him to do. He would even try and resist punching his occasional friend Gary, who had gotten him thrown off the original school tour of the *Titanic* and thus, arguably, had started off this whole mad adventure.

The road descended into an area where the trees stood so thick and tall around them that the glow from Fort Hope was extinguished, leaving them to march along in an even more intense darkness than before. The road continued to lead them down for another ten minutes before levelling out for a short distance. Then it began to climb steeply, which was

111

the last thing their tired legs needed.

They missed the *glow*. It had lifted their spirits. You could almost feel a weight settling on their sodden shoulders as they trudged uphill. Jimmy, though, had learned a thing or two about leading a team in his short time on the *Times*. These guys and girls he was marching with, he decided were no different than the rag-tag group of lost souls he'd encountered onboard – scared of what lay ahead, but probably brave enough if they got the right encouragement. (With the exception of Rain Man, of course, who remained his Mortal Enemy.)

'Won't be long now,' said Jimmy, 'then I bet there's hot dogs.'

'Yeah!' said someone.

'How'd you know?' someone called.

'I can smell them.'

Urgent mutterings and sniffings came from the troop.

'I can smell 'em too,' someone called out.

'And pizza!'

'There'll be hot baths,' someone called.

'*Playstation 5!*' laughed another.

'Hot dogs, pizza and *Playstation 5* all together in the bath!' one shouted.

Laughter rolled through the troop.

'Probably get electrocuted,' said Rain Man.

'Shut up, Rain Man,' said someone, and they laughed again.

'*Quiet back there!*' It was Mohican, from the front. 'It's not safe out here – keep your voices *down*!'

They fell silent, very quickly. Why wasn't it safe? They had *guns*. What was there to be scared of? They all had these same thoughts. They moved closer together as they marched, peering fearfully into the night.

The trees finally began to thin out and the glow returned, this time much more intensely, growing brighter until they finally reached the brow of the hill. Without being ordered to they came to a natural halt, looking at the vista below.

Jimmy had seen many ramshackle settlements, choking on wood smoke and poisoned by disease and bad drainage, while reporting for the *Times* – but this was quite the opposite. He was looking down the hill and across a flat plain on which a settlement perhaps the size of twenty football pitches joined together had been built. Long wooden huts were laid out in a perfectly symmetrical pattern, perhaps as many as fifty of them, surrounding a pentagonal-shaped group of larger buildings. There were open parks marked out for sports on every side. The whole, massive area was surrounded by a high wire fence and guarded by watchtowers, set into it at intervals of perhaps twenty metres, from which intensely bright spotlights swept back and forth. It was *really* impressive. Jimmy could sense the excitement around him. The group's fatigue and misery were instantly forgotten as they surged forward, breaking into a jog.

Mohican led the way, pointing ahead. 'Welcome to Fort Hope!' he cried.

Jimmy knew he was grinning as widely as everyone else; his legs definitely felt lighter, his head was now clear. Fort Hope – the Promised Land! Yet . . . yet . . . as they drew closer and its massive gates began to swing out, and he saw the guns bristling on the watchtowers and poking out of the wire fence, he couldn't help thinking that it was not only supremely well equipped to keep people out – but also to keep them in.

The Minister

Claire lay frozen as the minister bore down on her. She could not scream, she could not even make a sound. The shock was total. The man who had shot her, who had quite possibly killed Jimmy, was here on the *Titanic, here* in front of her, *here* almost right on top of her . . .

. . . and then he passed by. If he even noticed her, he gave no indication; there was just that humming, the slow solid footsteps on the deck, his eyes staring straight ahead under that wide-brimmed hat. Claire hardly dared breathe. Her eyes followed him as he continued along the deck towards the doors at the far end. She put her hand to her chest, trying to still her racing heart.

What if he turns back?

He can't fail to see me, the second time.

But he stepped inside, was visible for a few moments through the glass, then disappeared from view.

Claire counted to thirty. Then sixty. She got up from the sun bed and cautiously approached the doors. She peered into the area in front of the elevators, and along the corridors leading away. No sign of him. She pushed the elevator button.

What if they open and he's standing there?

I haven't the strength to fight him off.

She glanced behind her. There was a small, red, glass box attached to the wall – fire alarm. If she smashed that then everyone would come running and he wouldn't have the chance to . . . she stepped back as the elevator doors opened.

Empty.

Claire jumped in, pushed the button, and prayed that he wouldn't suddenly appear and trap her inside before the doors closed. She went down one level then hurried along to the bridge. When she peered through the door she saw Captain Smith and First Engineer Jonas Jones bent over a computer screen, looking tense. She scanned the rest of the room for First Officer Jeffers. He was easier to talk to, he would understand, he would do something. But there was no sign of him. She asked one of the passing crewmen where he was, her voice high, quivering – part fear, part adrenaline.

'He's off duty, love,' said the crewman.

Claire nodded. 'Don't call me love,' she said.

'All right, darling,' said the crewman. Ordinarily she would have laughed it off – or reported him, depending on her mood – but she just stared at him. 'You all right, love? You look a bit pale?'

'Fine.' She turned away. Jeffers' quarters were six levels below.

Keep calm. The minister is one man. This is *your* ship. She started walking. A cold sweat plastered her blouse to her back. Her arm ached more than it had since she'd returned to the ship. When she reached the elevators her heart skipped again as the door opened and a man stepped out, but it wasn't him, it was one of the chefs going off shift. The *Titanic* was huge and she knew that the chances of running into him again so quickly were slim, but still she jumped at every movement around her, every sound. She made sure to stay in the interior of the ship. She knew if she ventured out on to deck he might simply step out of the shadows, pick her up and throw her overboard.

When she eventually reached Jeffers' quarters she knocked lightly on his door. She would have hammered on it, but what if that drew the attention of the minister and he came thundering down the corridor and killed her before Jeffers could answer?

She knocked again. After what seemed like an eternity Jeffers opened the door, his eyes bleary and his hair sticking up at a mad angle. He tutted the moment he saw who it was.

'Claire, what the——?'

Claire threw herself forward, pushing the door fully open and thrusting past him right into his cabin.

Jeffers' mouth dropped open in surprise. But he recovered quickly. 'Claire! I'm tired, I haven't time for your . . .' He stopped. His eyes had cleared now, and he could see the horror etched on her face; her bottom

lip was quivering, her eyes were wide with fear. 'Claire
– what is it?'

'He's here!'

He moved towards her. 'Who is, Claire?' He put
his hand on her shoulders and bent slightly so that
she was looking straight into his face. She collapsed
against him and burst into tears. Words came out in a
torrent, but they were incoherent, jumbled half-
sentences. 'Claire! Claire, shhhhh . . . just slow down –
I can't . . .'

He led her across the cabin and eased her on to
the side of his bed. 'It's OK,' he said gently, 'you're
safe now.'

'But . . . he's . . . out . . .' She squeezed her words
out between snorts and wheezes and cries. 'What . . .
if . . . he . . .'

'Shhhhhh. Breathe. Deeper. That's it . . .'

Slowly, slowly, she regained control of herself. He
got her a Coke from the mini bar. 'I'm sorry . . .
sorry . . . it's just . . .'

'Tell me.'

She told him. She tried to remember Scoop's
journalistic training. She kept it as simple and succinct
as she could. When she was finished she apologised
again for getting into such a state.

'It's fine.' He stood up. He rubbed at his jaw. 'I know
who you're talking about,' he said. 'He came on board
at Cooper's Creek, the last stop. In fact, I interviewed
him. His name's . . . his name's Calvin something . . .

Cleaver, I think. Some kind of Presbyterian minister. Said he got stuck at a church convention in New Orleans when the plague broke out, been trying to make his way back to his congregation in New York ever since.'

'He's a murderer.'

'Claire – are you absolutely sure?'

'One hundred per cent.'

'Because that type of minister, they all wear those outfits, the big hats, you could easily have mistaken him for someone—'

'It's him. He's not a minister, he couldn't be.'

'And according to what you've told me, you only ever saw him at a distance.'

'It's *him*! You have to arrest him!'

Jeffers shook his head. 'No, Claire. At least, not yet. I'm going to have a little chat with him.'

'But—'

'Claire, you're perfectly safe. He didn't approach you up top because he didn't recognise you. If it *was* him in the woods then the chances are he didn't get a proper look at you. And besides he would have no reason to suspect either that you're alive, or alive and onboard this ship.'

Claire shook her head incredulously. 'But he could find out! He could talk to someone! He'll come looking for me! You need to lock him up, you need to . . . you need . . . !'

There was no convincing him. And, deep down,

Claire knew he was right. There were ways to do things. She would be perfectly safe. Or reasonably so.

Now that she had a job with the *Times* and felt pretty grown up, Claire had stopped living in her parents' suite – with their approval, because she drove them to distraction. So they were quite surprised when she arrived back at their cabins in the company of First Officer Jeffers and informed them that she was going to spend the night.

Mr Stanford, who was wearing a scarlet dressing gown and smoking a cigar, immediately jumped to the usual conclusion. 'What has she done now, Mr Jeffers?'

Claire sat quietly while the first officer explained. Mrs Stanford, listening from the bedroom, emerged towards the end and gently put a comforting arm around her daughter. Claire would normally have shrugged it off – but this time she allowed it to stay in place. It was actually quite comforting.

'Why don't I make you a nice cup of hot chocolate?' her mother asked.

Claire managed a smile. 'Mother, you've never made hot chocolate in your life.'

'Well, I can order one from room service. It's the same thing, isn't it?'

Her father stubbed out his cigar in an ashtray and turned back to Jeffers. 'You've done the right thing, Mr Jeffers. But if there's the slightest proof that this might be the man who shot my daughter, then by God we'll put him overboard, won't we?'

'Yes, sir. Absolutely.'

Claire lay in her room, but insisted that the door was left open. Hot chocolate was duly brought and consumed. She tried to sleep, but couldn't. When, after an hour, she heard Jeffers' voice at the main door she sprang from her bed and hurried into the lounge. He was just removing his cap and accepting a tumbler of whisky from her father.

'Well?' Claire immediately demanded. 'Is he behind bars?'

Jeffers took a sip of his drink before answering. 'No, Claire, he's not.'

She exploded. 'You believe HIM before you believe ME?'

Jeffers raised his hands. '*Listen* to me, Claire. Please.' Claire took a deep breath. 'OK. So, I found him in the restaurant. Reverend Cleaver. He seems like a perfectly nice man—'

'He's—'

'Quiet, Claire!' Her father waved an admonishing finger. 'Let Mr Jeffers speak.'

Claire bit down on her lip. Her cheeks were *burning*.

Jeffers nodded at Mr Stanford before continuing. 'As I was saying, he seems very nice and quiet. But he was truly shocked by what I told him. And he sends his apologies for shooting you.'

'Good God!' This time it was Mr Stanford who exploded. 'He actually admitted—'

'Shhhh, dear.' Mrs Stanford put a calming hand on her husband's arm. 'Let Mr Jeffers speak.'

The first officer nodded gratefully. 'He didn't deny it at all,' he continued. 'He told me he was passing through the woods east of Tucker's Hole when he stumbled across a young man lying on the track who seemed to be injured – except when he went to help him the man pulled a gun and tried to rob him. There was a struggle, the gun went off and unfortunately the young man was shot. Revered Cleaver was absolutely distraught at this, and also terrified – he tried to save the robber's life – kiss of life, heart massage – but it was no use . . . Then when he heard what he now knows must have been you and Jimmy in the bushes, he was convinced you were part of this man's gang and that you'd take revenge – so he grabbed the gun again and fired blindly into the trees before running off. He had no idea that he had shot anyone, he was just trying to frighten you off. He was so scared that he bypassed Tucker's Hole completely, just kept going until he managed to pick up a lift on the far side of the woods. It took him as far as Cooper's Creek. And that's how he got to us. He was very upset, Claire. He wants to know if he can come and see you to apologise personally.'

All eyes turned on Claire.

'That's . . . *not* how it was . . .'

'Are you absolutely sure, Claire?' her father asked.

'He's a minister, for goodness' sake, why would he want to shoot you?'

'Yes, of course I'm sure . . .'

But the truth was that there *was* a slight hint of a doubt creeping in. Since she'd become a journalist she'd learned that you could look at a story you thought was one hundred per cent true from a different angle and suddenly it didn't make any sense at all. And it was complicated by the fact that her memory of the events in the forest was somewhat hazy – she *had* been shot after all, she'd lost a lot of blood. She rubbed at her brow.

'It *was* him . . . He's a murderer . . .'

She wasn't even convincing herself now. She desperately tried to remind herself of the detail of it. Hearing the gunshot in the woods with Jimmy, sneaking up, seeing the minister going through the man's pockets . . . Jimmy accidentally making the noise . . . the minister looking spooked . . . raising his gun . . . coming towards them . . . they'd started running . . . She sighed. He *could* be telling the truth. They had, quite naturally, run before he had the chance to shoot them – but the minister might just as easily have been the victim of an attempted robbery. He might not have been going through the dead man's pockets, he might actually have been trying to save him and, yes, if you'd just killed someone by accident, of course you'd be nervous, of course you'd fire at the first noise you heard. And he must have run off instead of pursuing them, otherwise he would surely have found her and killed her?

Claire sat down heavily on a leather sofa. 'Oh, I don't know any more!' she wailed.

Her mother raised her eyebrows at her husband. 'Presbyterian ministers,' she observed, rather haughtily, 'are not known for their shooting ability. Perhaps we should have him for dinner.'

Mr Stanford rubbed his stomach. 'You keep me so well fed, darling, I'm not sure if I could actually eat a Presbyterian minister!'

Both of them exploded into laughter. Claire stared at them, aghast. Thankfully, Jeffers didn't laugh either. Sensing that she was about to scream something at them he neatly stepped in with, 'Claire, Reverend Cleaver is waiting outside. He really does want to apologise to you.'

Claire shook her head violently. 'No. Please. Tell him I'm asleep. Too tired. I just couldn't, Mr Jeffers. What if he really did shoot me? What if he really did kill Jimmy? I just *don't know*. But I don't want to meet him, I don't want to shake his hand, I don't want him to apologise. Just tell him to go away, please?'

Mr Jeffers nodded. 'It's done,' he said. 'Get some rest.'

Jeffers turned to the door. Claire slipped into her room without a further glance at her parents. Partly because she was mad at them, but mostly because she didn't want the minister to be standing there when Jeffers opened the door.

She tossed and turned for ages. She kept replaying the events in the woods. After a while her mother came into the room with another hot chocolate and apologised for being insensitive earlier – she had just been so relieved that the minister had turned out to be innocent and her beautiful daughter was safe.

Claire sipped her drink, and said nothing. When her mother got up to go, Claire again insisted that she leave the bedroom door open, and the light on in the lounge.

'Of course, darling,' said her mother, and kissed her brow.

Some time after midnight she finally drifted off to sleep. She was dreaming about her ponies when something disturbed her. She opened her eyes. Her room was dark, save for little moonlight coming in through the porthole. But the lounge was also dark – although she had demanded that the light be left on.

Movement.

There was something in the doorway.

Someone!

And then, drifting towards her, a very soft, melodic humming.

'Give me oil in my lamp . . .'

Louder, closer, a black figure moving . . .

Claire screamed and screamed and screamed and . . .

Training

At exactly five a.m., and still dark, the barracks door was smashed open and Mohican strode in screaming: 'Out of your pits, you lazy bunch of good-for-nothing losers!'

He also had a small air horn in his hand, which he blasted three times. This is a contraption which sounds loud *outside*; inside it was deafening. But it certainly had an effect – everyone was instantly awake. What it didn't create was any kind of order – they sprang from their beds and began to run about like headless chickens, panic stricken, disorientated, convinced they were under some kind of attack. In short: uproar.

The horn blasted again, but this time, with the sleep driven from them, they were more inclined to notice Mohican standing calmly in their midst. He dominated everything. Beside him, even the biggest and strongest of them felt small and weak.

'All right, you have ten minutes to get showered, into your uniforms and eat breakfast! Today, ladies and gentlemen, you become United States Marines!'

He strode out, leaving them all stunned – for about

three seconds. Then there was a mad scramble to get dressed and out and fed. That is, apart from Jimmy. And Rain Man.

Jimmy said (but not to Rain Man) – 'Do you think you can order breakfast in bed?'

Rain Man said (but not to Jimmy) – 'I'll have my eggs sunny-side up, wholemeal toast and a glass of milk fresh from a fat cow.'

The rest of them were now bolting out of the door. Jimmy lay back on his bed. Rain Man lay back on his.

'United States Marines,' said Jimmy (although not to Rain Man). 'I'm not even American.'

'I wonder if they do room service?' Rain Man asked (although not of Jimmy).

They had been well fed on arrival at Fort Hope, in what Mohican called the mess hall. Then they'd been shown to this barracks hut, which had been enticingly warm; the long rows of bunk beds were fresh and comfortable and smelled of new pine. He had told them to get a good night's sleep because they'd be up quite early for some light training. It was all very welcoming, like arriving at a summer camp (except, obviously, it was cold and damp outside). Jimmy had fallen asleep at once, his immediate doubts assuaged. Now, with bright sunshine steaming through the open door, feeling refreshed and revitalised, Jimmy stretched and yawned and turned over for another sleep.

He had been lying there for perhaps ten minutes, and was just slipping into a nice hazy dream state, when his feet were grabbed and he was dragged off the bed. The back of his head hit the floor with a loud thump; he let out a shout, but neither one of the young soldiers who'd taken hold of him paid any attention. He was pulled across the floor, down four steps – banging his head again on each one – then thrown down into the mud. He was wearing only his boxer shorts, which had seen better days. He heard two groans of pain – one was his own, and the other came from Rain Man, lying in a heap beside him.

Dazed and hurting, Jimmy blinked up. Mohican was standing over them. The rest of the troop was now spilling out of the mess hall and milling nervously outside the barracks.

'I gave you an *order!*' Mohican screamed, his face flushed with anger.

'I thought it was like . . . a *request . . .*' Jimmy mumbled.

Mohican's lips curled up in disgust. He drew his black army boot back to kick him. Jimmy tensed as he swung it forward – and then stopped it just short of impact. He lowered his foot, snarled down at Jimmy and turned to address the anxious onlookers.

'This is your first day at Fort Hope. I want you to remember where you are! The name is HOPE! H – O – P – E! The world as you know it is no more! The only H – O – P – E for any of us is to stick together, to learn discipline, to train hard so that we can serve the President and rebuild this great country of ours! Behaviour like *this* will not be tolerated! You are all now part of a team! If one member of that team disobeys orders, then the whole team gets punished! That means no lunch today for any of you!' A moan rolled through the troop. Mohican returned his attention to Jimmy and Rain Man. 'Get up and get changed! The mess hall is now closed!'

Mohican strode away.

Jimmy and Rain Man climbed somewhat painfully to their feet, well aware that they were being scrutinised with obvious contempt by their comrades.

'Do you think,' Rain Man said quietly (although not to Jimmy) 'that that means there's no room service?'

Mohican's concept of 'light training' was light years away from everyone else's. Of course, in every group there are going to be natural athletes – *jocks* – but even *they* were in a state of shock. It was torture. They started with running around the perimeter of the fort, four laps, all under the gaze (and guns) of the guards in the watchtowers. Then there were press-ups and squats and step exercises. After an hour of this the gates were opened and they were marched out to the woods, where they were forced to run up and down the steep hill they'd painfully ascended the night before. Worst of all, when they got back to base, they had to sit and watch while hundreds of soldiers queued up and ate lunch in the mess hall.

Jimmy and Rain Man could feel eyes burning into

their backs as they sat alone. They spoke, but not to each other.

'I didn't sign up for this,' said Rain Man. 'In fact, I didn't sign up at all.'

'I have no interest in becoming a Marine,' said Jimmy. 'I wonder who you complain to?'

'They can't just not feed us,' said Rain Man.

'They can't treat us like dogs,' said Jimmy. He was angry and hungry. 'Who does Mohican think he is? Big bloody bully.'

'I'll bet the President doesn't know what he's like,' said Rain Man. 'I bet he'd sort him out.'

'That's it,' said Jimmy, getting to his feet. 'I've had enough of this crap, I'm taking it to the top.'

He pushed his way out of the mess hall and began to march away across the yard.

'Give 'em hell,' Rain Man called out, while remaining exactly where he was.

Jimmy was seething. And when he was like that he didn't always wait for his brain to get into gear before he sprang into action. He'd sometimes been like this on the *Titanic*, where, mostly, he'd gotten away with it. One thing about being the boss of something, the way Jimmy felt he was boss of the *Times*, is that you get used to giving orders, not taking them. Now he was being ordered about like he was a little kid and *he wasn't going to take it any more*. He was Jimmy Armstrong, editor of the *Titanic Times*, and he had a lot to offer that didn't involve press-ups and running around in circles. Or rectangles.

He didn't know exactly where the President was, but he headed for the group of larger buildings and hoped it would become obvious once he got there. But they all looked pretty much the same — all set in a pentagon shape around a central yard. A kid who looked about four years younger than Jimmy but in full army uniform and with a pistol in a holster on his belt, was just hurrying across the yard.

'Hey, kid,' said Jimmy, 'where's the President?'

'In the White House.'

'No you idiot — where's *our* President?'

'In *our* White House, you idiot.'

The boy soldier pointed, and true enough, there was a wooden hut, slightly larger than the others, painted with a bright white gloss.

'All right, smart arse,' Jimmy snapped back, already marching towards it.

There were two armed guards outside, standing on either side of the door and at the top of a short flight of steps. As Jimmy hurried up and then tried to go between them, they quickly closed ranks.

'What the hell do you want?' one asked.

'I'm here to see the President.'

'You have an appointment?'

'No — but he'll see me.'

'How'd you know that, then?'

'I just — just tell him Jimmy Armstrong wants to see

him *right now*.' Even as he said it, Jimmy realised how stupid it sounded. But it was already out. He added a belated, 'Please.'

The guards smirked at each other. One bowed his head a little. 'Wait here, *please*.'

He went inside. The other guard continued to smirk at him. Jimmy wiped his boots on the steps, trying to remove at least some of the thickly-caked mud on them. A few moments later the first guard reappeared. 'This way, sir,' he said meekly, holding the door open and waving his arm in an exaggerated fashion to indicate that he should enter. Jimmy was fast running out of the steam that had propelled him here. Nevertheless, there was no turning back. He took a deep breath and stepped into the White House.

There was a nice, bright, outer office, with half a dozen young women sitting at computer terminals. One stood up and indicated for him to follow. She led him to a door at the end of a short corridor with another guard standing outside it. He frisked Jimmy for weapons, nodded at the young woman and she tapped lightly on the door.

'Mr President – Private Armstrong to see you, sir.'

It was the first time he'd been called that, and it caused him to swallow.

The young woman opened the door and motioned him in.

The President's office could not have been more different than the reception area. Just like it had been on the train, curtains were firmly closed over the windows, and the reading light on the desk was barely sufficient to dispel the resultant gloom. This time the President was facing him, sitting behind a desk with his hands clasped on top of it.

He looked at Jimmy, without smiling. 'Private Armstrong?'

Jimmy thought he had better get it all out before his nerve deserted him completely.

Right. Here goes.

'Mr President – I'm sorry to trouble you . . . but . . . look – the thing is, I never intended to be part of any . . . you know, *army*. That's not what I'm about . . . I'm more sort of . . . you know – freewheeling . . . a bit of a free spirit – do you know what I mean?'

What on earth are you talking about? Shut up now!

But he couldn't stop himself.

'The thing is, I thought I was coming to your new . . . city . . . and I want to contribute and all, except . . . not really like this. I'm no soldier, I'm a newspaper man . . . you probably don't think I'm old enough – but I've been editing a daily newspaper on the *Titanic* for ages so I thought I could do something similar here – you know, start a newspaper? It's important that a record's kept . . . I mean, you're like the President of the United States – this is history – one day people will want to know how you started to rebuild . . .'

The President held his hand up to stop him.

Jimmy chewed on a lip.

'What do you mean, the *Titanic*?'

Jimmy hesitated. He hadn't previously mentioned his old home. Now it had just slipped out. 'Yes – the *Titanic* . . . I was on it, for a while.'

'The new *Titanic*? The one they launched just a few months ago?'

'Yeah . . .'

'She's in full working order, captain and crew?'

'Yes, sir.'

'Where is she now?'

'I don't know, sir, she sailed off and left me behind – by mistake, obviously . . .'

'This was off where, Tucker's Hole?'

'Yes . . . yes – we've been working our way up the coast, but that's not really the point. What I'm saying is I want to work for you, but in a different way, I want to write about what you're doing here and . . . and . . . and if you don't want me to do that . . . well, that's OK . . . But I can handle a camera, you'll want a photographic record for the history books as well . . . and . . . and . . . you know . . . if you don't want that either, then maybe I can just . . . you know, go on my way . . . Mr President. I'm no use to you as a soldier. But before I go, I really think you need to know about that guy out there, you know, the one who's training us, the one with the Mohican. He's just a compete sadist – some of us haven't eaten all day, he's working us into the ground. One or two of us are pretty fit, but some of the young ones, you'd think he was trying to kill them the way he's working them. He's a bully, sir. Anyone who wanted to help you out with this great . . . plan . . . well, they're going to be put right off by this – this *arse* . . .'

For the second time the President raised his hand. 'I think I've heard enough, son.'

'So, you'll . . . you'll do something about him? I know in the grand scheme of things it's not that important but maybe just a quiet word or . . .'

The President smiled. 'Oh, it's important enough, Private. In fact I'm going to have my son look into it straight away. That OK with you, Kyle?'

For a moment Jimmy didn't get that there had been someone else in the room all along. He had walked straight to within a metre or so of the President's desk without realising that there were chairs against the wall behind him.

'Yes, sir, Mr President . . . Father.'

Kyle stepped forward, into the light.

Jimmy saw a rather familiar haircut.

'Private Armstrong,' Mohican snarled, 'you have a problem with the way you're being trained?' Jimmy swallowed. 'You just want to breeze out of here, go on your merry way, leave the rest of us to rebuild this country?'

'Well I—'

'You shut your god–damn mouth!'

Jimmy jumped at the venom of it.

135

Mohican was suddenly right in his face, jabbing a finger *this* close to his eyes.

'One thing I hate more than punk kids who can't follow orders,' Mohican spat, 'is punk kids who go crying to Daddy every time someone shouts at them. You're a pathetic little worm, Armstrong, that's what you are, and I'll tell you this – you're going *nowhere*! By the time I'm through with you you'll walk and talk and kill like a Marine . . . or you'll be buried out there in the graveyard we reserve for cowards like you. Now you get back to that rabble I'm trying to turn into soldiers and you tell them they're getting no dinner tonight either!'

Throughout this verbal assault the President had said nothing. But he had nodded with approval.

The size of Jimmy's mistake was beyond colossal. And he didn't have a clue what to do about it. If Mohican didn't kill him, the rest of his troop would as soon as they found out about the food.

Jimmy sighed, saluted, then turned to go.

'One moment, Private,' said the President.

Perhaps, perhaps a ray of hope . . .

Jimmy faced the President again. 'Sir?'

'Private, I want a full run-down of the *Titanic's* defences, weapons, how many men at arms there are on board.'

'Uh . . . Yes, sir – but why?'

The President nodded at his son. 'Kyle – if a ship's in United States territorial waters and we're going through a national emergency, then we're perfectly within our rights to seize it, aren't we?'

'Yes, Father.'

'Excellent. There's your answer, Private Armstrong. Your arrival at Fort Hope is indeed fortuitous – not only do we gain a soldier, but he brings us the mighty *Titanic* as well. Well done, son!'

The Nightmare

After twenty minutes of arguing against all logic that it could not *possibly* have been a nightmare, Claire finally had to concede first that it *could* have been one, then that it *probably* was one, before eventually admitting that yes, it *definitely* had been a nightmare. The minister, Rev. Calvin Cleaver, could not possibly have entered the locked Presidential Suite to attack her; he could not have ghosted past her father, sitting smoking a cigar in the lounge, or vanished into a puff of smoke when he raced into her bedroom moments after she started screaming.

'OK, *all right*.' Her pyjamas were damp from the cold sweat that had drenched her. Her chest was tight with anxiety. 'It *was* a nightmare. But Dad, don't you see? It *means* something.'

'It means you're still weak after your injury,' said Mr Stanford, patting her shoulder reassuringly. 'It's obviously far too soon for you to be back at work . . .'

'It's not that – it's . . . it's like – a sign.'

Her father sighed.

'Dad – I'm serious, he—'

'I blame it on the cheese.' It was her mother, coming to lend her support.

Husband and daughter looked at her, still not quite used to the fact that she was from another planet, where logic had not yet been invented.

'*What?*' asked Claire.

'Cheese, it gives you nightmares. That's what they say.'

'Mum – I haven't had any cheese.'

'No, but you had two cups of hot chocolate. It's made with milk. So is cheese. I'm sure there's a connection.'

She drifted back out of the room. Father and daughter looked at each other and smiled. He ruffled her hair. 'Try and get some sleep, and then take it easy tomorrow, all right?'

'All right, Dad.'

Of course, Claire had no intention of taking it easy. She had a paper to run – and a killer to unmask.

Claire was proud of that morning's paper. They all were. It was packed with good news stories and features. There was a glowing tribute to Jimmy – under the headline *Jimmy Armstrong: Missing In Action.* On her way to work she was stopped several times and congratulated on the production. This, she knew, was a rare event in newspapers – usually you only heard from the general public when they had a complaint. When she reached the office the team was all there, busy chatting amongst themselves.

'You all did a really good job last night,' she said,

sitting on the edge of her desk. 'Now we've got to do it all over again today.'

They let out a resigned groan.

'I want a pay rise,' said Andy.

'Double pay for everyone,' said Claire, then pretended to do a mental calculation. 'What's the double of nothing?'

They laughed politely. Claire liked them. She liked being in charge. If Jimmy returned he would have a fight on his hands if he wanted his old job back.

She shook herself. *When* Jimmy returned.

Claire clapped her hands together. 'OK, let's take a look at what we've got today. Ty?'

'I have some more from Jonas Jones. The problem with the engines – I'd thought we were looking for some massive replacement part, but it turns out it's about *this* size . . .' He held up his thumb and forefinger, about ten centimetres apart. 'Don't quite understand what it does although Jonas spent about an hour explaining it to me, but that's what we need. It's manufactured in two places in the whole world – Belfast, where the ship was built, and a place in New Jersey not far from New York. That's where we have to get to.'

'OK,' said Claire, 'we're a couple of days out of New York yet. I'll do the photos, but I'll need a reporter along as well. Any volunteers?'

Everyone raised their hands, including the idiot who made the tea.

'If . . . you don't mind?' It was Ty again. 'I'm from New Jersey – I know the area, and I'd kind of like to see if any of my family . . .'

Claire nodded. His parents had both died during the plague, here on the ship. She hadn't asked if he had other family. That's how it worked on board, you rarely asked friends and colleagues about family – it was too painful.

'Of course, Ty.'

She spent another ten minutes discussing stories and handing out assignments before arriving at what was really on her mind.

'OK, I have another assignment here. We have a minister on board, Reverend Calvin Cleaver, came on yesterday. Looking for a profile of him, nice big interview, any volunteers . . . ?'

'*Boring*,' said Debs.

'I know. But it'll be good to have on file in case we have a quiet news day.'

'Remind me of the last time *that* was.' Debs laughed.

Claire was deliberately trying to make it sound boring. She was uncomfortable doing this, but she didn't want to let them know her real reason for wanting the story in case the interviewer inadvertently tipped Cleaver off that she thought he was a murderer.

'So?'

Nobody was interested. They were all keen to get started on their own assignments.

Then slowly, slowly, the idiot who made the tea

141

raised his hand.

'Alan,' said Claire.

'Brian,' said Brian.

'Yes, of course . . . ahm, you want to do this?' Brian
nodded. 'You haven't written anything for us yet, have
you?' Brian shook his head. He looked at the floor.

Claire wasn't sure if she'd ever actually spoken to
him. She couldn't quite recall how he'd ever arrived in
the first place. He had just started hanging around,
sitting in the corner, watching mostly, until someone
ordered him to make the tea or get lost. She thought
it was Ty who'd started calling him *the idiot who makes
the tea* – behind his back, of course – and it had just
kind of caught on. She should have put a stop to it. Or
Jimmy should. But they weren't perfect.

None of them had known how to write a story
when they'd started, but they'd all been given their
chance. Most of their first stories had been awful. But
they'd learned how to do it and were now reasonably
good at it. Brian deserved his chance.

'OK, Brian,' said Claire. 'Why don't you take a shot
at it?' She glanced across at Ty, who was looking
surprised. She smiled at Brian. 'Just remember, I want
as much detail as possible – don't be afraid to ask him
anything.' Brian nodded. 'You have a notebook?'

'I have a tape recorder.'

'OK, Brian. You go for it. Good luck.'

He smiled, without once raising his eyes to Claire,
and turned to the door. As he passed Debs' desk she

gave him the thumbs-up. When he was gone Ty looked across at Claire.

'Are you sure he's up to it?'

'We'll soon find out.'

Ty shrugged. 'I just thought he was stupid.'

Debs tutted.

'He's just shy. He has an IQ of 140. That means he's a genius.'

'How do you know he has an IQ of 140?'

'He told me.'

'And you *believed* him? Well I'm pretty sure *you* haven't an IQ of 140, if you fell for that. Anyway, if he was that smart he'd know how to make a decent cup of tea.'

'Well who knows, maybe Einstein couldn't make tea either.'

'Any idiot can make tea.'

'Well I don't see *you* making it, Ty.'

'Well, I'm not any idiot.'

'No, you're in a class of your own.'

Claire left them to it. She had her replacement camera with her, and a telescopic lens. She was both fascinated and repelled by Calvin Cleaver. She wanted to get close to him, but also remain at a distance. She would take his photo and study it. She would study Brian's interview and learn from it. There was something about Cleaver that was just plain *wrong*.

The Punishment

It was safe to say that Jimmy was not the most popular member of the troop. In fact, it was also inaccurate to say that he was the least popular, because any sentence containing the words 'Jimmy' and 'popular' should be regarded as unsatisfactory, such were the negative feelings engendered by his behaviour. Simple words like 'hatred' and 'loathing' would fit much more neatly into any sentence you could care to construct in reference to Lucky Jimmy Armstrong. Most of this had to do with hunger. When you've been worked into the ground in the morning, then missed your lunch, then trained even further into the ground in the afternoon, then missed your dinner and spent an evening lying about, exhausted and starving – well, one can understand just how you might feel about the boy responsible. One would also understand why you hurled him out of the barracks – incidentally, showing splendid teamwork in the process – so that he landed face down in the mud, and why you slammed and locked the door behind him so that he had to spend the next six hours wandering miserably around the fort by himself, aware that he'd made a big fat idiot of himself and that he'd not only betrayed his new comrades but also his *old* comrades on the *Titanic* as well. Even Rain Man joined in, and they hated him only marginally less than they did Jimmy.

Jimmy was still tramping around the camp as darkness fell and the floodlights snapped on. Searchlights began to rove across the plain and up into the hills surrounding Fort Hope. The guards in the watchtowers changed shift; those coming off duty appeared relieved, those going on looked nervous. Jimmy remembered Mohican's warning to be quiet as they'd approached the fort the previous night and wondered what could possibly be out there to cause such fear amongst those defending Fort Hope.

It was only as Jimmy wandered between the barracks that he began to fully appreciate the scale of what the President was undertaking – there were literally thousands of soldiers here, all undergoing similar training. There were armoured vehicles, missile launchers, even several tanks. It was an *army*. But what he didn't quite understand was what it was *for*. An army represents the citizens of a country; it defends that country, or attacks on its behalf. But there were no ordinary 'citizens' here – there were no mothers, wives, children: no bankers, carpenters or newspapers to protect, there was just the army. *Everyone* was in the army.

Fort Hope was completely different to any of the other settlements Jimmy had seen – as pathetic and disorganised as they had been, they'd also been determined attempts by survivors to put down fresh roots, safe havens where families could live together, start again. But Fort Hope felt . . . *temporary*. It was massive, but it wasn't permanent, it was more like a camp, somewhere you expect to move on from. It seemed clear to Jimmy that the President had a plan, and he was building an army with which to execute it. The *Titanic* now featured in that plan – although almost as an afterthought.

Guilt sat heavily on Jimmy's shoulders. He had more or less given up hope of ever returning to the *Titanic*. If he did see it again, it would most probably be as part of an army sent to capture it. He cursed himself for being such a big mouth. He *must learn* to keep his trap shut. He seethed inside. He *would not* be responsible for the *Titanic* falling into enemy hands – he would have to do *something*.

Jimmy stared at the perimeter fence. The chances of scaling it, cutting through it or digging under it without attracting the attention of the guards were minuscule. He had watched movies about prisoners of war escaping from camps like this – but such daring feats were always undertaken by large groups of inmates working in highly organised teams. Any individuals who tried to escape were usually discovered very quickly – and invariably shot.

But there had to be a way to escape.
Or to warn the Titanic.

In trying to keep as far away as possible from the delicious smells emanating from the mess hall, Jimmy found himself on the far side of the camp and outside a hut with a red cross marked on both sides of a slanting roof. As he wandered past it he could see through the open doors a dozen beds inside, with half of them filled. There was a nurse standing by one of the beds, and someone he supposed was a doctor sitting at a table, studying charts. As he moved around the back of the hut he saw that something like a picnic table had been set up in the fresh air. A girl of perhaps twelve or thirteen was sitting there, with a tray of food in front of her. She wasn't eating, just staring into thin air.

Jimmy wandered casually over. 'How's it going?' he asked.

The girl continued to focus on something invisible and far away.

Jimmy sat opposite her, directly in her line of sight. She stared straight through him. He might as well not have been there.

'I'm Jimmy,' he said.

She was *very* pale. Her eyes were green, but they were set in a face that looked sunken and starved. Her blond hair sat dank and tangled. Jimmy had often seen this vacant look in the settlements; it spoke of unseen horrors and tragic loss. Jimmy wasn't unsympathetic, his focus was just elsewhere.

'Jimmy Armstrong,' he said. 'Only arrived last night. You here long? What do you think of this place? What's wrong with you? Are you not eating your pie?'

His mouth was watering. It was a great big hunk of *something* pie. He didn't care what it was. There were potatoes and vegetables and a dessert bowl with custard swimming over a sponge cake. There was a can of Coke.

'Do you mind if I take a nibble? Just a teeny bit of crust? Been training all day and I'm absolutely…'

The girl didn't react at all.

Jimmy liberated a generous handful of pie and crammed it into his mouth. It was delicious. That said, he was so hungry that cardboard with gravy would also have qualified as delicious. The girl continued to stare right through him.

'What's that?' he said, playfully cupping a hand to his ear. 'Help yourself to some more? Don't mind if I do.'

He was just reaching across for a second helping when he saw the nurse glance out of the window behind her, then do a double take.

'What *on earth* do you think you're doing?' she demanded.

Jimmy choked down his mouthful of food. 'Nothing – she said I could help myself.'

The nurse's eyes narrowed. 'That poor girl hasn't spoken since she arrived here.'

'In that case,' said Jimmy, 'I'm lying.'

He grabbed the tray and took off.

Mohican stood in the middle of the barracks, resting his foot on Jimmy's back and glaring around the gaunt, starving, exhausted troop.

'Charge one – stealing food from a starving child. Charge two – refusing to halt when ordered to do so by a superior officer. Charge three – resisting arrest. Charge four – bleeding on an officer's boot without permission. Charge five – possession of a smart mouth. Have you anything to say in your own defence, Private Armstrong?'

Jimmy knew exactly what Mohican was doing. He was willing Jimmy to say something sarcastic, something defiant, to just open his bloody lips – he'd put up a bit of a fight when they'd eventually cornered him – and come out with something to make matters even worse. Jimmy knew it, and he also knew he couldn't resist, he couldn't help himself. He was Lucky Jimmy Armstrong, guaranteed to make a bad situation even worse.

'*Well?*' Mohican demanded. 'Anything to say, Armstrong?'

The words felt thick and unwieldy in his swollen mouth. 'Yes … sir. I just wanted to say . . . that the pie . . . was really, really . . . nice . . .'

Mohican thumped his boot hard into Jimmy's back. Jimmy couldn't stifle the cry of pain.

149

'Five charges, Private Armstrong, and I find you guilty on all counts. Once again the punishment applies to this entire troop. You will learn your lesson, Private Armstrong! No breakfast for anyone!'

There was no reaction. They had expected it. They stood silently. Only one emotion filled the air.

Pure hatred.

'OK,' Mohican snapped, 'six o'clock start tomorrow morning, so lights out in ten minutes. We begin with a boxing competition. Private Armstrong will be first in the ring. He will have both hands tied behind his back. Now I need someone willing to punch his stupid head off. Any volunteers?'

Every single hand was raised without hesitation.

Arrival

There were, of course, some people on the *Titanic* who simply weren't interested. Hard-bitten crew who'd seen everything before; passengers who'd lost interest in pretty much everything since the plague had struck – or who might just have been like that anyway. But *virtually* everyone on board was outside, lining the rails, for the mighty ship's arrival in New York.

It had limped along so slowly over the past few days, and with daybreak the coast had been swathed in mist, so nobody outside of the captain and his officers on the bridge really had a firm idea of how close they were – but then the mist had lifted and there she was, the Statue of Liberty, torch aloft. There was something magical about seeing her. She still spoke of hope and welcome, even though the people looking at her from every deck now knew not to expect anything. Claire was on the top deck, surrounded by her team, all genuinely excited, chatting away and pointing. She was looking at Lady Liberty through her telescopic lens – the only one amongst them who could actually pick out the weeds snaking up the green statue and the birds' nests lining her crown. She supposed in the good old days someone would have been employed to stop the old lady looking like she was homeless. But Claire said nothing. Instead she trained her lens on the harbour, before moving it up and across a skyline familiar from a thousand movies. She wished Jimmy was with her. They would have had a grand adventure on the streets of Manhattan.

Though they were *busting* to get ashore, Captain Smith, as ever, was taking no chances. It had been a battle just to get the ship this far, so no detailed planning had yet been made as far as shore visits were concerned. He would not be rushed. The *Titanic* dropped anchor just off Liberty Island. The captain, showing how much he respected what the news team were doing, chose to address the passengers and crew alike through a special edition of the paper instead of addressing them over the PA or just printing off his own message. Claire was quite proud of that. She devoted the whole of the front page to his statement. And even rewrote part of it, because it was dead boring.

His main point was – millions of people had died in New York. It was probably rife with disease. If there were survivors, *they* were probably rife with disease. If you got ashore and became infected with anything, you might not be allowed back on. The safety of the ship was paramount. Teams would go ashore to ascertain conditions in the city and secure the vital part required to fix the engines, which was the primary reason for coming to New York. Then the *Titanic* would continue its voyage.

One of the reporters, Andy, stood beside Claire, looking wistfully at the city. 'Do you think FAO Schwarz qualifies as essential supplies?'

'FAO Schwarz?'

'Toy store. They say it's the biggest in the world. There's lots of young kids on board, we could do with getting a load more toys. You know, the latest electronic games, loads of cool stuff.'

'Would this be for you, Andy, or the kids?'

'Oh the kids, definitely. But you know, if you want someone to go and check it out, well, I'm happy to volunteer.'

'You'd put your life on the line for some computer games?'

Andy thought about it for a few moments. 'For the kids, definitely.'

'You're very brave,' said Claire. 'And misguided, if you think the captain is going to let you off to go shopping for toys.'

Andy grinned at her. 'Talking of misguided, how did Alan's interview with that minister turn out?'

'You mean Brian's?' she asked. Andy shrugged. 'I don't know, haven't seen it yet.'

'Probably still working on it,' said Andy. 'Are you sure he has an IQ of 140?'

'I'm not sure of anything.'

'If he's so smart, how come he can't make a better cup of tea?'

'Wait'll you see,' said Claire. 'He'll surprise us. The interview will be brilliant.'

'I'd prefer better tea.'

Everyone on the *Times* was feeling upbeat about the arrival in New York, despite the captain's warnings. Certainly they would have to scramble later on to have their reports from the city in time for publication, but that was part and parcel of being a journalist. Deadlines! But there were a number of mundane tasks to be completed prior to going ashore – Claire wanted to run a series of features about passengers who'd been with the ship right from the start but were now going to leave its relative safety and take their chances onshore. A number of these interviews had been carried out already, but her journalists hadn't quite gotten round to writing them up. Now that they were needed it was proving difficult to get her staff focused on the task. All they were really interested in was New York.

Ty was finding it particularly hard to settle. He had no idea what he would find if and when he made it as far as New Jersey – or if he would return to the ship. Since his parents had died the people on board had become his family. But if he found survivors of his real family out there he would find himself torn. Blood was thicker than water. Now, every time he tried to continue with his article, he only managed a few words before sitting back and sighing.

'This is impossible,' he said. 'And now there isn't even anyone to make the tea.'

'Make it yourself,' said Debs.

'Where is Wonder Boy anyway?'

'Give him a break, would you?'

Ty made a face. Debs made one back.

'Ty,' said Claire, 'if you really can't work, go to Brian's cabin and find out how long he's going to be.'

'Me? Do I look like a messenger boy?'

'YES!'

From everyone in the office.

Ty pretended to huff off.

Three inflatables were to make the initial approach to New York. The first ashore would carry First Officer Jeffers, Dr Hill, Jonas Jones, Mr Benson – relieved to finally be off farmyard duty – and half a dozen other armed crewmen. Their job would be to secure a base at Battery Park and establish a perimeter before cautiously probing further into the city to try and establish what the conditions there were. Claire had tried her best to be allowed on to this first boat, but had been refused. If Jeffers decided it was safe, then she would be permitted to land with the second and third boats, which would contain additional armed crewmen and the passengers who wished to disembark. After that the plan was that vehicles would be commandeered and a convoy would make its way through the city towards the factory in New Jersey where Jonas Jones hoped to secure the part that would allow the *Titanic* to continue on its voyage. Along the way, passengers leaving the ship would be dropped off to begin their journeys home. If they chose to return to the ship they would be picked up on the way back at prearranged pick-up points. While all of this was happening the inflatables would bring more crew ashore to search for oil and supplies, which would be ferried back to *Titanic* using larger vessels abandoned at the docks.

Claire couldn't wait to get ashore. Yes, of course it would be dangerous, but she desperately wanted to know what had happened in New York. She had a reporter's insatiable curiosity. Standing on the lower deck, with the waves lapping softly against the mighty ship and the even mightier city laid out in front of her, she was gripped with excitement.

'First boat – away!' cried First Officer Jeffers, and the inflatable began to speed towards shore. The other two inflatables continued to fill with passengers.

'If you're going ashore, now's the time to get on board, ma'am.'

Claire nodded at the coxswain and glanced anxiously along the deck – Ty had not yet reappeared after going to check on Brian.

'Just a few more minutes,' said Claire.

The coxswain nodded reluctantly. Claire glanced

down at the inflatables, which were set slightly below her and waiting to be winched down to the water. One was completely full, the other had just the two places left. Her eyes settled on a familiar, wide-brimmed black hat. At that very moment the Reverend Calvin Cleaver raised his head and their eyes met. A shiver ran through her and she looked quickly away, but not before she registered the look he was giving her: cold hatred.

A hand came down on her shoulder and she jumped.

'Claire . . . sorry!' It was Ty. Andy and Debs were with him. 'We were looking everywhere for Brian, but nobody's seen him. His parents are frantic, we've been everywhere we can think of . . .'

Claire had a knot in her stomach. She looked back down at the minister. She could only see the top of his hat. 'OK, Ty, climb in. Andy, Debs – keep looking. Have him paged over the PA. *Find him* – and keep me posted.'

Claire stepped into the inflatable and took her seat beside Ty. A few moments later the craft was lowered into the water. With the noise of the engine it was impossible to be sure, but Claire thought she could hear someone humming a familiar tune as the inflatable began to speed towards New York.

Pain and Laughter

Jimmy's nose was definitely broken, but he was refusing to have it reset – partly because he wanted something to remind him not to be such an idiot in the future, to keep his big mouth shut, but mostly because he knew it would be extremely painful to have it physically snapped back into place. Anyone who had seen him climb repeatedly from the floor of the makeshift boxing ring would not have dreamed of saying that he was scared of pain, but everyone has their limits. They had all seen him knocked down for the sixth time. Much as they hated him, they could not help but be both sympathetic and impressed. Even though his eyes were swollen almost shut; his nose broken, his lips thicker and bloodier than they had ever been before and he was weaving around the ring like a drunk, he had kept coming back for more. Even the boys who hated Jimmy the most were beginning to rebel against Mohican's screamed instructions to hit him again, and harder. One, who'd acquired the nickname Thumper from somewhere, simply refused to hit Jimmy again; at which point Mohican jumped into the ring, hurriedly pulled on a pair of boxing gloves and flattened Thumper. Then he laid Jimmy out cold.

Jimmy lay flat out on his back in the dirt of the yard outside the barracks. The rest of his troop stood looking down at him, not sure what to do. Then Mohican appeared with a bucket of freezing water and threw it over him. The shock of it forced his eyes open as wide as they could go, which wasn't very wide at all. He coughed and spluttered and coughed up blood.

'OK!' Mohican cried. 'All of you have worked hard. Go eat!'

Jimmy lay where he was while the others *ran* towards the mess hall. They hadn't eaten in twenty-four hours, largely thanks to him. Mohican crouched down beside him. Jimmy tensed up, expecting a dig in the ribs or a poke in the eye.

'You did well, son.'

Jimmy grunted.

'Brave. Now listen to me. In a war you have to be able to depend on the man next to you. You have to work as a team. Disciplined. Follow orders. We don't need mavericks. Mavericks get killed, and cause others to get killed. You understand?'

Jimmy nodded. It hurt.

'Now get over to First Aid, get yourself cleaned up.'

Mohican stood up and walked away. Jimmy lay where he was. He was a little groggy still, and a lot confused. Mohican had sounded almost human.

No, I was probably mistaken. Perhaps I have brain damage.

Jimmy lay where he was for another five minutes before forcing himself up on to his knees. He was groggy. He stood. Dizzy. He began to stagger along towards the First Aid hut. His route took him past the mess hall. The food smells almost made him throw up. He was aware of being watched as he passed the open doors. He looked straight ahead. It took all of his strength to walk in a straight line and upright.

When he reached the First Aid hut the nurse who'd scolded him previously took one look at him, then quickly guided him to a bed and made him lie down. She fetched a sponge and a basin of water and began to wash the worst of the mud and blood from him. He thought he heard her mutter, 'He's a monster,' under her breath. She definitely said, 'I will need Dr Moore to come and reset that nose.'

That's when he told her no, to leave it as it was.

'It'll set crooked,' she said.

'Fine,' said Jimmy.

'Up to you.' She gave him some painkillers and told him to try and sleep for a while until they took effect.

'Don't need to,' Jimmy whispered. She turned to pick up some ointment for his lips. When she turned back he was fast asleep.

It was late evening when Jimmy woke, stiff and sore. His nose was thick with dried blood and his head ached. A single bare bulb hung from the ceiling, inadequate for the size of the room and leaving a third of it in shadow. The other beds were empty, the nurse's station deserted and, when he checked, the doctor's small office at the far end was locked. But he heard the scrape of a chair from outside, and when he peered out he saw that the wild-looking girl he'd previously stolen food from was back, sitting in exactly the same place and position – or perhaps she'd never left. He didn't remember her being there earlier but, truth be told, he remembered very little from earlier – besides the fact that he'd taken a beating.

Jimmy opened the First Aid hut's door and stepped on to the wooden surround. He shuffled along to where the girl was sitting at the white plastic picnic table. She had an identical tray of food before her, again untouched.

'It's OK,' said Jimmy, 'I'll not be stealing your food tonight, not with these lips – unless you mash it up and blow it into my mouth through a straw.'

She continued to stare into the distance.

'Do you mind if I sit down?'

There was no reaction. Jimmy pulled out a chair and sat. It was a pleasant, warm evening, with a light breeze. The girl was wearing a plain white nightdress. Her hair was still as dank as before.

'So, what's your problem? A wee touch of the plague? No?' Nothing. 'Ah well, sometimes silence is best.'

He looked out across the camp. The floodlights were on. The barracks huts were shut up for the night. The plain beyond the perimeter fence was dark and uninviting, except for when the spotlights swept across it, when it became bright and uninviting. How was he ever going to be able to escape? And if he did attempt it, what would they do if they spotted him – drag him back into the fort, or shoot him as he fled?

He smiled across at the girl. 'Maybe the two of us could dig a tunnel? Or I could send you out first, then when they're busy shooting you I could slip away? No? You don't say much, do you? They looking after you OK? You know – you're quite pretty, aren't you? I wouldn't normally say something like that in a million years to a girl I'd never met before, but seeing as how you seem to have all the brain activity of a plank of wood, I don't see how it can do any harm. Of course you'd probably need to comb your hair. And wash the dried-on drool off your face. But look at me – what an oil painting *I* am, eh? Hey relax, seriously. I have a girlfriend. She's just not aware of it yet.' Jimmy drummed his fingers on the table and stared into the distance. 'In fact, chances are she's dead. Still, that's no big thing these days, is it? Everyone's dead. Mum, Dad, family, friends. Yours as well, do you think? No – you don't have to tell me. Claire, that's her name. We hated each other at first, then we liked each other, then I put my two big feet in it and she hated me again, and then we got split up and...'

He pictured her lying in the woods, helpless, bleeding to death. He imagined the minister finding her, raising his gun, finishing her off.

'. . . I think it may have been my fault.'

A few hundred metres away the guards were just climbing down from one of the watchtowers, and their replacements were waiting to go up. If all of the towers changed at the same time, that might have given him an opportunity to dash across the plain unnoticed. But they weren't that stupid. The changeovers were staggered five minutes apart so that the surveillance was never interrupted. Jimmy sighed.

He studied the girl again.

'You know something? I bet I could make you smile.'

Nothing.

'I'll bet you a kiss I can make you smile.'

Nothing.

'I know one of the worst jokes in the history of the world, but I bet you won't be able to resist it. OK – if you smile, I get a kiss, deal?'

She stared ahead.

'Right, if you say nothing, I'll take that as a yes. If you shake your head, it's a no. So, do we have a deal?'

There was no reaction.

'OK, excellent. You're a challenge, I'll give you that – but I reckon I'm up to it. Here we go, are you ready?' Jimmy moved his chair slightly and leaned forward until he was so close that she could look nowhere else but straight into his eyes. 'Anyone ever tell you you've got nice eyes? Well, one of them anyway. The other's a bit crossed. Only joking. Can you have one crossed eye? All right – here we go. What did the big chimney say to the little chimney?' He waited. Ten seconds. Nothing. '*You're too young to be smoking!*'

Nothing.

'OK,' said Jimmy. 'A tougher nut to crack than I thought. I'm going to have to wheel out the big gun. This joke – *this* joke makes the other joke look really pathetic. *This* joke saves lives. Are you ready? I'm warning you – you may die laughing.'

Nada.

'OK. Did you hear about the fella went to the doctor's and said he thought he was turning into a pair of curtains? *Doctor told him to pull himself together!*'

Jimmy examined her pale face right up close. Not a flicker. In fact, she didn't even appear to be breathing. He might well have been talking to a corpse.

'Soldier!'

Jimmy jumped. The nurse was hurrying towards them. 'What're you doing? Leave the poor girl alone!'

'I wasn't doing anything, I was only—'

'Leave her alone and go back to bed now – or if you think you're well enough, return to barracks.'

Jimmy wasn't ready to face his fellow soldiers just yet. He pushed his chair back and stood up as the nurse mounted the steps and approached the table.

'Sorry,' he said. 'I didn't mean any harm.'

The nurse took the girl by the hand and gently pulled her up. The girl didn't blink.

'I'll, uh, go and have a lie-down, then,' said Jimmy. 'What's wrong with her anyway?'

'She was picked up in the woods just like this, traumatised. God knows we've tried everything to bring her out of it.'

Jimmy nodded sympathetically.

'Have you tried a good slap in the face?' he asked.

The nurse scowled at him and began to turn the girl. But as she moved slowly past him, Jimmy was certain that he saw a little flicker of movement at the sides of her mouth, the merest sliver of a hint of a suggestion of a possibility of a smile. It was gone as soon as it appeared, and it might just as easily have been a spasm of pain, or wind. She allowed herself to be slowly walked along the wooden surround, and back into the hut.

Jimmy followed them in. The girl stood immobile beside her bed while the nurse turned back the sheets, guided her down, lay her back and lifted her legs up on to the mattress. She then pulled the covers up and tucked her in. The girl lay flat on her back, staring at the ceiling.

Jimmy lay on his own bed at the far side of the room as the nurse turned for the door, then glanced back at him.

'I won't turn the light out,' she said. 'She's frightened of the dark.'

'How can you tell?' Jimmy asked.

The nurse just shook her head. 'Rest while you can, soldier. You'll be back at training tomorrow.'

She closed the door behind her.

Jimmy stared at the girl for a long time. She did not turn restlessly. Or yawn. Her eyes did not flicker. But eventually, his did. He began to drift. He had already slept for most of the afternoon and evening, but his body needed time to recover from the pounding it had taken, both in the ring and over the past few days. Soon Jimmy was in a deep sleep. So deep, in fact, that he was not aware of the girl pushing back her covers. He did not know that she climbed out of bed and padded across the floor to his bed. He would never know that she bent over him and kissed him on the forehead.

Battery Park

It became clear within minutes of landing at Battery Park that they wouldn't be forming a convoy to take them anywhere.

The inflatables tied up between two Circle Line ferries that had once ploughed back and forth to Liberty and Ellis Islands packed with tourists, but which now creaked and rattled and rusted at the foot of a short jetty. As Claire climbed up on to it she immediately detected an unease amongst the first landing party. First Officer Jeffers was pacing back and forth, a radio clamped to his ear, in urgent discussion with Captain Smith. The armed sailors had set up a perimeter at the entrance to the park and appeared jumpy and nervous. Then there was the smell – not the stench of death she had expected, but something that reminded her of . . . a barbecue. Yet there was nothing reassuring about it. The remains of fires were dotted across the park and some of them were still smouldering. Hundreds of what appeared to be recent footprints scarred the grass. But it was deadly quiet.

So if there were people here recently, where are they now?

If there are survivors, why aren't they making themselves known the way the inhabitants of other settlements always do as soon as the Titanic *appears?*

Claire spotted Benson standing near the entrance, supervising two sailors as they pushed the metal gates closed.

'What's the problem?' she asked, nodding at the gates.

'Nothing – just a little extra insurance.'

'Against what?'

'Not sure,' said Benson. 'We thought we saw people here on the way in, but they've gone.'

Claire scanned the open space beyond, which continued for several hundred slightly elevated metres to the foot of Broadway, the famous avenue which ran all the way up the island of Manhattan. She knew immediately that the convoy idea would have to be rethought – the road ahead was thick with abandoned vehicles, and was for as far as she could see.

Jeffers was still talking to the ship; as he paced, his every step was repeated by Jonas Jones. The passengers who'd disembarked were milling around, anxious to be on their way. Calvin Cleaver stood off to one side, his bony white hands clutching a small Bible, which he was studying intently. Dr Hill had crouched by one of the smouldering fires. He had picked up a stick and was poking around with it.

Ty came up beside her. 'It's so quiet,' he said. They gazed up towards the city – although now that they were so close they could no longer see the epic skyline they'd been enthralled by on the way in. 'Every Saturday, my dad used to take me downtown – we'd go catch a movie, play in Central Park. It was my special time with him. It was never quiet, always this buzz, always cabs blasting their horns, it was just *noisy* . . . not like this...' He shook his head. 'Not like this.'

'You know, Ty, you don't have to come with us. If your family are all . . .'

She didn't finish.

Ty sighed. 'Yes. Yes I do.'

And then, almost as if God or someone equally important had been listening, they heard it – a distant, echoing call, something utterly strange in the circumstances but also instantly recognisable.

'That was an elephant,' said Claire.

'Yes it was,' agreed Ty.

The passengers and crew gathered together, alert, as if half expecting to see the mighty creature lumber into view. But nothing moved.

'You know what this means?' Ty whispered. Claire shook her head. 'It means the elephants have taken over the city. They've enslaved the survivors. We have entered the Kingdom of the Elephants.'

'Did anyone ever tell you you're a complete idiot?'

'Many people,' said Ty.

'It probably just escaped from the zoo.'

Ty nodded. 'That makes sense. Elephants have never

enslaved anyone. If any creatures have taken over the city and enslaved the humans and set up their own kingdom, it's probably the monkeys. They have thumbs.'

'Right,' said Claire. 'Excuse me.'

She had spotted that Jeffers was off the radio and crouching down by one of the old barbecues, conferring with Dr Hill. She hurried up.

'So, what's the plan?' she asked, sinking to her knees and looking eagerly from one to the other. Dr Hill was turning a charred lump of wood over in his hands.

An exasperated expression swept across the first officer's face. He had never been happy with either Jimmy or Claire tagging along on what were occasionally dangerous missions.

'Well, Claire,' he said, 'if it was up to me, I'd pack you back to the ship.'

'Why, what's happened?'

He took a deep breath. He lowered his voice. 'Well, for one thing, we're going to have to walk most of the way to Newark – that's where this damn factory is – because the roads are impassable to vehicular traffic.'

'That's cars,' said Dr Hill, helpfully.

Jeffers gave him a brief look. 'What it means is that we're going to be here a lot longer than we expected.'

'So what's the problem with that?'

'It means crossing the city. And I don't think it's safe.'

'Why?'

Jeffers' eyes flitted back to Dr Hill. The doctor looked away.

'It's just *not*,' said Jeffers. 'Not for a large party like this. If we were mobile, if there was just a few of us, we could zip in and out – but some of these guys are old, most of them aren't fit . . . we'll be too slow, we'll be . . .' He looked at Dr Hill again. 'It's just dangerous.'

Claire looked from one to the other. 'I work for the *Times*, it's the paper of record, it's my responsibility to report what's going on, if you *know*, you should tell—'

'Enough!' snapped Jeffers. 'I don't want to hear *the speech* again, Claire. I know why you're here, and I know the captain thinks it's important that you are kept informed. I don't agree, I won't ever agree, but I have no choice.'

'*So?*'

Dr Hill spoke before Jeffers could respond. 'I think one word will probably cover it, Claire.'

He held up the piece of charred wood, except that now that she looked at it up close it no longer looked like wood.

'Cannibals,' said Dr Hill.

Ham

Jimmy entered the mess hall with his head up, shoulders back, eyes front. Though he looked battered, he was determined to show everyone that he was not beaten. But, in fact, 'everyone' was not that interested. The hall was packed with hungry soldiers intent on filling their faces with as much food as they could before another hard day of training. They weren't bothered about one soldier's miserable experience. Many of them had their own hard-luck stories. The din of plates and cutlery was deafening, the chatter incessant. It seemed to be one of the only places in the fort where they were free to let their hair down. Nobody paid him any attention as he joined the queue for food.

He may not have been beaten, but he had changed. Or, at least, he *thought* he'd changed. He had decided it wasn't fair on his fellow troopers to keep getting into trouble – otherwise they'd all starve to death. And, if he didn't keep his mouth zipped, then attention would remain focused on him, which would make it much more difficult to escape from the fort.

He needed to quieten down, blend in more.

With his plate piled high Jimmy found a space at one of the long trestle tables that filled the hall. The soldiers around him weren't any older, but they had clearly been at the fort for a lot longer; they looked lean and fit and had something of a confident swagger about them. Maybe the training regime here wasn't all bad. Or perhaps they hadn't been trained by Mohican.

As he tucked into eggs and ham, another boy he recognised from his own troop sat down opposite him – clearly by mistake, to judge from the surprised expression on his face when he noticed Jimmy. His immediate response was to look around for somewhere else to sit. But there wasn't anywhere close by, so he decided to make the best of it. He kept his eyes on his food.

'So how's it going?' Jimmy asked.

The boy, with short black hair and round, black glasses, looked up. 'OK,' he said, rather flatly. His eyes darted about to see if anyone was watching.

'What do they call you?'

'Harry Potter.'

'*Seriously?*'

'My real name's Christopher Carter. But they started calling me . . .' He shrugged. 'Stuck with it now.'

'I'm Jimmy Armstrong.'

'I know that.' He took a mouthful of food and chewed it methodically. When he'd swallowed and allowed ten seconds for digestion, he glanced up at Jimmy. 'Your face – must hurt.'

'A bit.'

'You kept getting up.'

'Stubborn, I suppose.'

'When it was my turn, I got hit once and stayed down. Hit by a girl. She's half my size. Mohican says that if we go to war, I can carry the First Aid kit.'

'It's important to have First Aid,' said Jimmy.

'I faint at the sight of blood,' said Harry.

'Well, maybe we won't go to war.'

Harry blinked at him. 'Then why build an army?'

It was a good point.

An officer stood up at the far end of the hall and blew a whistle. There was an immediate scramble to finish off, deposit the empty plates and get back to barracks. Jimmy, his mouth full of ham, had intended to return with his new friend, but Harry magically lost him in the crush.

This time, when he walked in, all eyes were immediately upon him. They were already getting changed into the training kits they'd been issued with, but all movement stopped.

Jimmy stood in the doorway.

'I'm back,' he said.

He held his hands up in what he hoped looked like an apologetic gesture.

A big guy called Gomez walked up to him. 'Here,'

he said, and thrust a fresh set of T-shirt and shorts into his hands. 'You'll need these.'

'Cheers,' said Jimmy.

'You take a good punch,' said Gomez. He nodded once and returned to the side of his bed to continue changing.

'Mohican was mad as hell!' someone shouted from the other end of the hut.

'You just wouldn't stay down!' someone else called.

Jimmy smiled crookedly. 'Next time I will,' he said. Laughter rolled around the barracks.

'There won't be a next time.' It was Rain Man. The lightness evaporated immediately. 'We all went hungry because of you.'

'Yeah, well,' said Jimmy.

He moved to his bed and began to get changed. He could feel Rain Man's eyes on him.

'Give Frankie a break,' someone shouted.

'Yeah – Frankie took his punishment, and now he's back, so give him a break.'

Jimmy looked up. 'Cheers,' he said, 'but the name's Jimmy.'

'Have you looked in the mirror lately, Frankie?' Gomez asked.

The penny dropped. Frankie for Frankenstein. His face was so battered he looked like a monster. Claire, who was well-read, could have pointed out that Frankenstein was actually the name of the guy who built the legendary monster out of body parts and not the monster itself. Jimmy was none the wiser. And it didn't matter.

He laughed. 'Frankie,' he repeated. 'Frankie.'

Training didn't get any easier. In the morning, and then again in the afternoon, Mohican worked them like dogs over an assault course built at the northern tip of the fort. They climbed mock cliff-faces, swung on ropes across imaginary gorges, balanced on narrow beams and crawled through mud while being screamed at to keep their heads down to avoid invisible bullets. Jimmy threw himself into it all enthusiastically. He helped out the slow and the lame and the exhausted and, in turn, when he faltered he was helped out by his comrades. They were learning not just to help themselves, but to help each other. They were becoming a team, a troop, a well-oiled machine.

When the sun finally began to dip Mohican ordered them back to the barracks for a shower. They were all exhausted, but it was a good kind of exhaustion. They'd all come through a tough day. When they crossed to the mess hall it was as one big group. On the way there it was all, 'Frankie this,' and 'Frankie that'. His sins had been forgiven, if not forgotten. Only Rain Man stayed clear of him.

Just as Jimmy finished eating, Mohican appeared at his shoulder and said he was wanted over at the White House. Jimmy made a surprised face at his comrades and rose. They marched over together, silently. This time, instead of being shown into the President's office, he was led along a corridor and told to wait outside while Mohican went on in. As he stood he studied a series of framed photographs hanging on the wall. The President featured in all of them – there he was raising his right hand and taking the oath of office; there he was helping to build Fort Hope; another showed him standing with young recruits, overseeing their training; yet another pictured him with his senior officers – Mohican standing proudly on one side and . . . another somehow familiar face on the other . . . Jimmy knew it, he definitely knew it, but he just couldn't place . . . and then a shiver of recognition coursed through him. It was the Minister . . . the man who had so recently tried to kill him . . . even though he had only observed him at a distance, there was something so striking about him that Jimmy was absolutely certain that this was the same man, the same murderer. Except that here he was wearing an army uniform . . . he wasn't a man of the cloth, he was a soldier. But what on earth had he been doing then, dressed as . . . ? Jimmy jumped as the door opened suddenly behind him and Mohican was back, clicking his fingers at him to enter. Jimmy, his thoughts still jumbled, stepped into a large, bright room. Each of its walls was covered in maps; different coloured pins were stuck in them. He had seen rooms like this in movies.

It's a war room.

They're planning a battle or an invasion or . . .

'Ah, Private Armstrong.' The President, who was standing with several of his officers before a street map of New York City, indicated for Jimmy to walk with him. He led him to a large-scale map showing the eastern United States. The President's officers stood behind Jimmy. 'I'd like you to show me, if you could,' said the President, 'the ports that the *Titanic* has stopped at in the past few weeks.'

Jimmy stepped calmly forward and pretended to examine the map, but his mind was racing. He already knew that the President planned to seize the ship, but he would have to find it first. Jimmy was determined not to give anything away that might help him track it down, but he had to do it in such a way that he appeared to be trying to help. If he was cooperative then he could continue to plan his escape; defiance would only land him in more trouble and place him under even more intense scrutiny.

He shook his head slowly. 'I'm sorry, but most of the places we stopped at, they're new settlements, they're not on any map.'

'You must have a rough idea,' said one of the officers.

'Not really. Last one we stopped at was Tucker's Hole.' He waved vaguely at the map. He wasn't giving anything away – that was where he'd first encountered the President, and the President knew it. 'I'm not even sure where it is . . .'

The President jabbed a finger at the map. 'Here.'

'A ship that size,' said one of the officers, 'is going to need hundreds of thousands of gallons of oil to refuel. You don't pick those up at the settlements. What cities has the ship stopped at?'

Jimmy looked helplessly at the map. It wouldn't be hard for them to discover where the *Titanic* had started her voyage – it had been well publicised before the plague struck that she was bound for Miami for the first leg of her journey. So he pointed at it on the map. 'After that, I'm not too sure, there were a couple of stops, but I didn't pay a lot of attention.'

'I thought you were a reporter, Private,' said the President. 'Wasn't it your job to know?'

'We weren't told. The captain didn't want to upset the passengers and crew who had families ashore. I think the plan might have been to cross the Atlantic, you know, back to Belfast. I think that's where they've probably gone now.'

The President's eyes bored into him for what felt like an eternity, before he turned suddenly away and studied the map again. 'OK. Miami to Tucker's Hole, travelling north. If she's crossing the Atlantic she's going to have to fill her tanks. So the next major port she'll arrive at would have to be . . .' He traced his finger up the map. 'New York. Agreed, gentlemen?'

The officers nodded. 'Absolutely, Mr President,' said one.

The President clasped his hands behind his back.

'That is indeed fortunate. If we get the timing right we may have the opportunity to kill two birds with one stone. Private Armstrong – that will be all. Gentlemen, we have a battle plan to consider.'

Jimmy tramped unhappily away from the White House. He had tried to mislead them, but it hadn't worked. From what he had overheard, from the maps and the pins stuck into them, it was clear that the President intended to lead his army into New York. But why were they discussing a *battle plan*? The plague had devastated all of the major population centres – who was there left to fight? And if a battle was brewing in New York, was the *Titanic* sailing right into it? And if the minister was really a soldier, what on earth was he up to?

Thought processes are rarely linear – they're a jumble of ideas and questions and half-formed answers, and Jimmy was trying to puzzle his way out of this maze when a voice to his right made him jump.

'Say, friend, you got a light?'

A boy of about twelve years was sitting on a bench outside one of the administration buildings, a cigarette in one hand and a lighter, which he was repeatedly flicking, in the other.

'Sorry, no,' said Jimmy.

'Damn,' said the boy.

Jimmy would have walked on, but in pausing to answer he'd caught a glimpse through the open door beside the boy and spotted an array of radio equipment set against the far wall.

'Are you not a bit young to be smoking?' Jimmy asked, but in a friendly way.

The boy shrugged. 'Am I not a bit young to be carrying a gun and learning how to kill people with my bare hands?' he asked. 'Times have changed, my friend.'

Jimmy smiled. 'Suppose they have.' He nodded through the open door. 'You the radio man?'

'One of them. I've pulled the night shift.'

'Cool.'

'You into radio?'

'A bit, yeah. I was on the new *Titanic* for a while, hung around with the radio operators.'

He hadn't, actually. But he had interviewed them for a feature article in the *Times*. Now he was desperately trying to remember what he'd learned.

'*Titanic*? Excellent. We had an amateur radio club in school – not very fashionable, but it got me out of gym. You want to take a look?' Jimmy nodded enthusiastically. The boy led him inside. 'They call me Ham, by the way.'

'Jimmy. Or Frankie. Whatever you like.'

The radio equipment on the *Titanic* had been state of the art. *This* stuff looked like it had been rescued from a museum.

'So is there much traffic out there?' Jimmy asked, bending to examine the equipment.

Ham pulled out a chair and sat down; he pulled on a pair of earphones, but secured them just above his ears so he could chat. 'Very little – mostly it's just communication with the other forts.'

Jimmy looked at him in surprise. 'Other forts? I thought there was only Fort Hope.'

'Oh no – there's five others. Fort Perry is the closest – it's about thirty miles away. They're all in a kind of semi-circle around New York. We're hoping to establish telephone communication soon, but in the meantime radio's the best we have. But we also use *this* little nightmare a lot.' He tapped a small machine beside the main radio transmitter.

'Morse code.'

'You know about Morse? Not many kids know about it.'

'I'm no expert, but I know a bit.'

He knew a reasonable amount, again from writing about it for the *Times*. It was a nearly two-hundred-year-old method of transmitting messages, using a series of dots and dashes to represent letters and numerals and punctuation. These short electrical pulses were originally sent along a wire between two points by being tapped into a hand-operated device called a telegraph key, but after the invention of radio these were transmitted over the airwaves as a high-pitched audio tone – it was, he recalled, the only form of digital communication that could be used without a computer, which made it ideal for emergency signalling. Jimmy had never physically written or sent a message by Morse code, but he had watched it being done. And now Ham was busy sending one himself.

'This is what I have to do all night,' he moaned. 'Tap tap tap – it drives me mad, but they insist on it. And now I can't even light a cigarette to see me through.'

'What's the big important message? And who's it going to?'

'It's going to anyone who can pick it up, my friend – we broadcast on all the old amateur radio bands – LF, MF, HF, UHF and VHF – and what we're basically saying is don't give up, the President is alive and rebuilding civilisation. The catch is that we don't give our location. That's the way he wants it done – he thinks that only the best people will find their way here. But he also gets idiots like me.' Ham sucked on his unlit cigarette. 'I'm not convinced that one single person has ever heard it. I mean, who the hell listens to Morse code these days?'

Ham began to tap in the coded message. There was a chart showing the Morse letters and numerals pinned above the transmitter, but Ham didn't refer to it once.

'Do you not have another lighter, or matches?' Jimmy asked.

'Yeah, but if I leave my post, they'll shoot me.'

'Seriously?'

'Well, I don't really want to find out.'

'What if I stand guard and you nip out?'

His eyes brightened considerably. 'I shouldn't.'

'If anyone looks in the window, I'll be sitting in your seat, earphones on, pretending to transmit.'

'I . . . *really* shouldn't . . .' He took the cigarette out of his mouth and rolled it back and forth between his fingers. 'I smoke seventy-five of these a day. My dad got me started. I was the only one in my class at school who smoked. They all died of the plague, and it never touched me. Far as I'm concerned, smoking saved my life.' He took a deep breath – then coughed raggedly. 'Sorry . . . OK, deal – my barracks is just around the corner. I'll be like, two minutes, tops.'

'No problem,' said Jimmy.

Ham hesitated. 'So why exactly are you helping me out?'

'Because soldiers help each other. We're all in this together now, aren't we?'

Ham nodded enthusiastically. 'We sure are, friend.'

Ham hurried to the door while Jimmy took his seat at the transmitter and slipped on the earphones. He gave Ham the thumbs-up and the young radio operator winked and hurried out, closing the door firmly behind him.

Jimmy immediately stood and ripped the Morse chart off the wall. He propped it up in front of him and with his left hand gripped the top of the telegraph key and began to tap out his message as his eyes repeatedly flicked up and then down again . . .

—...•— ...•••—•• •••••—••• —•—•——

He was tapping as fast as he could, but he was still frustratingly slow. He couldn't be completely sure that he got the dots and dashes completely right. As soon as he finished his short message he began to send it again.

—...•— ...•••—•• ••••••— ••• —•—•——

He was just starting through it a third time…

—...•—

…when rapid footsteps announced Ham's return. Jimmy jumped up, stuck the Morse chart back on the wall and rapidly sat again just as the door opened. Ham entered, slightly out of breath, and closed the door behind him. He slipped his cigarette between his lips, removed a shiny red lighter from his pocket, tossed it up into the air, caught it, flicked it and lit up. He inhaled deeply, held it for ten seconds, then exhaled.

'That feels *soo goooood*,' he said.

Jimmy slipped the earphones off and stood away from the transmitter. 'You found it then?'

'Sure did.' Ham happily flipped the lighter into the air again, but before he could catch it Jimmy stepped smartly across and grabbed it.

He held it up and nodded admiringly. Then he abruptly dropped it to the floor and before Ham could move or protest he brought his heel down on it hard, crushing it.

'*What the . . . ?*'

As Jimmy stepped away from it Ham dropped to his knees and tried to pick up the shattered pieces.

'Why the hell did you do that?'

Jimmy pulled the door open, but then paused and looked back. 'Ham,' he said, 'you seem like a good kid. But take my advice. I'm the big chimney, you're the little chimney. You're too young to be smoking. Understand, *friend*?'

Jimmy winked at him, and strode out of the room.

22

The City

The column snaked forward through the ruined city, the passengers flanked by the armed crewmen. The passengers, many of them labouring for breath, thought the crewmen were going too fast; the crewmen, anxiously eyeing the surrounding buildings, thought they were going too slow. Jeffers was at the front with Jonas Jones; Dr Hill stayed at the back, encouraging those who were finding the going tough.

Claire moved back, and forth: sometimes at the front, aware of the tension; sometimes at the back, using her telescopic camera lens to scan the way they'd come.

Ty shadowed her all the way, aware that she was jittery. 'What's Jeffers so scared of? Monkey enslavement?'

Claire grinned at him. 'Something like that.'

But when he looked away the grin faded and her eyes flitted up the sides of the concrete valley they were passing through.

The devastation was immense. The plague must have struck New York very suddenly – so many cars were crashed off the road; hundreds of skeletons lay on the sidewalk and in stores, as if they had just dropped down dead rather than becoming ill and lingering for days the way they had on the *Titanic*. It reminded Claire of the many tourists they'd found dead on their deckchairs on the beach in St. Thomas, but on a hugely greater scale. Millions of people had died in this city, but some had survived – and apparently the only way they'd been able to feed themselves was by . . .

She could barely contemplate it.

Cannibals.

When Dr Hill had shown her the bone her immediate reaction was to laugh. Surely they were just cremating the bodies to cut down on disease? But then he'd shown her the grooves and chips in the bone where the meat and flesh had been cut away.

'OK,' she'd argued, 'so a couple of people went mad. It doesn't mean that every survivor is—'

'Claire,' Dr Hill said gravely, 'I've checked all of the bonfires and there are *hundreds* of bones, maybe thousands. This is cannibalism on a *massive* scale . . .'

Jeffers nodded beside him. 'Presuming that they've now developed some kind of a taste for human flesh, and if they're not eating each other, then they're going to be constantly on the lookout for fresh meat.'

'That's us,' said Jonas Jones.

Now they were walking through the ruined city, getting further and further away from harbour, the inflatables and the safety of the *Titanic*.

'I get the feeling we're being watched,' said Dr Hill, as Claire fell into step beside him.

'Me too,' said Claire. 'I wonder what human flesh tastes like?'

'Chicken. I'm told it tastes like chicken.'

Claire grimaced.

Five minutes later, First Officer Jeffers called a rest halt. Bottles of water were passed. As the crewmen formed a loose perimeter, guns ready, Jeffers warned everyone else not to wander off; despite this some poked into stores on either side of the broad avenue. Jeffers then checked in with Captain Smith. When he was finished Claire asked to use the radio and was patched through to Andy in the newsroom.

'Has Brian turned up yet?' she asked.

'No,' said Andy.

Claire tutted. 'I should have given the story to someone else. He may have an IQ off the scale, but it doesn't mean he knows how to write a decent—'

'Claire. We found his cell-phone. He was using it to tape his interview with that minister guy.'

'What do you mean you found it? Did he lose it or . . .' There were several long moments of speechless radio static. 'Andy?'

'We found it on the top deck at the very back of the ship by the rails. It was smashed to pieces. We've searched every inch of the ship, Claire. There's no other sign of him. If we found it there, then maybe he . . . you know, fell . . .'

Claire was momentarily stunned.

I sent a shy kid to interview someone who might be a killer, and now he's disappeared. I should have confronted Cleaver myself, not sent some green kid to do it.

But then she thought, no, that's jumping to conclusions. There could be a dozen reasons why Brain had disappeared. Maybe he'd dropped the phone by mistake, realised he'd lost the interview, and was too embarrassed to show his face in the office. Andy might well have claimed to have mounted a thorough search, but that was impossible in the short time that had passed – the ship was massive. It would take an organised team weeks to check every nook and cranny. Brian could quite easily just be hiding out. Or, if by some chance he *had* gone overboard, it didn't mean he'd been murdered. He might have been in some kind of freak accident – or he might even have killed himself. It wasn't unheard of for people to throw themselves off the *Titanic*. Losing loved ones, your home: even losing treasured mementoes had been known to drive people to suicide. There was no way of knowing if Brian was 'the type' to kill himself, because there *was* no type. It could affect anyone. One moment they were there, the next they were gone.

Claire sighed. 'OK – look, we need to keep looking. Inform Captain Smith, he'll organise a proper search.'

'Will do. What's it like out there?'

'Interesting,' said Claire.

She talked for a few more minutes, while Andy

wrote her observations down. It looked like they were going to be ashore for several days, and there was still a daily paper to produce, so she would have to take opportunities like this to file her reports. When she was finished she handed the radio back to Jeffers, grabbed a bottle of water for herself, and was just turning to look for Ty when she jumped suddenly.

The Rev. Calvin Cleaver was right beside her. *Centimetres* away.

'Sorry,' he said, his voice a cold rasp. 'I didn't mean to frighten you.'

'You – you didn't . . .' Claire took a step back. She glanced around to make sure someone was watching.

'We haven't been introduced . . . apparently I shot you.'

His eyes were pale and tinged with red, his teeth sharp and crooked. Claire had time and again counselled herself not to judge a book by its cover, but it was impossible. Cleaver might as well have had *evil bad guy* printed on his head. It just seemed that nobody else was aware of it.

'Yes . . . yes . . . you . . .'

She found herself involuntarily rubbing at her arm. It *ached*. Like it knew that the monster responsible was right there.

'I'm really dreadfully sorry.'

He reached out, and before she could do anything, he had taken hold of her hand. He clasped it between his own. His flesh was cold and clammy.

'I wish I could make it up to you.'

'No . . . no . . . it's quite . . .'

She wanted to *run*, but he wouldn't let go.

'I couldn't help but overhear . . . has something happened to that little fellow sent to interview me?'

She was trying to read his eyes. Were they cold and gloating, or were they just *like that*?

'We're . . . not sure – he seems to have disappeared.' She took a step back, and in so doing managed to free her hand from his grasp. It just slipped out. 'The interview – you did it with him?'

'Oh, yes. He asked all sorts of interesting questions. He was really awfully smart. Nervous, but intelligent, I thought.'

'His cell-phone was found on the top deck, smashed.'

'Really? How odd. He interviewed me in the restaurant on the eleventh. Do you really think something has . . . happened to him?'

'I . . . don't know.'

At that moment Cleaver was distracted by First Officer Jeffers calling on them all to get ready to move out again. There were groans from some of the older passengers as they got to their feet. Claire hurried towards the front of the column. She felt odd – unclean. The hand he had held was moist with her cold sweat *and* his. She wiped it on her jeans. He had acted pious and innocent, but he knew something, she was sure of it. But again, it was just a feeling – intuition, no cold hard facts.

They were just about to move when one of the passengers cried out: 'Not yet – my wife isn't here.'

Jeffers shook his head impatiently and hurried down the column. 'Well where is she? We haven't time to hang around.'

The passenger, a bald man with a paunchy belly was wearing a Hawaiian shirt, and standing in the doorway of an optician's store. 'She was looking for a new pair of sunglasses. She was thirsty, I went to get her another bottle of water . . . I only left her for a minute . . .'

Jeffers studied the store for a moment, before moving past the passenger and into the interior, removing his pistol as he did so. Two crewmen followed him in. Claire peered through the front window at display cabinets full of designer glasses caked with thin layers of dust, before following the passenger inside. She immediately noticed a slight breeze coming from the rear of the store where a door lay open. Jeffers cautiously approached this and looked out into the alley beyond. It was empty. He bent and lifted something from the ground. He held up a pair of glasses, with one cracked lens. The passenger hurried up and examined them.

'These are Mary's! These are her glasses . . .' He looked about him, his eyes full of panic and desperation. 'I don't understand – I was only gone for a minute! Where is she?'

Jeffers moved back into the store, closing the door behind him.

'What're you doing?' the passenger demanded. 'She must be out there – she's—'

'She's gone.' Jeffers' voice was as hard and cold as Claire had ever heard it.

'What do you mean she's . . . ? She must have just popped to the next store – she's . . .'

Jeffers led the way out of the optician's. 'We're leaving, we're leaving now!' he cried. He strode straight up to the head of the column, geeing people up along the way. 'C'mon, let's go!'

Claire stepped into the column about halfway along, beside Ty and a little way behind Cleaver.

The passenger whose wife had disappeared remained in the store doorway. 'We can't just leave her!' he cried.

But that's what was happening. As the column moved out, passengers and crew alike avoided eye contact with him.

'*Please!*'

They kept going.

'What do you think happened?' Ty whispered, glancing back.

'Don't know,' said Claire.

'Jeffers looks spooked.'

Claire nodded.

'Those damn monkeys,' said Ty.

The River

Jimmy had no hopes at all for his stunt with the Morse code. He had only tried it because it was *something*. He wasn't worried about Ham being suspicious or reporting him for smashing his lighter – he'd left his post while on duty, so he'd only be getting himself into trouble. But he still felt like a prisoner. The Morse code wasn't enough. He wanted to charge at the wire fence. He wanted to dig a tunnel with his bare hands. He wanted to convince his fellow soldiers to stage a revolution. Yet he couldn't understand why nobody else seemed to feel the same way. The rest of his troop all seemed so content – yes, the training was hard, and of course Mohican was a monster, but otherwise they seemed quite happy with their lot. In the darkness of the barracks that night he told them about the plans he had seen on the walls of the war room, of the battle that was being planned. He meant it to scare them. He meant for them to realise that this wasn't a game, that soon some of them might be dead. But they welcomed it. They whooped and hollered and predicted how many bad guys they were going to kill, even though they had no idea who the bad guys were.

Jimmy couldn't sleep. He felt claustrophobic. Quite often on the *Titanic* he would sleep on the balcony outside his cabin, wrapped up in a blanket with the sea air whistling around him. He tried it here, dragging his sleeping bag out of the barracks and on to the wooden surround outside the hut. He stubbed his toe in the darkness. He cursed to himself. He lay down on the floorboards. He looked up at the stars, but they were obscured by a cloudy sky. The wood smelled of damp and mud. He tossed and turned. One of the search lights crossed above him, and it was only in following its trajectory that he became aware of a single, small red light, just a few metres away. It moved.

He wasn't alone.

Someone sitting in the corner, smoking.

Jimmy groaned inwardly. Ham. 'What, are you stalking me now?' he hissed. Then added, 'You little creep,' for good measure.

The light was extinguished. For ten seconds everything was black.

'Oh, you're scaring me.'

All the same, he tensed, in case the little chimney took a run at him in the dark.

Then there was a *click click*, a little roar of flame, and Ham bent into the sudden brightness to light his cigarette.

Except it wasn't Ham.

It was Mohican.

Time to backtrack . . . *quickly*.

'Of course, when I said *little creep*, I meant *most wonderful leader*.'

'Relax, Armstrong,' said Mohican. He closed the lighter and they were plunged back into darkness again. 'What's wrong, can't sleep?'

'No. I mean yes. I mean, I can't sleep.' Silence. 'Can you not . . . either?'

The cigarette brightened for a moment as Mohican inhaled. He ignored the question. 'I heard you earlier. Talking about the coming battle.'

'Oh.'

'You're different than they are, Armstrong. I'm sure you've seen some bad things, but you seem to have come through them pretty unscathed. Those guys in there, I know their stories. Terrible stories. Torres – you know what he had to do? He had to shoot his parents. They were in agony from the plague and they begged him. Ramon – with the black glasses? He had little brothers, twins. His parents were gone. He only had enough medicine to give to one of his brothers – he had to choose which one lived. Imagine doing that? And then they both died anyway. Marissa, girl with the long blond hair? Fifteen days without food, turned into a slave by bandits, do I have to say what they did to her? They all got stories like that. So when they find something like this, what we have here, they embrace it. Sure it's tough, but it's not tough compared to what they've been through. They have friends here.

They have food and heat and hope. And if they have to go into battle to keep this, then they'll do that, they won't question orders, they'll do exactly what they're told.'

Jimmy could see exactly how attractive Fort Hope, the President and the camaraderie of army life would seem to someone who'd endured and survived the plague.

But at the back of his mind he also knew that that was how dictators got started. Jimmy had been one of the worst students in East Belfast High, but he wasn't stupid. If he'd appeared lazy, if he seemed to lack application and seldom paid attention – well, that was all pretty true; but he took things on board, he thought about them when he wasn't *forced* to think about them. He knew about Hitler's Germany – that when people were down, if you promised them great things and then delivered at least some of them, they would follow you even if, ultimately, what you were doing was wrong. Germans hadn't been bad, but they had been led to badness by bad men. And by the time they realised their mistake, it was too late.

Jimmy might have pointed this out, but part of surviving a dictatorship is knowing when to keep quiet. He was only learning this *slowly*. As Mohican smoked in the darkness, Jimmy merely asked:

'Who are we fighting?'

'The enemy.'

'In New York?'

'Wherever we tell you.'

Mohican stubbed the remains of his cigarette out on the wooden floor and stood. 'You should get some sleep, Armstrong. You're important to this troop, you show some good leadership qualities, they respect you. Don't let them down.'

He stepped off the surround and walked away.

Jimmy felt pretty good about what Mohican had said. For about ten seconds.

Then he shook himself and muttered: 'What a lot of crap.'

It was raining heavily by morning. Jimmy had slept only fitfully on the surround, and felt stiff and sore. He showered and dressed before the rest of the troop was awake. He decided to make himself useful by taking a plastic bag full of trash out to the garbage disposal unit on the far side of the Fort. On the way back he splashed past the First Aid hut. The girl was sitting outside. Her tray was on the table in front of her as usual – but this time the food had been devoured. She continued to stare ahead. She did not acknowledge him. But there was something definitely softer about her face.

'Starting to get your appetite back, eh?'

He leaned on the wooden fence and smiled at her.

'I'm going for breakfast myself in a minute, anything else I can get you? I can smuggle out most things, although I'm not sure what I'd do with scrambled eggs. No?'

No reaction.

The whistle sounded for breakfast; immediately barracks' doors all around the camp began to open and their hungry occupants spilled out.

Jimmy winked at her. 'See ya later,' he said.

The rain had not let up when Mohican marched them out of the fort an hour later. And they did *march*. They really were starting to look like a cohesive army unit now. He led them south across the plain until they came to the banks of a river. The grass on both sides had been trampled down, and a series of ropes and pulleys set up. He lined them up in two rows and called them to attention.

'Today, ladies and gentlemen, we will be learning how to cross a river at speed. You will see that the ropes have already been set up. I want you to examine them, work out how it has been done, and then the ropes and apparatus will be removed. It will then be up to you to get the ropes, and then yourselves, across the river. The first time you do this will be in uniform alone. The second time will be carrying a full pack. The third time will be carrying a full pack, under enemy fire. This will show whether you can operate as a team, it will show whether you can remain calm under attack, it will show whether you have what it takes to become a United States Marine. If any of you fall into the water – that is allowed – *once*. If you fall twice, then you are on a warning. If you fall three times, then you are not a team player and you will be removed from the unit and reassigned. Do you understand?'

'YES, SIR!'

'Very well. But before we start, Private Armstrong – step forward!'

Jimmy gulped. His eyes darted from left to right and all places above and below.

He stepped forward. 'Sir?'

Mohican, marched up to him. His eyes bore into Jimmy's.

'Armstrong, you've been trouble since you arrived.'

'Sir.'

'You have constantly questioned authority and disobeyed commands.'

'Sir.'

Mohican stepped behind him.

'But you have spirit, and you're brave, and you have provided vital information to our President.'

Jimmy said nothing. His eyes remained fixed front.

'Therefore I have decided to promote you to the rank of Corporal.' For the first time Jimmy's eyes flitted to the side. 'This is your troop, it is your responsibility to get them through training, to make sure they work hard.'

Mohican stepped back in front of him. He produced two pointed yellow cloth bars, like two mountain peaks, one behind the other, and pinned them loosely to his arm. He stepped back, and saluted.

Jimmy returned the salute and backed into the ranks.

'Well done,' someone whispered.

'Arse-kisser,' whispered someone else.

There was no let-up in the rain. They were wet and miserable *before* they started falling into the river.

Jimmy had always thought of himself as being fairly hopeless at logical thinking, but the troop was looking to him for leadership and he surprised himself by remaining calm and organised and coming up with some sensible ideas. In truth, it wasn't rocket science, and soldiers had been fording rivers for thousands of years. It was more the conditions than the task that were providing the biggest challenge; the ground was slippery, the mud seeped into everything, getting a firm grip of the ropes on the riverbank was one thing; maintaining it as you tried to cross the river was something else.

The rope was fitted to a grappling hook and hurled across. It took four attempts to secure it with enough certainty to allow two soldiers to pull themselves across through the water trailing secondary ropes. Once on the other side they established the connection between the two banks and raised the ropes out of the water. Jimmy, trying to instil confidence into some of his doubtful-looking troop, was the first to clip himself on and haul himself across. He waved back across the river to the next trooper to begin her attempt. She nodded, gave him the thumbs-up and, suitably inspired, slipped straight down the bank and into the water.

But she climbed out and tried again.

They all kept at it. Mohican watched without commenting as their confidence grew. Finally they managed to fire the rope across the water and get everyone across without incident. Then they broke for lunch, tired but feeling good. They returned to the fort, ate well, laughed and joked, then emerged to find that the rain had become torrential. When they reached the river the water had risen and was now flowing past exceptionally quickly.

This time they had to cross wearing packs. They had not actually been issued with enough equipment yet to make them particularly heavy, so Mohican thoughtfully weighed them down with rocks. Their grip on the bank and the ropes became even more precarious. Jimmy moved back and forth, shouting encouragement, making sure the team (and the ropes) were secure, leading from the front; crossing the river half a dozen times. Confidence grew again. The only one who didn't seem to respond was Rain Man. When Jimmy offered advice or a helping hand he snapped back or slapped it away. Jimmy could see the pulse in the side of Rain Man's head racing. It was either intense concentration – or fear.

When they came to make their final effort to get everyone across with full packs, Jimmy personally checked that every one of them was clipped securely on to the line across the bulging river. If someone fell, they might hit the water, but they would remain securely fastened to the bridging rope. It would be up to the others to haul him or her back in.

Jimmy had managed to get half of them across and they were shouting encouragement back for the others, when there was a ripping sound, and Marissa's backpack strap snapped. Marissa let out a yelp, and held tight to the rope. Her backpack fell into the river and was flushed hundreds of metres away in a matter of seconds.

It was a grim warning as to what could happen – especially during the next task, getting everyone safely across under gunfire.

While Mohican supervised the setting up of the machine guns that would provide a steady stream of fire to the left and right of the ropes and over their heads, the troops stood anxiously on the far bank. This was different. This was more like the real thing. Jimmy saw Rain Man whispering to Torres; Torres gave him a reassuring punch on the arm. When Jimmy went over and asked if he was OK, Rain Man told him to get lost. Jimmy shrugged.

The rain had eased up a little, but the water, if anything, was flowing faster and stronger as Mohican, standing behind the gunners, blew a whistle to begin their crossing. As the gunfire began Jimmy crouched down with the others.

'Come on, we can do this!' he cried.

Two soldiers darted forward, heads low, and fired the rope and grappling hook across. It caught first time! Jimmy himself made sure it was secure then clipped the same two soldiers on to the line and urged them forward as bullets ripped into the mud on either side of them. They plunged into the water, struggled against the current but finally made it across to properly secure the ropes and raise the line. The remaining soldiers scuttled forward, hauled themselves up on to the rope, secured themselves and began to race across. If they were frightened they showed no sign of it; their concentration was intense – even Rain Man, ducking down on the bank, waiting his turn, looked like he meant business. They were so keen that Jimmy even had to slow them down so that no more than four were on the rope at any one time – with their full packs and the extra weight caused by them being absolutely saturated by the rain, the rope bridge was beginning to sag in the middle.

Jimmy gave Rain Man a hand up, then Torres. Jimmy clipped himself on last and moved out. The gunfire was loud, even above the roar of the river, but not as loud as the yells of encouragement coming from the far bank. They were the last three. If they made it across the troop would have successfully completed its mission.

Jimmy was filled with an immense pride as he reached the halfway point. Between them, Mohican and he had turned a gang of lost souls into a troop of soldiers, a finely-tuned unit that could fight together, serve the Pres—

Wait a minute – what the hell am I thinking?

There, hanging precariously to a rope, gunfire all around him, soaked to the skin, he suddenly caught sight of what he'd become. It wasn't quite an out-of-body experience, more like out of his mind. He was turning into exactly the opposite of what he had intended. A yes-sir, no-sir soldier preparing for a war he had no interest in. He'd been planning his escape, but instead had been sucked into soldiering by Mohican's simple device of promoting him to Corporal.

Jimmy stared at the water.

That's it!

My escape route!

All he had to do was unclip from the rope and fall in. He'd be swept miles downriver. Of course there was a strong possibility that he would drown. The current was vicious and if he wasn't sucked under, the speed and strength of the river would probably smash him on the sharp rocks jutting out of the water. But it might be his only chance to get away. He absolutely did not want to be part of the President's bloody army, and he had to get to New York before it did to warn the *Titanic*.

Jimmy stared at the water. He was a good swimmer, but wherever the water took him, whatever it did with him, it would be beyond his control.

The others were nearing the far bank. He had to decide *now*.

Bullets continued to yip above his head.

Jimmy's damp finger curled around the clip and released it.

Jump on three.

One—

There was a metallic crack to his right – but not a bullet. Rain Man let out a panicked yell as his clip snapped and he was hurled backwards into the water.

'Rain Man!' Torres yelled.

He had already been whisked fifty metres away.

'He can't swim!' Torres screamed.

If anything, the gunfire intensified, drowning out the concerned shouts from the far bank. Rain Man's head disappeared under the water.

His one chance of escape and Rain Man *couldn't swim.*

Jimmy dropped his pack and let go of the rope.

In a second the river swallowed him.

Grand Central

They heard the elephant before they saw it – not just its trumpet roar, but also a metallic dragging sound. Then they saw it, and thanked God that the street to their right was completely blocked with abandoned vehicles so that the creature, huge and mad, with the remnants of a heavy anchoring chain still attached to its leg, could not barge its way through. It tried – with the brute strength of its massive shoulders, with the pointy end of its razor tusks.

'Cool!' said Ty. 'Do you think if I offered him a peanut he'd take it?'

'Of course he would,' said Claire, 'along with your arm, your neck and your head.'

First Officer Jeffers urged them on – although he practically had to drag Claire, who was busy taking photos, and Ty, who just liked elephants.

He kept them moving all morning, every one of them aware, despite the distraction of the elephant, that they were being watched and followed. It wasn't that they caught many actual glimpses of their pursuers – though they did occasionally see shadowy figures

208

ducking down behind abandoned vehicles, or moving back from overlooking windows – it was a feeling, an intense awareness that they weren't alone, that someone, somewhere, meant them harm: had already struck once and would strike again.

Jeffers led them up Broadway as far as 42nd Street and the entrance to the Grand Central Terminal. It was, as far as Claire knew, the largest railway station in the world. Over half a million passengers and tourists had once passed through it every day, but now it was empty of everything but skeletons and birds. Their footsteps echoed around like gunshots on the marbled floors. The main concourse, huge and cavernous, was dominated by a massive American flag, which drooped down, tattered. As they walked along, Ty nudged Claire's elbow and pointed up at the ceiling: it was completely covered in an elaborately decorated depiction of the night sky, an astronomical guide to the stars. 'Though it's completely wrong,' said Ty. 'It's based on some medieval map, and they didn't know anything back then.'

'You've been here before?'

'All the time, with my pa. Loved it. You couldn't move, it was so alive! Man, we'd buy hot dogs and just sit over there and watch . . .'

He stopped. There were tears in his eyes. Claire didn't know what to say. They'd all run out of the right words *months* ago.

Jeffers waved them forward, down a ramp on to the

lower concourse and gathered them in a food court. Some of the tables were still occupied by people who would never finish their meals. A small amount of food had been brought from the ship, and they were able to supplement this with sealed items recovered from some of the many fast food outlets dotted around and about. They drank warm Coke and snacked on potato chips. But they didn't have much of an appetite. The whole area stank of rotting food. Guards were posted at the top of the ramp while Jeffers, Jonas and Dr Hill spread out a free tourist map of the station, one of hundreds lying scattered about, and debated their next move. When they'd come to a decision Jeffers took two crewmen with him and returned to the upper concourse, and from there back outside, trying to get the best radio signal he could in order to inform Captain Smith of his next move.

Claire kept an eye on Cleaver, sitting at a table by himself, the brim of his hat pulled down to leave the top half of his face hidden so that she couldn't tell whether he was reading the small Bible open before him or sleeping. As she watched, the man in the Hawaiian shirt, whose wife had disappeared earlier that morning, sat down opposite him. The minister's head scarcely moved up as the man began to speak. Within a few moments he abruptly jumped back up and stomped away. Cleaver's head remained bowed.

Claire slipped out of her seat and approached the Hawaiian man where he was leaning against a pillar on the far side of the food court. His cheeks were flushed and he kept firing angry glances towards the minister's table.

'Is everything OK?' Claire asked.

'What do you think?' the man snapped. He glared at her for a moment, before sighing and shaking his head. 'Sorry. It's just – I asked that . . . that *reverend* to say a prayer for my wife, and he just refused … he just said if she was gone it was the will of the Lord! You imagine that?'

Claire was trying her best to calm the man down when there was a sudden commotion as Jeffers reappeared with his gun out and one of his crewmen supporting the other, who now had a rough bandage around his arm. His white shirt was ripped and soaked in blood. Dr Hill hurried up to examine him as Jeffers helped ease the injured man on to the floor.

'He's been shot,' said Jeffers. 'There's a lot of people moving out there, coming this way.'

'Why're they shooting at us?' one of the passengers asked in panic.

Jeffers glanced at Dr Hill, but didn't immediately respond.

'Maybe they don't realise that we can help them,' said another passenger. 'If we just try and talk to them maybe—'

'No,' Jeffers said firmly, climbing back to his feet. 'It's not safe.'

'We have to at least try,' continued the passenger.

Jeffers took off his cap and wiped his brow. He looked around the passengers. 'Listen to me, all of you. Whatever survivors there are out there, they're not friendly. Whatever happened in this city after the plague has reduced them to cannibalism.'

He let it sit in the air. Claire already knew, but she still felt a shiver run through her.

'You're not serious…' said one of the passengers.

'Deadly serious. Dr Hill and I have both seen the evidence. We're not safe out there – which is why we're not going back out.' This set off a flurry of questions, but Jeffers quickly held his hand up for silence. 'Folks – *you* are here out of your own choice. *We* are here because we need to retrieve a vital part for the *Titanic*. If *you* wish to travel on to your homes in different parts of the city or beyond, if you wish to try and track down relatives, then I believe this station provides you with your best chance – perhaps your *only* chance of getting to your preferred destination safely. I'm going to split you up into small groups. You will use the underground rail tracks to traverse the city; we have a detailed map here, we have a supply of flashlights, and I am prepared to assign two armed guards to each group to get you as far as possible. But they may not be able to take you all of the way. After a while you're going to be on your own. That's a decision you have to make. What I will say is this – it's going to take us a full day to get to *our* objective and back. I plan to be at this exact location twenty-four hours from now. If you decide to return to the *Titanic* for whatever reason, I would suggest that you do your best to make it here for this time tomorrow and then we can escort you to the ship. But we're not going to hang around. Now, any questions?'

As with any large group of diverse people, there were *loads* of questions, some stupid, some bright. Jeffers answered them all as well as he could, but he was honest enough to answer, 'I don't know,' to many of them. There was a crushing lack of information about what the rest of the city was like – this cannibalism might well be confined to one small section, or there might be thousands of them. Yes, the railway tunnels could also be teaming with cannibals.

Eventually Jeffers called a halt to the discussion and gathered the passengers around a map of the station which showed the platforms and tunnels and routes, and then split them into groups according to their destinations and assigned guards to each. There were six groups in all – the smallest with four passengers, requiring only one guard: the largest with ten, which included Jeffers himself, Jonas Jones, Dr Hill, Claire, Ty, a husband and wife, the Robinsons, an elderly man on a walking stick called Morgan, the man with the Hawaiian shirt, whose name was Rodriguez – and the Rev. Calvin Cleaver. The three remaining crewmen, including Mr Benson and the wounded man, joined this group.

When they were all ready to set off, Jeffers addressed them all. 'On behalf of Captain Smith and myself,' he said, 'I want to wish you the best of luck with your journey. I hope you find what you're looking for, be it family or friends, or perhaps just a little bit of closure. Remember, you have twenty-four hours to make your minds up about returning to the *Titanic.*'

The groups began to move out. As they passed each other, they shook hands solemnly. Only Cleaver failed to partake. He sat by himself, waiting.

Ty nudged Claire. 'Looks like he's with us.'

'In a dark tunnel,' said Claire, shuddering.

'I'll watch your back,' said Ty, 'you watch mine.'

'I think I'd rather be caught by the cannibals than be stuck with him,' said Claire.

'Don't say that,' said Ty.

Jeffers came up to her. 'Claire – I don't want you wandering off to take photographs, OK?'

'I *know*,' said Claire, rolling her eyes.

Jeffers smiled, and was just about to move on when he suddenly remembered something. 'Oh, and Claire – when I was on the line with Captain Smith, I also spoke to your newspaper office . . .'

Claire immediately looked towards Cleaver. 'Have they found Brian?'

'Brian? No, it wasn't about that. As you know, the communications centre monitors radio traffic, and it seems they picked up some Morse code they thought might be of interest to you.'

Her brow furrowed. 'Morse . . . ? Why would—'

'Just two words – *Babe lives*, with an exclamation mark. Mean anything to you?'

The Plan

They were found clinging to a rock two miles downriver, frozen, unable to move, on the verge of passing out and slipping back in, two almost-drowned rats. They could not feel their arms or legs. They were hauled out by their comrades, with Mohican yelling commands, and then rushed away in an ambulance. In the back, drifting between lucidity and coma, Rain Man whispered, 'You saved my life. Why did you do that?'

'Because I'm stupid,' Jimmy whispered back.

He blacked out.

For a long time he wasn't sure where he was. Or if he was alive or dead. He kept thinking he was awake and he was talking coherently to Claire, but then she vanished, or grew trotters. And then he realised he was asleep – but if you realise you're asleep, are you really asleep? – that puzzled him, while he slept. When he did wake, he ached. He felt as if a dwarf with a very small sledge-hammer had whacked every single bone in his body. He didn't want to ever move again, but then the nurse brought in a tray of bacon and eggs and toast and he immediately sat up and ate everything.

Rain Man was asleep in the bed opposite. There was an IV tube inserted in his arm. The girl with the constant stare was awake – but constantly staring at some far-off imaginary planet.

The nurse beamed down at him. 'Our hero,' she said. She nodded beyond him and he turned to find that some kind of a medal had been pinned to the wall. 'The President himself came by last night and presented it to you. He was going to wait until this morning, but thought it was better to do it immediately in case you died.'

Jimmy swallowed. 'Was that likely?'

'Likely? It was *probable* – but you didn't.'

'What about him?' Jimmy nodded towards Rain Man.

'You both surprised us. You're made of strong stuff.'

Jimmy glowed, just a little bit. And then he remembered: that's how they operate. They praise you, they promote you, it's how they win your loyalty.

Escape – you have to escape.

But he was going nowhere just yet. When the nurse left he tried to stand – his legs were like jelly. He sat on the edge of the bed instead, slowly flexing his muscles, forcing the blood to flow back. He graduated to standing upright, then shuffling along. It was exhausting, but he knew he had to do it. He *had* to escape. But how? The river had been his best

217

opportunity and he'd blown that by . . . doing something good. He would try and avoid being good in future. He'd had a lifetime of practice.

As the morning wore on Jimmy found himself being drawn again to the girl. There were crumbs on her top sheet and an empty plate on her locker, so she was now clearly capable of movement, but she appeared as lost as ever. Jimmy sat in a chair beside her bed and just looked at her.

Eventually he said: 'I talked to you a while back about escaping. Just wondering if you'd had any further thoughts, or if you've managed to dig that tunnel while I've been out saving lives. I have a medal, you know? I'm pretty great. But I need help. I have to get out of here. I have to get back to *Titanic*. You'd love it there. Biggest cruise ship ever built. Everything on board, a real luxury liner. And we have chickens and pigs. Well, we *had* some pigs . . .'

He told her about Babe. He couldn't help but laugh when he started in on the anxious wait for Babe's execution and how he'd returned to the newsroom with a bag of sausages. 'They weren't really made out of Babe, you know? But if you'd seen her face . . .' He sighed. The laughter was gone. 'I just need to get back there. It's the only home I have. The newspaper is . . . everything. Can you understand that?' He looked for some response. Nothing. He sighed again. 'Oh, what's the bloody point?'

Jimmy stood to go, but as he reached the end of her

bed, the girl said very quietly: 'Take me with you.'

Jimmy stopped, stunned, as her eyes flitted towards him, just for a second, before returning to the ceiling.

Jimmy stepped right back up to her. 'You can . . . ?'

She nodded slowly.

'The whole time you could . . . ?'

She nodded again.

'So you've listened to all my crap and never said a . . . ?' She nodded once more. 'But *why*?'

She smiled. 'Do you think I want to become a soldier either?'

It was a show of bravado. She had been very seriously ill and badly traumatised when she'd been found wandering in the forest six weeks previously. And she clearly wasn't completely right yet. When Jimmy pulled his chair closer to the bed and asked her how she'd come to be lost in the forest she just shrugged.

'Well, where were you before that?'

She shrugged again.

'Can't remember, or don't want to talk about it?'

'Both. Either.'

Jimmy had interviewed enough people for the *Times* – kids and adults alike – to know that many of them had been through such horrific experiences that they literally *couldn't* talk about them, without seriously jeopardising both their mental and physical wellbeing. They built protective walls around those memories, sometimes so tall and strong that even they could no longer access them.

'So, anyway, you were sick when you came here, but then you got better – but you never let on because . . . ?'

'. . . because it's all about fighting and conquering and . . . stuff. I like the sound of the *Titanic*.'

'You have a name?'

'Ronni. Two *n*s, one *i*.'

'Ronni. What's that short for?'

'It's not short for anything.'

Jimmy nodded. 'Ronni,' he said. '*Ronni*. OK, Ronni. Do you really want to escape with me?'

'Yes. Definitely.'

'OK then. All we need now is a plan. And an opportunity. And some luck.' They heard footsteps outside. Ronni's head fell back on her pillow and her eyes glazed over. 'Start thinking,' whispered Jimmy, and stood just as the nurse re-entered, carrying a large pile of fresh linen. She looked surprised to see him up.

'Jimmy, should you—'

'I'm confused,' he said quickly, nodding down at Ronni's bed. 'She never moves a muscle, yet her plate's always empty. I think we have mice. Big ones.'

The nurse smiled indulgently. 'Jimmy, she eats. But only in the dark, in the middle of the night. She's getting better, but it's going to be a long, slow process.'

Jimmy shook his head. 'If you ask me, she's faking.'

He turned for his bed.

'*Jimmy!*' scolded the nurse.

★ ★ ★

220

One thing he was pretty sure of, he needed to stay in the First Aid hut for as long as possible. If he returned to the troop there would be less opportunity to plan or execute the escape. So in the midst of more verbal sparring with the nurse he faked a dizzy spell and collapsed down on to his bed. She rushed across, pulled the covers up over him, took his temperature and tutted. In fact he *was* feeling rather hot, but he played it up. Later in the afternoon, several of his comrade troopers visited, but he pretended to be asleep. They cooed over his medal and talked about his heroics and remarked on how ill he looked.

'He's definitely not going to be fit for tomorrow,' said Torres.

One of the girls said, 'I can't imagine going into battle without him.'

Through all of this Rain Man continued to sleep.

After five minutes the nurse shooed them away. Then she went off for dinner, allowing Jimmy to climb back out of bed. Ronni stood with him by the window while they tried to puzzle out a way to escape. She was slightly more practically minded than he was.

'We'll need food, clothes and medicine,' she said. 'We'll need a tent and pots and—'

'We're not going *camping*,' said Jimmy. 'We just need to get *out*. There's a whole world full of stuff out there that nobody needs any more — we can pick it up as we go.'

'And what if we wander around lost in the woods, what if we're wet and hungry and—'

'We won't be. Or if we are, we'll figure out what to do. But none of it matters anyway, because there's no way out.'

Jimmy stared through the glass at the wire fence thirty metres away. It wasn't quite dark yet, but the search beams were already crisscrossing the plain beyond. Trucks filled with supplies rumbled back and forth; soldiers sat in little groups, taking their guns apart and putting them back together, checking and rechecking. Some alredy had camouflage painted on their faces.

What did they say earlier? '*He's definitely not going to be fit for tomorrow.*' '*I can't imagine going into battle without him.*'

They were preparing for war.

Jimmy drummed his fingers on the window.

We haven't even trained with guns yet. What kind of a crazy war is that? If we're fighting another army, we're going to get slaughtered!

Not 'we'!

They. They'll get slaughtered.

It has nothing to do with me.

I have to get out of here! There must be a way.

And it has to be tonight.

'There must be a way! There must be a bloody—'

'There is a way.'

It wasn't Ronni.

It was Rain Man, sitting up in bed.

Jimmy gave him a hard look. 'I thought you were sleeping.'

'How can I with you two plotting your escape?'

'You weren't supposed to hear that. And there's no plotting going on. And if you squeal on us I swear to God I'll—'

'You'll what? Kill me?' Rain Man laughed. 'You've just *saved* me. Anyway, I figure I owe you.'

'Whaddya mean?'

'Don't get me wrong, Frankie . . .'

'Frankie?' said Ronni.

'It's a long story,' said Jimmy.

'Short for Frankenstein,' said Rain Man.

'Are you some kind of monster?' asked Ronni.

'No!' He glared at Rain Man. 'What are you talking about?'

'Well, Frankie, I still think you're an arrogant, disloyal, disruptive son of a . . . but I still owe you. And I think I know how you can escape. Both of you, if that's what you want.'

Jimmy stared at him.

'That's what we want,' said Ronni. She nudged Jimmy. He nodded begrudgingly.

'What's the big idea?' he asked.

Rain Man pushed his covers back. He took a deep breath and stood. He immediately sat down again. Ronni went across and offered him her arm. He took it and she helped him up then supported him as he crossed to the window. He leaned on the sill and nodded out. 'Through the fence . . .'

'*Through the fence?*' Jimmy exploded. 'Do you not think—'

'Will you give me a chance?' Rain Man snapped. Jimmy glared at him again. They would never be friends. 'OK. So all of the lights are powered from a central generator. If I find a way to disable it then it's going to be pitch black out there. You'll have at least five minutes before they get the backup working.'

Jimmy blinked at him. 'You would do that?'

Rain Man nodded. 'If it makes us even, sure. Anyway, chances are they'll get the lights back on and you'll be shot before you make the woods, but if you think you can do it, why not?'

'And what if *you* get caught?' Ronni asked.

'I'll act all delirious and they'll think I did it by accident. Or something. It doesn't matter, I owe him.'

Jimmy shook his head slowly. 'Maybe you'll just switch the generator off for a minute, long enough for us to get out there, and then you'll switch it back on again and we'll be sitting ducks. Maybe *that's* your plan. How do we know we can trust you?'

'You don't,' said Rain Man.

Tunnels

They were being followed, they knew that. Footfalls echoed along the tunnels; they caught flashes of light in the darkness. First Officer Jeffers repeatedly whispered for them to be quiet, but it was difficult, with huge brown rats nipping at their ankles every few metres. They too had developed a taste for human flesh since the plague, but with it running out above ground the Rat Gods had seen fit to deliver a nice fresh dinner below. Or something like that. They were relentless.

'I hate this, I hate this, I hate this…' Claire repeated over and over in a frozen whisper. She'd always hated the dark. Now she hated the dark *and* rats. The dark and rats *and* cannibals. And the fact that their radios no longer worked so far underground. She tried to focus on the one good thing she was holding on to – Jimmy was alive! *Babe lives!* What else could it mean? But where was he? Was he trying to get back to the ship? What if he'd been alive when he sent it, but was dead now?

C'mon, Jimmy you can make it.
Even if we don't.

She'd thought Jeffers' idea to use the underground tracks was a good one. But the reality was something else. Cannibals behind. Rats all around. Flashlights beginning to weaken. All they needed now was for the cannibals to appear in *front* of them as well and they'd be trapped. And eaten. She wanted to run, sprint, make it back to daylight, but they had miles to go and they had to keep the speed down because the other passengers couldn't keep up.

The slowest of them all was the Rev. Calvin Cleaver.

The minister started to cough and splutter almost as soon as they entered the tunnel that would take them on the first leg of their journey underground to Penn Station. Every few minutes he would bend double and dry retch, forcing Jeffers and the crewmen to call a halt until he had recovered sufficiently to continue.

Cleaver was apologetic and blamed his illness on an allergy to rats. 'You go on – leave me . . . I know I'm slowing you down . . . I'm sorry . . .' and he looked fearfully back down the track.

'I'm not leaving anyone behind,' said Jeffers.

It was a good and noble thing to say, but it didn't sit well with Rodriguez. 'You left my wife behind!'

'Mr Rodriguez, your wife was *taken*,' said Jeffers, his voice calm but firm. 'To have spent any longer looking for her would have endangered our entire mission. We are all together here now, and I intend to keep it that way. Now keep your voice *down*.'

Rodriguez seethed, but said nothing further.

Cleaver pushed himself erect. 'I think I can go a bit further now,' he rasped.

As they moved on Claire whispered to Ty, 'Maybe if we left Cleaver behind the cannibals might forget about us and have him for lunch.'

'There's not much meat on him,' observed Ty. 'Barely enough for a sandwich.'

'Don't be ridiculous,' said Claire. 'Where are they going to get bread for a sandwich?'

They giggled. But then there was a cry, a flash of light, and the shadows of perhaps fifty pursuers all jumbled together, were briefly illuminated on the tunnel wall perhaps only a quarter of a mile behind them.

Already the giggling seemed like a distant memory.

'Come *on*!' Jeffers urged.

Two of the crewmen grabbed Cleaver and bundled him along. Claire found herself jogging along beside Jonas Jones. He was a large man and not terribly fit, but he was still quicker than most of the passengers.

'This isn't going to work,' Claire moaned. 'They're too fast, we're too slow!'

Jonas smiled grimly. 'I'm sure the boss has a plan.'

'It better be a good one.'

About a hundred metres further on Jeffers stopped abruptly and shone his torch, which was scarcely larger than a pencil, to the left. Then he quickly consulted the map of the network of tracks he'd kept folded in his left hand. As Claire and the rest of them approached she registered the slightest breath of cool air on her face.

'Mr Benson!' Jeffers barked urgently.

Benson, hurried up. '*Sir?*' he asked, a little warily.

'Benson, you've been a thorn in my side ever since you joined the *Titanic.*'

'Sir.'

'You're always on punishment duty.'

'Sir.'

'Well, if you do this properly, you'll never be on punishment duty again.'

'Sir? What if I do it wrong?'

'Then you'll be dead, Mr Benson, and it won't matter. We all will. Now listen carefully – to our left here is a service tunnel. The entrance is marked on the map, but not how long it is or where it goes. However, there's fresh air coming from somewhere. I want you to run down there and make plenty of noise; take your flashlight and *make sure* they see you.'

'I'm a decoy, sir.'

'That's it. We will continue on along the tunnel in the dark, hopefully we'll confuse them for long enough to get a proper head start. You understand what you're doing?'

'Yes, sir. You're sacrificing me for the good of the company.'

'No, Mr Benson, you're volunteering to sacrifice yourself for the good of the company. Aren't you?'

'Yes, sir.' He turned to go, but immediately turned

back. 'Sir, if I always screw things up, how come you're trusting me to do this?'

'Because, Mr Benson, if it comes down to a fight, I want my best sharp-shooters here with me. You couldn't hit a barn door with a cannon from a distance of one metre. Right – off you go. You lead them on, you do your best to lose them. If you make it, you know where the rendezvous point is – we'll see you there in twenty-four hours. Now get moving!'

'Sir!'

Benson darted into the left-hand tunnel.

'Lights out, everyone,' hissed Jeffers. They were plunged into darkness. Jeffers immediately called out as loudly as he dared: 'Not you, Mr Benson!'

'Sorry!' echoed back towards them.

His light blinked on.

'OK, let's move out everyone,' Jeffers whispered. 'Quietly, carefully, and when I give the word, freeze and don't move again until I say so.'

They walked cautiously along the railway tracks, Dr Hill in the lead, the next man with his hand on his shoulder, the next on his, and right back. They didn't make a sound when they stumbled. They bit their lips when something furry brushed their legs. Jeffers stayed right at the back, urging stragglers forward, watching the advance of the cannibals behind. There was nothing as disciplined about their pursuers. They were a tumultuous, ravenous horde.

Jeffers passed the word back and they flattened

themselves against the wall as the cannibals reached the entrance to the service tunnel. A dull, metallic hammering reached them – Benson at work, attracting their attention by banging on the tunnel walls. The rest of them held their breath as the cannibals' lights, most from burning torches, flickered in the sudden breeze from the service tunnel. It was the first time Claire had been able to glimpse their pursuers. She was surprised by their appearance. She had imagined crazed, blood-spattered zombies, but they looked so *ordinary*. Men, women, even children she might quite easily have passed in a supermarket or sat beside in a cinema. Ordinary people, who wanted to have her for dinner.

After a brief hesitation the horde surged into the service tunnel. One by one the lights disappeared as they crowded through the narrow entrance. Soon there were only two distinct lights remaining – one elderly man holding a burning torch and a child in short trousers with a flashlight – and Jeffers was on the verge of ordering them to press ahead, when there was a sudden clattering sound from behind Claire. A moment later a torch, having rolled across the ground and struck the far wall, turned itself on. In the brief moment before Jonas Jones threw himself upon it to block out the light Claire saw Cleaver with his hands raised in abject horror and mouthing the word '*Sorry!*'

The old man and the child turned from the service tunnel entrance to look in their direction.

The old man pointed.

The child yelled to the rest of his kind.

'Run!' Jeffers barked.

He grabbed hold of Claire and propelled her ahead of him into the darkness, pushing the other passengers after her.

Cleaver stumbled forward. 'I'm sorry, I'm sorry, I'm sorry . . .'

'Just keep going!'

Jeffers and the remaining crewmen held back. They had their guns out and were aiming back down the tunnel towards the cannibals, who were now pouring back out of the service tunnel.

Jonas drew his own weapon and came to join them. But Jeffers quickly sent him away. 'You must press on,' he ordered, 'we'll hold them for as long as we can, but you must reach the factory.'

Jonas raised a hand and saluted. 'Good luck!'

First Officer Jeffers nodded grimly, returned the salute and then turned to join his men. The shooting started a few moments later.

Escape

'Cut it! Cut it! Cut it!'

'I am bloody cutting it!' Jimmy hissed.

'Cut it harder!'

They were at the wire fence surrounding Fort Hope. Rain Man had done what he'd promised to do. The generator was down and this was their one chance to escape. Hand-cranked sirens wailed. Officers screamed orders. Soldiers stumbled out of their barracks. It was utterly black. There wasn't even a moon to give them some guidance. It was total chaos, and exactly what they wanted, but it wouldn't last for ever – and they couldn't cut the damn wire and vital seconds were storming past.

With the nurse gone for the night Jimmy and Ronni had gone through the surgical equipment stores in the First Aid hut and found a stout pair of jagged-mouthed scissors which cut cleanly through everything they tried them out on – wood, plastic, iron bed springs – but now that they really needed to work they were absolutely *useless*.

'Jimmy – do it!'

'I'm doing my best!'

But his best wasn't good enough. Jimmy flung them down. He looked up at the fence – the barbed wire that topped it was thick and razor-sharp, there was no way they'd be able to wriggle through it. Nor could they dig under – the fence was tight against the ground and sealed in with cement.

Ronni pulled at his arm. 'Jimmy – the gates, we have to go through the gates . . .'

'Too far away – too many soldiers!'

'We have no choice!'

In those last few moments before the lights went out they'd been anxiously scanning the perimeter as far as they could see so they knew the gates had been open *then*, but the guards' first reaction to the sudden darkness would surely have been to shut them to prevent what must be an enemy attack from penetrating the fort. But Ronni was right – what choice did they have?

They turned and they ran. The gates were easily two hundred metres away. They collided with other soldiers, running about confused. They picked themselves up and charged on. Someone was yelling, 'Protect the President! Protect the President!' Jimmy was sure he heard Mohican's distinctive tones.

They came to the gates.

Open!

There were guards there, dim outlines against the blackness, but not close enough together. And they were facing the wrong way – *out*.

A better army might have had night-vision glasses and could have shot them dead. But these soldiers couldn't see more than a metre in front of them. Jimmy and Ronni slipped between two nervous sentries.

'You see anything?' one of them hissed. Jimmy could almost feel his breath.

'I can't see nothin', but there is *somethin'* there.'

'Should we shoot?'

'Not me, I don't give orders!'

'Sir! Somethin' movin' – *can we shoot*?'

'What is it?'

'Don't know!'

'Where is it?'

'Not sure!'

'Hold your fire!'

Jimmy grabbed Ronni's hand – there was too much chance of losing her in the dark – as they raced away from the fort. Jimmy's legs, so recently sucked of all strength by the river, wobbled beneath him. Ronni had lain largely immobile for weeks and her muscles now strained and threatened to rip apart. But they kept going. The plain seemed to roll on for ever. Their feet, rushing though the knee-length grass, sounded incredibly loud purely because they were trying to be so quiet.

'We . . . must . . . nearly . . .' Jimmy wheezed.

'We . . . *have* to be close . . .'

And then, as simple as someone flicking a switch,

the lights of the fort came on – just bright enough to turn them into running shadows, and they still had a hundred metres of the open plain to cross before they reached the relative safety of the woods.

For a few achingly long seconds they ran on, unobserved, but then the searchlights began to sweep back and forth. They passed in front, then behind, before finally converging on the escapees.

Without speaking or even looking at each other Jimmy and Ronni began to zigzag. The beams lost them for a moment, then caught up again. They let go of each other's hands; Jimmy veered left, Ronni right. There was blessed darkness for another ten seconds and then they were found again, and this time they couldn't shake them.

A shot rang out, then another and another, then the steady clatter of a machine gun. The soldiers of Fort Hope were not trying to capture them alive.

Jimmy threw himself the last few metres, crashing through undergrowth and rolling over three times before coming to a dead halt up against a gnarly stump. Although he was just a few metres into the trees it was suddenly absolutely black again, as if a giant wooden curtain had been pulled behind him.

'Ronni!' he shouted. 'Ronni . . . !'

There was only silence. For a moment he feared that she was still out on the plain, shot down as she ran, but then he heard a low groan.

'J-jimmy – are you . . . ?'

'I'm here!'

Jimmy scrambled sideways. 'Keep talking, I'm coming!'

He'd moved about a dozen metres when he collided with her.

'Are you OK?' he asked breathlessly.

'Sore . . . sore but fine. Just fine. We did it!' cried Ronni.

'We really did it!'

They hugged each other, jumping up and down – and then abruptly found themselves very embarrassed about it and separated. Just as they did they heard the unmistakable rumble of a diesel engine. They hurried to the edge of the woods and peered out. A truck laden with solders was roaring across the plain towards them.

They weren't done with running!

Captured

Claire ran and ran, but it was no good. Not long after the shooting stopped the horde caught up with them. She screamed as they pounced on her, screamed as they pinned her against the wall and prepared to rip her to pieces and devour every inch of her. Inside she prayed harder than she could ever have imagined that they would kill her quickly and eat her later, that she wouldn't suffer too much, or at all. But there was one image that stayed with her through all the horror. In the moments before she was overwhelmed she caught sight of Cleaver standing with his hands clasped before him like a martyr. As they surrounded him and grabbed at him his eyes fastened on to hers and if she hadn't been so concerned with her own impending death she might have sworn that she saw him smile.

Death was . . .

. . . *not instantaneous*. Instead, the horde, once it was certain that it was in control, quickly calmed itself. The prisoners were herded against one of the walls and counted. The Hawaiian-shirted Rodriguez was begging not to be eaten. They just laughed at him. Cleaver stood at the end of the line. He appeared unfazed. Ty, standing beside Claire, touching her shoulder, was physically shaking. Or maybe it was both of them. She tried to get her heart to stop racing. Steady breaths. She darted a glance up the line of prisoners and realised that Jonas Jones wasn't amongst them. Had they killed him? The last time she'd seen him he'd been struggling to keep up. She wondered whether he'd collapsed from a heart attack. Or could he possibly have escaped? He was the only one amongst them who knew what part was needed to save the *Titanic* – his duty was not to think of them but to try and retrieve it. She crossed her fingers.

'Just do what they tell you to do,' Dr Hill whispered. 'Keep calm. We're not done yet.'

They were marched down the tracks. They weren't restrained in any way, but with the cannibals walking on either side, prodding and pinching them, there was no hope of escape. When they reached the entrance to the service tunnel Claire was surprised to spot First Officer Jeffers and the two crewmen sitting on the ground with their hands clasped on their heads and a single guard watching over them.

'Mr Jeffers!' Claire gasped. 'I thought you were . . .'

'Ran out of bullets,' Jeffers replied. His voice was low and his face barren of emotion, but his eyes were darting back and forth. Even though their situation appeared totally hopeless she could tell that he was still thinking hard, planning, calculating; she knew that he would never give up hope.

They were herded forward again. It was difficult to establish who, if anyone, was in charge. After what felt like an eternity of walking in flickering shadows they began to move towards what was literally the light at the end of the tunnel. They emerged on to a station platform that in turn led them up a permanently-stopped escalator. They climbed over jammed ticket turnstiles and then blinked out into the late afternoon sunshine of downtown Manhattan. As they walked an amazing – but still very unsettling – thing happened. People began to emerge from the buildings – at first, just one or two ragged-looking individuals, but then more and more, lining the sides of the broad avenues and moving closer and closer until they were right up close against the prisoners. Then they began to cheer and clap as if it was some kind of a victory parade in Ancient Rome. There were hundreds and hundreds of them, perhaps even thousands.

'Where in hell did they all come from?' Ty whispered.

'There're not that many, if you think of the millions who lived here,' said Claire, trying to look on the bright side.

'Know what this reminds me of? The way they're looking at us? The all-you-can-eat buffet we had on the ship.'

'Thanks for that,' said Claire.

But Ty was right. It was *exactly* how people were looking at them. There were men and women and children; there were old men and little toddlers, there were teenagers with guns slung over their shoulders; ghetto blasters pumped out music. Everyone looked rough and dirty and undernourished; but they appeared comfortable in each other's company. They were a community surviving together. Claire thought that they probably didn't eat each other.

Maybe they just send out for dinner.

They came to the junction of Broadway and 7th Avenue and looked down into what once provided one of the most famous sights in the city: Times Square. Here garish, animated digital advertising displays decorated almost every building. Here were the theatres that had once drawn in tens of thousands of tourists. Here was where New Yorkers gathered in their millions to celebrate New Year's Eve. But now the neon signs hung lifelessly: a huge Coca-Cola legend, adverts for Panasonic and Budweiser and Pontiac, dead reminders of a different time.

Except for one sign.

In the very heart of the square a big pixilated cat leaped and roared above the New Amsterdam Theatre. It was dazzling, even in daylight. *The Jungle King* blazed above theatre doors which were open and a red-carpeted foyer which was swept clean. Two ushers in great coats and military-style hats stood, outside marshalling a queue which tailed back for several hundred metres.

'What the . . . ?' Ty whispered.

Claire could only shake her head. Jeffers, at the front of their column, was looking equally bewildered.

They were led past the queue and through the theatre doors. There was a concession stand directly in front where children crowded around and a woman in a green uniform was handing out buckets of popcorn. They moved up a short flight of stairs into the theatre proper. There were possibly a thousand seats inside – with half of them filled and more people coming in all the time.

'This is surreal,' said Ty.

They were guided down an aisle towards the stage, but then veered off to the left, through a door which hid them from the gawping audience and up into the backstage area. All around them there were men and women dressed in animal costumes or in native African outfits. A giraffe walked by, with a man on stilts inside. The sounds of an orchestra tuning up drifted towards them. They were kept there, surrounded by armed guards, while what appeared to be a full-scale theatrical production prepared to take to the stage.

The lights dimmed. The music swelled up and the crowd erupted as the curtain rose and the actors and dancers took to the stage. A musical number was energetically performed to wild applause.

'This is really good,' Ty said, having to shout to make himself heard. 'But I have the feeling I may be dead already and this is just a weird dream.'

Claire closed her eyes and was almost – *almost* – able to imagine that the weird dream was not what was going on on stage, but everything that had happened in the past few months. That her parents had taken her to see a Broadway musical but she was coming down with the flu so that while she was enjoying the show she was also drifting in and out of lucidity. The plague and the *Titanic* and the cannibals were all fantasies brought on by her fever. When the show was over her mother would shake her back to reality and they'd drift out into a neon-lit Times Square and her father would hail a cab and they'd go back to a nice, comfortable hotel.

Almost.

As the closing bars of music faded the crowd, clearly familiar with the performance, began to chant, '*Slash, Slash, Slash, Slash!*' Claire was quite familiar with the film version, she'd watched it repeatedly on DVD as a kid, but she couldn't place this moment in it. Not the darkening stage, not the huge throne now being pushed forward by heavily muscled men in loincloths.

'Slash! Slash! Slash!'

A man in a wolf mask stood at the opposite side of the stage and rammed a spear down on the fake savannah.

'All praise King Slash!'

'Slash! Slash! Slash! Slash!' the audience screamed. Many of them surged out of their seats to line the foot of the stage, clapping and cheering as the throne emerged into the brightness of a single spotlight.

Sitting regally – Slash, the Jungle King!

Or a man in a lion mask, with a rifle across his lap. He stood, he held the gun aloft, shook it at the crowd. In response they punched the air, yelling, '*Slash! Slash! Slash!*'

Slash turned towards his prisoners on the side of the stage. They could not see his real eyes, only the huge painted ones on his mask, and it made him even scarier. It was as if he was studying every single one of them individually, yet somehow also all of them at the same time.

'Oh God,' Ty whispered.

Slash raised his free hand and ushered them forward.

First Officer Jeffers led the way; jungle drums broke out as they stepped on stage. The crowd roared in response. But then Slash raised a hand for silence – and it came instantaneously, as if he had flipped a switch. They were totally under his spell.

Slash turned his false eyes upon his subjects.

'If you enter the city of the Jungle King,' he cried, 'you must suffer the wrath of the Jungle King!'

They roared in response. With the clapping and screaming and thumping of feet and drums it felt like the entire building was shaking.

'Prepare the fires! Tonight we feast!'

Decisions

Jimmy and Ronni, propped up against each other in the thick branches of a pine tree, woke damp and sore to a grey, misty dawn. They had just kept running until they could go no further. When, in the early hours, all sound of pursuit ceased, they could only presume that the soldiers had given up and returned to Fort Hope.

Jimmy lowered himself cautiously down on to the forest floor. As he yawned and stretched – while looking vigilantly around him, obviously – Ronnie slithered down the trunk, completely out of control, crashing through branch after branch and snapping each and every one of them before landing in a heap at his feet.

'In case any of you weren't aware until now,' Jimmy announced to anyone who might be in the general vicinity, 'we're over here. Hiding.'

'Sorry,' said Ronni.

By way of further apology she delved into one of the pockets of her khaki jacket and produced a small plastic bag, inside of which were two large, round, chocolate-chip cookies. She took one out and offered it to Jimmy. 'Breakfast?' she asked.

Jimmy took it and immediately bit into it. He gave her the thumbs-up. 'Well done,' he said, spraying her with crumbs. 'But is this all we have to get us to New York?'

'If you remember I tried to suggest—' And then she stopped. She swallowed a mouthful of biscuit, but having bit into it with enthusiasm it suddenly looked as if she was forcing herself to swallow sawdust.

Jimmy's cookie was *delicious*. 'What's wrong, has it gone off or . . . ?'

Ronni shook her head. 'I'm not going,' she said.

'You're not *what*?'

Her eyes flitted up, then down again. 'I'm not going – to New York. You never mentioned New York. Not once. You never said it. I'm not going.'

Jimmy gave a short laugh. 'Why not? What's the problem?'

She kicked at a dead fern on the ground. 'It's not *funny*!'

'OK – I didn't mean . . . it's just—'

'I'm not going. Not back there.'

'Oh. *Right*. I see. That's where you came from. That's why you were so upset when you arrived at Fort—'

'I wasn't *upset*! I was . . .'

'Traumatised. Yes. I know. I'm sorry.'

They both looked at the ground.

'Do you want to tell me about it?' Jimmy asked after a bit.

Ronni shrugged. Then, 'If you want.'

'Let's walk while you do. At least we'll be further away from the fort.'

'I'm not walking in the direction of New York.'

'That's fine. I've no idea which direction it is. We'll just go . . . *this way*.' He walked forward.

Ronni watched him for a moment, then shook her head. 'No.' She nodded in the opposite direction. 'That way.'

'That would be back to the fort. *This* way.'

Ronni changed her stance some forty-five degrees. '*This* way.'

'No – that's back where *I* came from. *This* way.'

'*That's* towards New York.'

'You don't know that.'

'No I don't,' she admitted. 'But you do.'

She studied him for several long moments.

Jimmy threw his hands up. 'OK, you got me – that way's *probably* New York. But Ronni, please listen to me. We escaped together. We're a good team. I think wherever we go we can probably look after ourselves pretty well. I *have* to go to New York. The *Titanic* might not even be there, but if there's even a small chance that she is, then I have to warn the captain that the President and his stupid army are going to try and seize the ship. It's my home, it's my life, and I think you'll love it too. To get there we have to go through New York. If you don't want to go, that's your choice. But I *have* to.'

Jimmy gave her an encouraging smile, but when she didn't respond he just gave a disappointed shrug before turning and walking away.

Towards New York.

She stood where she was.

He didn't look back.

Ten minutes later, walking down a hill only sparsely covered in trees, with a cold rain falling and a breeze making it feel even colder, Ronni fell into step beside him, only slightly out of breath, and said, quite simply, 'Cannibals.'

'Yeah, I heard there were odd bits of cannibalism after the plague.'

'Not odd bits!' she exploded suddenly. 'There were *hundreds* of them! I watched them! They chased me! They *caught* me! Jimmy, please, you have to understand what they're like, what you're walking into! They kept me prisoner in a dark hole! They fed me to fatten me up! Slash said he was going to have me for supper!'

'*Slash?*'

'Yes! He's like . . . he's like . . . a lion. He's their king!'

Jimmy cleared his throat. 'Their *jungle king?*'

'Yes, I know what it sounds like! But it's not a comedy, Jimmy, it's not a cartoon! They *eat people*! Slash has these two men — he calls them the Royal Butchers — and they're the ones who take people away and execute them, and then they're roasted on barbecues and served up . . . It's horrible and mad and I never want to go near them again – do you not understand that?'

'Yes, I understand . . .'

'But no, you're not going to change your mind.'

'I can't. And I should point out that you're still alive, aren't you?'

'Only just! I *escaped*! I was very lucky. I was in a cage. And the night they were due to . . . *eat* me . . . they fed me first and this guy didn't lock the door properly and I got out, but they spotted me and chased me, they hunted me for days and days and they came so, so close to catching me . . . Jimmy it's really, really awful – they're . . . they're . . .'

'Cannibals. Yes, I gathered that.'

At the bottom of the hill they came to a set of railway tracks. Jimmy looked along them, left and right.

'Left,' he said.

They turned that way, and began to skip along the overgrown sleepers, hugging their sides to try to keep warm.

'I hid in the sewers for days. There were *billions* of rats. If I fell asleep I'd wake up covered in them. There were wolves. I can't even remember most of it.'

He said nothing.

'Jimmy, please. Do you even have a plan? I can't go through that again. How do we get through to your ship without being captured? Please, Jimmy, what's your plan? You must have a plan . . .'

'My plan is to just keep walking.'

'That's no good!'

'Best I've got.'

They walked for another hour. Then they sat down on the track for a while to rest.

'No more magic cookies?'

'No more magic cookies.' She had her hands in her pockets. She was looking truly miserable. But there was nothing he could do.

They got up and started walking again. Perhaps another thirty minutes later they became aware of a dull vibration beneath them. At first they thought they were imagining the sensation and said nothing to each other, but then it became more pronounced and they exchanged glances before turning as one to look back down the line.

About a mile away: a train, coming towards them.

Wordlessly they darted off the tracks and into the trees. They threw themselves down as flat as they could and peered out from behind the thin pines as the train approached.

As it rattled past they saw that every carriage was filled with teenaged soldiers, bristling with guns. Missile launchers and mortars were mounted on the roof.

The President's army – or part of it – aiming straight for New York.

As it began to shrink into the distance Jimmy and Ronni raised themselves and scurried back to the track. They felt just the faintest of vibrations coming up through their boots.

Jimmy blew air out of his cheeks and looked at his friend.

'I have a new plan now,' he said.

'What is it?' Ronni asked.

'We walk faster.'

King Slash

They were locked into a dressing room somewhere in the bowels of the New Amsterdam Theatre. The music and singing and dancing thundered on for another hour above them. The tunes were familiar, but poisoned for ever. They sat disconsolately on hard wooden chairs or dressing tables stained by years of make-up. After a while a steaming pot of food was brought in to them by men in wolf masks, together with bowls and spoons and cans of warm beer. The food smelled wonderful. But nobody wanted to be the first to try it.

'It's some kind of stew,' said Ty, sniffing at the open pot. He had a big appetite normally. 'It's *someone*, isn't it?'

Dr Hill fished out a piece of meat. He held it up to his nose. He let it drop on to a dresser before pushing and prodding it with a spoon. 'Impossible to tell,' he pronounced. He nodded around the passengers. 'I'm sure it's *safe* to eat.'

'And you will all be damned to hell.'

It was Cleaver, his eyes blazing, his skin as pale as Claire had ever seen it.

Mr Rodriguez, who clearly despised the minister, took this as a challenge. He lifted a spoon and stepped up to the pot. 'We have to eat,' he said. 'As long as we don't know for sure, I think we can eat this with a clear conscience . . .' He looked round the little group for support. It was not forthcoming. 'Please yourselves,' he said and dipped his spoon in, briefly examined what he brought out, then closed his eyes and put it in his mouth.

'Perhaps it's your wife,' said Cleaver.

Rodriguez immediately gagged, ran into the corner and spat it out. Then he was sick. He collapsed and began to cry, repeating his wife's name, Mary, over and over again.

Ty shook his head sadly and turned away. 'I wish I'd had more fun,' he said wistfully.

'What?' asked Claire.

'Mom and Pop wanted me to be a lawyer, so ever since I was a little kid I was always studying. It didn't come easy to me. All the time I should have been out there being a kid I was working.'

'I thought you spent all that time with your dad. Central Station, the park . . . ?'

'Yeah. Well. Once a year, maybe.' He sighed. 'All that work, just to end up in a stew.'

Claire patted his arm gently. 'Maybe you won't end up in a stew,' she said. 'Maybe you'll end up in a pie.'

'That makes me feel better.'

They turned as the door behind them opened and

one of the Wolf Men entered. 'Slash wants to see you,' he barked at Jeffers.

The first officer studied him for a moment, then pushed himself off the dresser he'd been perched on. He fixed his cap. He nodded across the room. 'Claire, with me.'

Claire looked at him in surprise.

'Just you,' Wolf Man snapped at Jeffers.

Jeffers shook his head. 'She's our official historian, she comes too.'

Wolf Man's head moved stiffly towards her. Then he turned back to Jeffers, gave a short nod and indicated for him to follow. Jeffers looked at Claire and together they approached the door. Claire gave Ty a *what on earth is happening?* look as she jumped up to follow.

Wolf Man led them along a corridor and up a set of stairs into the backstage area. Although the show was over it was still busy with actors and technicians. The prisoners continued on through this, and then began to mount several flights of steps.

'I don't understand,' Claire said to Jeffers. 'Usually you never want me along.'

'This is different.'

'How?'

'Because they want to negotiate.'

'*What?* How do—'

'Shhhhh.'

There was a door at the top of the steps with two armed guards stationed outside. One of them opened it and they followed Wolf Man into a large, mostly empty space, with mirrors along one wall. As a child Claire had attended ballet lessons in a room similar to this. A throne like the one she'd earlier seen pushed on to the stage sat at the back of the room. It was empty, but men wearing cheetah heads stood on either side of it. Each of them gripped what appeared to be samurai swords. They stared straight ahead and didn't acknowledge either of the prisoners as they approached the throne. A tap could be heard running from a smaller room off to one side. Then it was turned off, and a moment later King Slash appeared, his lion head in place, wearing a flowing white gown with some kind of ceremonial dagger in a jewel-encrusted belt looped around his waist. He was wiping his hands on a paper towel, which he rolled up and threw to one side. He nodded at Wolf Man, who turned and left the room, closing the door behind him.

Slash mounted two steps to his throne and sat. 'Have you met the Royal Butchers?' he asked.

Claire shuddered as the two swordsmen stepped forward, in perfect time, until one was behind her, the other behind Jeffers. Then they performed an about turn, so that they were facing their king again.

'They will carve the meat from you while you still breathe.'

Claire swallowed.

'They will suck the marrow from your bones and—'

'Enough.' Jeffers' voice was quiet but steady.

Silence.

Claire wanted to scream at him, *Be quiet! Don't make them angry! They're going to slice me up alive!*

Slash rose slowly from his throne. He stepped down to their level. He stood in front of Claire. He moved his impassive lion face right into hers. Slash sniffed at her. Sweat dripped down her back.

'*Please . . .*' she whispered.

Pure dread.

He moved on to Jeffers. Two sets of eyes bore into him – the unmoving lion eyes and the brown human eyes, narrow, piercing. Jeffers stared straight ahead.

'What do you want?' Jeffers asked.

Slash began to laugh, but it sounded odd, hollow, through the mask. Suddenly, and with considerable speed, he whipped the dagger from its sheath and held it to Jeffers' neck just below the ear. Claire let out an involuntary cry.

'What do I want?' Slash hissed. 'I want *Titanic*.'

Hang On

They came to their second station platform of the afternoon, but they were still resolutely out in the country. They were exhausted. New York seemed as far away as ever. Jimmy knew they weren't going to be able to do anything to help *Titanic* if they didn't get a move on. The war had probably already started. The President versus King Slash. It sounded like something you'd dream up in a nightmare.

Ronni lay down on the platform and refused to budge. 'Just ten minutes,' she pleaded.

Jimmy stared up the line. He thought they were probably walking along a track that had only been used irregularly even before the plague had struck; it just felt remote, even though he knew the massive sprawl of New York could not be *that* far away. Possibly it looped right around the outskirts of the city, serving small outlying communities. There *must* be a connection somewhere up ahead which would have transferred the President's train on to the main line leading directly into the city. But it could still be miles away.

He returned to the platform, wandered past the ticket window and down a set of moss-tinged wooden steps into a small car park. There were three cars there, but they had been stripped of their essential parts and drained of fuel and now they lay with their doors open, windows smashed. It was a pity. A car would at least have gotten them as far as the outskirts of the city. If New York was anything like Miami or any of the larger cities he'd recently visited, that would have been the limit of it's usefulness – everywhere he'd been the streets had been impassable because of abandoned vehicles.

At the end of the car park there was a wooden shack with a sagging roof which had collapsed at one end. He pulled the bolt back on the door and looked inside, then nearly had a heart attack as a bird or a bat or something flashed past him. He took a deep breath and stepped in. It was a mechanic's workshop. Benches were piled high with spare parts and tools; it smelled of oil and paint. At the end where it had caved in there was a crumpled tarpaulin which had protected something from the cascade of rotten wood and rubble. Somewhat apprehensive of setting off a further collapse, Jimmy nevertheless cautiously raised the end of the tarp and peered beneath.

Ronni was out for the count. She'd only meant to rest her legs, but her exhausted body had overridden that intention and the moment she allowed her eyes to even flutter, she was gone. What brought her back was a *roar*. Her survival instincts had been so finely honed by her horrific experiences over the past few months that even before she was really awake she had rolled off the platform on to the track and was running with all the speed she could muster. But the roar was getting closer and closer. She daren't look back, she just had to escape, she had to—'

'Ronni, do you want a lift?'

Jimmy cruised effortlessly past her astride a gleaming red Kawasaki motorcycle. Ronni stopped, gasping for breath, as Jimmy turned the bike and came back towards her.

'Jimmy! You nearly . . . !'

He ignored her. He was in love. He'd occasionally ridden scrambler bikes over rough terrain with his friends back in Belfast, but this was something altogether different – fast, powerful and with half a tank of petrol. The bike was far from new, he could tell that, but someone long dead had lavished a lot of attention on it. It felt *fantastic*.

'So, what are you waiting for?' Jimmy laughed. 'Climb on!'

Ronni looked at the bike, and then at Jimmy, doubtfully. 'Crash helmets?' she asked hopefully.

'Yeah, *right*.'

In fact, she loved it too. She tucked her legs in and held tight to Jimmy, peering over his shoulder as they roared down country roads, the wind in their hair,

258

teenagers having fun. Even as they entered the suburbs of the city he was able to weave in and out of abandoned cars and mount sidewalks, and it barely slowed them down. Ronni wasn't quite so relaxed now – she shouted above the engine that the noise of the bike against the silence of the city was sure to attract attention. But he wouldn't listen. He was enjoying himself too much. Of course he didn't say that. He shouted back that the further they could get at speed the better. There was no time to waste. They would have to take the chance – and besides, it was a huge city and they'd barely entered the outer limits of it. She had no choice but to hold on. They skirted the edge of Newark Airport, the huge fleets of abandoned planes a stark reminder of the scale of the disaster.

A couple of miles further on the engine began to splutter and cough. Jimmy gunned it, trying to coax life back into it, but within a few hundred metres it died completely.

'Out of petrol,' he said as he dismounted.

He looked about him; there were strip malls on both sides of the street.

'OK,' said Ronni. 'It got us this far, now we start walking.'

Jimmy took hold of the handles and began to push it. 'Not yet,' he said. 'There'll be a petrol station further up.'

He was already straining to support the weight of the bike.

'Jimmy – now it'll slow us down. You have to leave it.'

'No.'

He pushed on. Ronni walked out in front, occasionally casting disapproving glances back at him. She was scared now. She had felt a certain measure of security with Jimmy, but now that he was acting so childishly the knowledge that he really wouldn't be able to protect her if the cannibals spotted them was growing with every step she took. What was she even thinking of, returning here? Why hadn't she stayed in the security of the camp? *What if they're watching us already? What chance would we have?* She tramped on, her eyes darting suspiciously from building to building.

They came to two petrol pumps in front of a 7-Eleven grocery store. But there was no electricity to work them. Jimmy thought if he could gain access to the underground tanks he might be able to siphon enough out to get them going again. While he tried to work out exactly how to do that Ronni quietly picked through what was left of the store – it had already been looted long ago – for something to eat. She was able to forage several bottles of Coke and a box of half-melted Hershey chocolate bars. She smiled to herself as she tucked in: if the plague and the cannibals didn't get her, the cholesterol probably would.

She was just emerging from the store to offer Jimmy a share when a hand was clamped roughly over her mouth and the muzzle of a gun was placed against the side of her head.

'Shhhhh.'

Jimmy used a discarded wrench to pry off the metal casing over the underground storage tank, and was just looking down into the darkness, trying to determine if there was actually any petrol left in there, when a shadow fell over him.

'Raise your hands, you cannibal monster,' said a ragged voice.

Jimmy raised them.

'Now turn around very slowly . . . and throw me the keys.' Jimmy started to turn. 'If you try anything I'll put a bullet in her.'

Jimmy completed his turn.

Ronni was bug-eyed with fright. The man with his hand across her mouth and gun to her head was overweight, steaming with sweat and covered from head to toe in grime.

'Hello, Jonas,' said Jimmy. 'Long time no see.'

Betrayal

They were given thirty minutes to think about it.

Jeffers remained silent as they were escorted from King Slash's throne room back to their prison below. Once the door was closed and locked behind them the passengers and crew clustered around Jeffers and Claire, demanding to know what had happened.

Jeffers asked for silence, his face grim.

'This . . . *Slash* — he wants the ship,' he said. 'He wants us to lure *Titanic* into port, and then he will seize her. If we do not agree he will kill one of us every thirty minutes and roast our bodies on the fire for supper. He will keep doing this until we give up the ship, or until there's none of us left.'

They all stared at him. They had expected to die from the moment they were captured, but when it hadn't happened instantaneously they had allowed themselves some small measure of hope. But now this situation seemed even worse. They were being offered a chance to save themselves — at the expense of the ship that had saved them.

Dr Hill was the first to speak. 'We cannot risk the

Titanic. There are hundreds of passengers and crew still on board – if they get the ship they will surely kill them as well as us. They have no reason to keep any of us alive.'

'We don't know that,' said Rodriguez. 'Maybe he just wants the ship – not the people inside.'

'If it buys us some more time,' said one of the passengers – Mr Robinson, clutching his wife's hand tightly – 'maybe we should agree. Captain Smith might be able to find a way to rescue us.'

Dr Hill shook his head. 'If Captain Smith becomes aware that we're being held hostage, he will not attempt a rescue. He will sail away rather than lose the ship.'

'But he *can't* sail away,' observed Claire. 'Not without the missing part.'

'We don't know that for sure,' said Dr Hill. 'Jonas may still be alive. He could still make it back to the ship.'

'He's gone,' said Rodriguez. 'If the cannibals didn't get him, the rats surely did. He could hardly walk when I saw him. The ship is dead in the water. We have to try and save *ourselves*.'

They argued back and forth. There was angry pointing and raised voices, threats and warnings and cries of despair. The only members of their company who did not contribute were First Officer Jeffers himself – and the Rev. Cleaver, who remained sitting, off to one side, hands clasped, eyes closed, his lips moving every so subtly, apparently in prayer. Claire looked at Jeffers two or three times; he was at the centre of the group, he appeared to be listening, but there was something about the distant look in his eyes that made her think he had zoned out, that he was thinking his own course through it all. Eventually, as they continued tearing each other's arguments to shreds, he pushed through them and went and stood in front of the door, just staring at it. Claire also detached herself from the group and stood by him.

Without looking at her, he said: 'There's something about this that isn't right.'

'There's *none* of it that's right.'

'No – I mean . . .I don't know exactly what I mean. It's about the show – the musical, the costumes – they're all . . .'

'Actors,' said Claire.

Jeffers nodded.

'Their language, the way they act – it's like a *performance* . . .'

Claire wasn't really sure what he was driving at, but she was prepared to trust his instincts more than most of those still arguing amongst themselves on the other side of the room. Dr Hill would go with whatever Jeffers decided. Probably the remaining crewmen would continue to obey orders. Ty would do the right thing, she was sure. The remaining passengers, though – they might do anything to survive, even if that meant betraying the *Titanic*.

Eventually, with everyone still arguing, the door opened and a Wolf Man entered. Silence fell immediately.

'Have you come to a decision?' He demanded. 'Are you prepared to give up the ship?'

They all looked to Jeffers. He nodded around them, then faced the Wolf Man. 'Yes,' he said, 'we will surrender *Titanic*.'

Claire's mouth dropped open. Although most of their group had argued for such a decision, to hear it coming from Jeffers was quite a shock.

'I am the senior officer present,' he said. 'I have made my decision. Dr Hill, you're in charge until I return.'

Claire never thought in a million years that Jeffers would give the *Titanic* up so easily. She was about to protest – though, she noted, nobody else was – when Jeffers addressed the Wolf Man again, 'The *Titanic* is yours, subject to one condition.'

The Wolf Man immediately barked: 'What?'

'That's between me and Slash.'

Because of his mask it was impossible to read his face. There was a long moment when nothing was said, before he angled his head to one side and snapped, 'This way.'

In turn Jeffers indicated for Claire to follow him. She hesitated, unsure if she wanted to be part of this great betrayal. But then she decided it would at least give her the chance to make one last effort to talk him out of it. As they were led back down the corridor she hissed: 'What are you doing? You can't give her up!'

He didn't look at her, and as he spoke his lips barely moved. 'I need you to trust me.'

Slash sat regally, with a Royal Butcher on either side. The Wolf Man bowed, approached and whispered in his ear; Slash nodded and the Wolf Man withdrew.

'A *condition*?' Slash sneered. 'You are not in a position to make a *condition*.'

'I believe I am.'

Slash bristled. The Butchers inched closer; Claire was aware of their hands moving to the hilts of their swords.

'I am giving you the *Titanic*', said Jeffers, 'I believe that deserves something in return. All I want you to do is kill me and to let the rest of my party go free.'

Claire spun towards him. 'You can't—'

'Be quiet! It's my decision.'

This then was his grand plan – a noble sacrifice to save their lives . . . or an easy escape from the guilt of giving up his ship?

Slash's real face was hidden, but he *sounded* like he was smiling. 'You have my word. Now, how can you be so sure that you can deliver the ship?'

Jeffers looked emotionlessly at Claire. She knew immediately what was coming. 'Don't—' she began, but there was no stopping him.

'This is the daughter of the owner. If she sends a distress signal, they will come ashore to rescue her.

They would only do it for her, not for me or anyone else. As long as you have her, you have the ship.'

Claire glared at him. 'You . . . you *bastard*! How *could* you?'

'Be quiet, Claire. It's done.'

Slash stood from his throne and stepped down, rubbing his hands together. 'It has been a pleasure doing business with you. Now, my Butchers, take him away and—'

Jeffers shook his head and said, 'No.' Slash stopped. 'That wasn't the bargain. My condition was that *you* kill me.'

Slash laughed. 'And get blood on my hands? I don't think so. Guards, take . . .'

Jeffers suddenly took a step forward and ripped the jewelled dagger from the sheath on Slash's waist. Before Slash or the Butchers could react he plunged it into his own neck.

Claire screamed.

But instead of blood spraying out, instead of Jeffers collapsing down dead by his own hand, he stood where he was.

No blood.

Unharmed.

He turned swiftly to one side and chopped one of the Butchers across the neck; as he fell, Jeffers spun and punched the other. As *he* tumbled backwards and Slash stood, stunned, Jeffers calmly bent and lifted one of the samurai swords, stepped forward and thrust it deep into the king's chest.

Slash took a step back.

But he remained standing.

Claire stared – shocked, mesmerised.

He has a sword sticking out of his heart. Why isn't he dead? Why isn't Jeffers?

Her questions were answered almost immediately as Jeffers pulled the sword out of the king – again there was no blood and no gaping hole – and showed it to her. 'See? Retractable blade! It's not real, Claire, it's a theatrical prop!'

He threw it down. Behind him the Royal Butchers were groggily getting back to their feet, but he ignored them and instead took hold of Slash's lion mask.

'No . . . !' Slash cried, but it was too late. Jeffers ripped it off his head to reveal – well . . . someone very, very ordinary.

Claire was looking at a quite pleasant-looking man, perhaps in his mid-thirties; he had short, sandy hair, a wispy moustache and a pair of glasses. His face was pale, and now that Claire could properly see his eyes she realised that they were wide and fearful and blinking uncontrollably. Instantly all of her fears and concerns evaporated.

'Please – don't hurt me . . .' Slash took a step back. Now that the wooden lion mask wasn't acting as a buffer to his voice, making it deeper and causing it to echo, it sounded really *ordinary*.

Jeffers spun towards the Butchers. 'Yours too!' he snapped.

The Butchers hesitated for a moment, looked at each other and then rather sheepishly removed their cheetah heads. If anything, the two men inside were even less impressive to look at than Slash.

Claire was utterly astounded. 'I don't understand . . . what . . . ?'

'You know already, Claire,' said Jeffers. He shook his head at Slash and the Butchers. 'You're actors – you put on your masks and act scary and people fall for it. Isn't that right?'

Slash nodded warily.

'*Please*,' begged one of the Butchers, 'you can't tell anyone.'

Jeffers ignored him and pointed at Slash. 'You. What's your name?'

Slash cleared his throat. 'Billy. Billy Whitehouse. I, uhm, received a Tony Award for my role in *The Jungle King*. I—'

Claire had heard enough. 'Let's just get out of here – stop even talking to them, they're still *cannibals* . . .'

'No,' said one of the Butchers, 'we're really not.'

'Honestly,' said the other.

Jeffers looked from one to the other. 'Tell me.'

But it was Slash – Billy who stepped forward. 'Please – this is all my fault. We haven't done anything wrong – we're just trying to, you know, get through this . . . You have to understand – we were rehearsing

269

up here when the plague struck, there were twenty of us . . . and somehow it passed us by. We knew there were other survivors out there, but we stayed hidden in here, scared and hungry and . . . well, there were rats down in the basement, we killed some of them and I . . . well, when I wasn't working I used to have a job in a restaurant, so I know how to cook, so I made this stew out of them, managed to rescue some spices, dried vegetables . . . and it was really not bad. Soon we were making it every day and word got out that we had fresh food and other survivors started to arrive and they ended up laying siege to the theatre and so we had to come up with a plan . . .' He shrugged helplessly.

'We put on our costumes,' said one of the Butchers. 'We opened the doors and let them all in, we put on our show for them, and then we fed them – and halfway through Billy told them that we were cannibals, that they were eating human flesh, and that we would continue to feed them if they followed our commands – and that we would eat anyone who didn't. You have to understand, we are *good* actors, we play *terrifying* very well . . .'

'They so absolutely believed us,' said the other Butcher, 'and there's an inexhaustible supply of rats down there – they come up through the sewers.'

'So they only *think* they're cannibals?' Claire asked.

'Yes!' said Billy. 'We are not monsters. We only have the appearance of monsters.'

'But what about the people you capture? The bones down at the harbour?'

'It's just a charade! If we capture someone, we tell them that they're going to be eaten, we turn it into a big party, we make a huge rat stew, and then right before we're *supposed* to kill them we "accidentally" leave their cell unlocked. They escape and when they get outside the city they tell everyone they meet that cannibals control New York, which scares people from coming in, so we're left in peace . . .'

'You're left *in charge*, you mean,' said Jeffers.

'It's not like that. Please believe us. Even the bodies that we burn, it's all stage dummies and special effects and make-up. There are millions of bones lying about, we just carve a few up to make it look like they've been skinned and toss them on the fire. It's all basic stagecraft.' He sighed. 'Look, we've . . . gotten used to doing it. It's been a real kick, but we knew it couldn't last. We honestly haven't harmed anyone, we just came up with a scheme to keep people in line as a way of protecting ourselves. The problem is, it's gotten a bit out of hand. It started out with just a few believing us – but now there's thousands of them and they *all* think they're cannibals. But if they find out it's all been . . . a *trick* . . .'

'They'll eat you alive,' said Jeffers.

Tunnels

Jonas Jones' directions were precise. There was a train station a short distance from the 7-Eleven. They were to follow the underground tracks through half a dozen minor stops to Penn Station, and then continue on to Grand Central. They should wait at the rendezvous point there to see if anyone showed up, and then make their way to the harbour for the prearranged pick-up by the *Titanic*. He tried to make it sound as if it would really be as straightforward as that, and they nodded as if there was a remote possibility that it might be. But they all knew the truth. They were still walking into the heart of Cannibal City.

Jonas roared off on the newly refilled Kawasaki, bound for a mysterious factory and carrying on his broad shoulders the *Titanic*'s only hope of escaping from New York.

As they watched him go, Jimmy said: 'I do believe that man just stole my bike.'

Ronni was still a little shocked – not only because she'd thought her time was up, but also at discovering

272

that the man who'd put a gun to her head was a friend of Jimmy's.

'What are the chances of that happening, city this size?' she asked.

'Slim,' Jimmy agreed. 'Then again – everything's so quiet, our bike could probably be heard for miles.'

'So others might have heard it.'

They both scanned the surrounding buildings. 'Let's get moving,' said Jimmy.

They hurried towards the station entrance. Though he didn't say anything, Jimmy's mind was racing.

Claire's here in the city.

Jonas had escaped capture by sheer luck. In attempting to outrun his pursuers in the dark he'd stumbled over a caved-in section of the tunnel and had hidden behind the rubble while the cannibals swarmed all around the other passengers and crew. He had then watched helplessly as they were taken away. But yes, last time he'd seen them, they were all still alive, including Claire. Jimmy had thought Claire had died in the woods, and that it was his fault for falling out with her over Babe. Now that he knew she wasn't dead – or hadn't been when Jonas had last seen her, which was, admittedly many hours ago – surely it was his responsibility to try and help her? Jonas had ordered them back to the ship, but how could he do that? On the other hand, he also had a responsibility to get Ronni to safety. Was there a compromise? Or should he just not tell her that he was going to try and help

Claire? Jonas had followed the captives at a discreet distance until they had exited the tunnels at Times Square, so Jimmy had at least a rough idea of what part of the city they were in. It was more or less on their way. Probably less.

As they entered the station's tunnel, Ronni said: 'You're very quiet.'

'Thinking,' said Jimmy.

'I had a friend like you, once,' said Ronni. 'Every time I said to him don't put your head out of that window, he put his head out of that window.'

'What happened to him?'

'His head was cut off by a passing train.'

'That's probably not a true story,' said Jimmy.

They walked on, their way lit by a torch one of the passengers had left on the rail tracks and which Jonas had recovered. It showed them the way ahead, but it also showed them thousands of rats.

'Better rats than cannibals,' was Ronni's opinion.

Jimmy wasn't so sure. Every time he kicked one, another tried to bite him. The ones on the ground weren't so bad, it was when they unexpectedly fell off the ceiling and landed on his head that they really got to him.

'And swearing at them isn't going to help,' said Ronni.

'It helps *me*,' said Jimmy.

They came to Penn Station and continued on their underground path towards Grand Central. In another ten minutes they came to Times Square.

Jimmy stopped. 'If we continue on from here, next stop we'll be in Grand Central.'

Ronni nodded and looked on down the line. 'So . . . ?'

'So if we arrive in Grand Central we're going to be kicking our heels all night until the rendezvous time.'

'So . . .'

'So I could quite easily take a wander upstairs here, see what's happening. You could wait down here, if you want.'

'With the rats?'

'Better rats than cannibals, you said.'

'Jimmy – your friend ordered us to keep going.'

'Yes he did. But I'm only talking about taking a look. I mean, they're probably all dead or in a pie. What harm can it do?'

'*We* could end up in a pie, that's what. I almost did already.'

'Not if we're careful. You told me yourself, the only reason they knew you weren't one of them was because you screamed. If you just, like, *zip it*, we'll be fine.'

'Jimmy – please, it's NOT SAFE. We're not going and that's *final*.'

Ten minutes later they walked out of the subway station and joined the crowds milling along the overgrown sidewalk, all moving in one direction – towards Times Square. They looked so *normal*, at least compared to the folks he'd encountered in the new settlements. *They* always looked permanently lost and deprived – this lot looked *together*. And they looked well fed.

All around him there were happy, jaunty people. Jimmy was pretty good at blending in; Ronni not so much. She walked stiffly, her eyes almost out on stalks, hardly daring to breathe.

He told her to relax.

'I *can't*,' she hissed. 'I keep thinking one of them is going to turn round and bite me.'

'Don't be ridiculous,' whispered Jimmy. 'They'd want to cook you first.'

'That's . . . not . . . *funny!*'

But she smiled a little bit, and it helped. She didn't look quite so robotic – at least until they saw and *smelled* where the crowds were leading them. Ronni searched instinctively for Jimmy's hand as they saw the flames licking up from three massive bonfires burning in the middle of the street outside the New Amsterdam Theatre. Spits had been placed across them, surely ready to receive whoever the cannibals had captured.

Claire.

What can I do even if I find her? I have no weapon – and there's hundreds of them, I'll be torn to shreds if I try anything.

They had expected the cannibals to gather around the bonfires, but instead they were entering the theatre itself, which was the only building in the entire imposing square which was lit up. Jimmy stared up at the glowing neon sign above the theatre.

The Jungle King.

'What do we do?' Ronni whispered.

'We follow them in.'

'But we don't have…'

'Tickets?' It sounded ridiculous. 'If they ask just keep smiling and act dumb. That shouldn't be hard. Let me do the talking.'

They stepped into the theatre foyer.

Box office straight ahead.

Concession stand to the right.

The smell of popcorn.

Young ladies in smart uniforms giving out programmes.

No tickets required.

Everyone giddy with excitement.

Up red-carpeted steps and into an auditorium.

What is this? What's going on?

How can it be so normal?

They're cannibals!

An announcement came over the PA – 'Ladies and gentlemen, boys and girls, please take your seats for the *wildest* show on earth!'

The Death of Slash

They could hear the pounding music coming from the stage above, but it was distorted by distance and echo and stone floors and wooden beams so that it sounded like a remote signal from another world. It was just about discernible as 'Food Chain', a song, Claire thought, about the survival of the fittest.

That's what we are.

We're going to pull through this.

Jeffers is a class act: he's turned the tables, he's in command.

There was still, however, just a nagging doubt caused by the fact that they were still imprisoned in the bowels of the theatre; that upstairs was heaving with people who believed they were cannibals; and that they were all still obliged to go through with a bizarre charade to ensure that they made it out alive.

What could possibly go wrong?

King Slash and his cronies – the Royal Butchers, the Wolf Men and the other members of the cast of the Broadway production of *The Jungle King* – had wanted to bargain. They wanted out of New York. Their position was that those hundreds of people who *thought* they were cannibals, who had resigned themselves to it and accepted the terrible guilt of what they'd done, would not take kindly to suddenly being told that they'd been suckered into believing it all, that they'd been eating rats and obeying the sometimes brutal and often arbitrary commands of a bunch of *actors*. Although they might be relieved to discover that they weren't as bad as they thought, they were bound to react angrily and seek vengeance on those who had hoodwinked them.

Slash was still in a strong bargaining position. He remained the king, and one royal command could result in Jeffers and Claire and all of the other prisoners *really* being eaten. Slash was quite blunt – if that was the only way to save their own skins, then that's what he would order.

So the plan was this: the prisoners would be paraded on stage at the climax of that evening's performance of *The Jungle King*. They would then be taken away to be killed by the Royal Butchers and prepared for the barbecues outside. (Claire, rather stupidly, asked why they weren't killed on stage. One of the Butchers replied, 'Because we're cannibals, not barbarians!') While the crowds partied around the bonfires, awaiting the arrival of the 'meat', the prisoners, together with Slash and the members of the theatre group, would sneak into the sewers beneath the building and escape. They would make their way to *Titanic* where they would be offered safe passage to a port of their choice.

Jeffers had agreed to this – but had insisted that the detail of it was kept secret from the other passengers and crew. 'They're too fragile,' he told Claire. 'If they blab it out, if they act differently, they could jeopardise the whole escape. I'll only tell them what I have to – that we have a way out but that it absolutely depends on them following orders.'

Claire agreed, though she didn't envy Jeffers having to tell them.

Naturally, when he did, they *demanded* to know.

Rodriguez was the most vocal. 'You've sold us down the river! You're saving your own skin! That's why you want us to be quiet, that's why you want us to—'

One of the crewmen stuck a finger in Rodriguez's face and snapped: 'Shut up, or I'll eat you myself and save them the trouble!'

Rodriguez went quiet.

'I think we should trust him.'

It came from what Claire though was the most unlikely source of all. Cleaver. Throughout, he had remained calm and collected but withdrawn, so this sudden support for Jeffers' plan, even though he too was largely ignorant of it, had a settling effect on those doubting members of the party.

Ty nudged Claire's arm. 'What's he up to?' he whispered.

Claire shook her head. She had given up trying to fathom what the minister was about.

When the door was finally unlocked and Wolf Man appeared, all Jeffers said was: 'Keep calm, follow orders, everything will be fine.'

And so they were escorted out in single file, First Officer Jeffers following Wolf Man, Claire behind, and the other passengers and crew tailing back. As they rose through the levels towards the stage the music grew in clarity and volume, with the building vibrating both to it and to the frenzied stamping and clapping of the audience. Those nagging doubts were beginning to multiply in Claire's mind. What if the bargaining really had just been a way of keeping them quiet? What if Jeffers' exposure of King Slash and the Butchers as a fraud had merely prompted them to pull off another scam – making them think they were going to be released while all the time the plan was to shut them up until they could be executed? Were they, even now, walking placidly to their deaths? Killing them would allow Slash to continue his reign. Killing them was *expected*. Even if they hadn't actually murdered or eaten anyone before, if they started now nobody was going to know the difference, or punish them. There was no law but Slash's law. They could do exactly what they wanted.

The passengers and crew reached the backstage area. They were corralled into a tight group and prodded forward as the roars from the audience, prompted by a Wolf Man on stage, grew in intensity. Claire wanted to bolt, to hide, but there was nothing she could do but emerge blinking into a blaze of stage lights and the wall of sound.

'Ladies and gentlemen, boys and girls! I present to you . . . *dinner!*'

Jimmy could hardly believe his eyes. Claire was there on the stage before him, together with Jeffers and Dr Hill and . . .

Oh my God . . . the minister!

How was *that* possible?

Up until then Jimmy had actually been quite relaxed. They had sat unrecognised and undisturbed in a theatre, enjoying a musical. Even Ronni had been chilled enough to actually tap her feet and sing along. For a few minutes they'd been able to drift into a land of make-believe, to imagine that everything that had happened to them in the past few months might actually be some kind of bizarre fantasy, that what they were doing now, what they were seeing on stage, wasn't bizarre or surreal, it was the real world and they were just a boy and girl enjoying a night out at the theatre.

But then Claire had stepped into the spotlight, pushed and harried with the others, while King Slash strode around, revving the crowd up further as he sniffed and pawed at them, roaring his pleasure, stamping his feet. He lifted an arm here, a leg there, pretending to bite at it. The Royal Butchers moved along the back of the line, swords drawn, teasing and delighting the audience as they feigned stabbing their victims, their supper.

Slash came to the minister. He knocked the wide-brimmed hat from his head, bent and picked it up, then skimmed it through the air into the crowd. It floated back five or six rows until someone jumped from their seat and grabbed it, to universal applause.

The minister hardly reacted at all – at first. Slash moved closer. He began to sniff up and down him. He pawed at the minister's dog-collar. The minister moved for the first time. Jimmy thought he was just moving his arms to protect himself, but then there was a flash of metal, a blur of movement and suddenly Slash wasn't sniffing at him any more.

The Jungle King staggered backwards. He pawed uselessly at the air. Then he collapsed down on to the stage.

The crowd jumped to their feet, cheering, convinced it was all part of the act, even as blood began to seep out of his costume and across the floor. It was only when the minister stepped forward, and they saw a long, thin dagger in his hand; when they saw him wave it in the air and shout something out, once, twice, again and again, that they finally began to fall silent, that the music ceased and the relentless druming of feet faded and they at last began to understand what had happened as they heard the words of the wild-eyed man holding the bloody knife aloft and screaming:

'Long live the President! Long live the President!'

First Officer Jeffers was the first to react. He stepped forward and grabbed Cleaver's arm; he snapped it back, causing him to release the dagger. As it clattered on to the stage floor Jeffers twisted Cleaver's arm further up, and at the same time kicked at the back of his knees, which gave way, forcing him to the ground. The Royal Butchers, the Wolf Man and the rest of the cast all crowded around Slash; the audience surged forward, screaming and howling. They began to clamber on to the stage. As they advanced Jeffers yelled back at Claire: 'Get out of here! Move it!' Claire was frozen to the spot. Until Dr Hill clamped a hand on her arm and began to pull her backwards she hadn't realised that the others had already begun to move off the stage. Jeffers himself now bounded away as the mob descended on Cleaver. As fists and boots began to rain down on him there was a massive *clump* of a noise, and the entire building shook. Masonry showered down on the stage and across the seats in the auditorium. Another dull explosion came, even louder, with shock waves strong enough to throw half of them to the floor.

Jimmy and Ronni, caught up in the surge forward and now picking themselves up, might have been the only ones in the entire theatre who realised what was happening.

Artillery.

A familiar sound from Fort Hope.

The theatre was under attack by the President's army.

The war had begun!

Panic gripped everyone as more shells began to land.

A hole was blown in the ceiling and when the smoke cleared the night sky was clearly visible.

They heard an urgent rat-tat-tat of gunfire. People were running everywhere – some towards the exits, others swarming across the stage looking for a way out.

Only Jimmy seemed to know exactly where he was going – he kept his eyes firmly fixed on where Claire had disappeared backstage and charged after her, dragging Ronni along with him. They ducked as the theatre was struck again and scenery crashed to the floor all around them. Jimmy would not be stopped, but there was a moment of confusion when he got backstage and he couldn't see Claire any more. Then he caught just a glimpse of Jeffers' baseball cap as he disappeared down a set of stairs on the far side. With people running everywhere it took them a while to get across, but soon they were on the stairs and taking them four and five at a time, sliding down using the hand rail for support.

Another explosion – and the lights went out. There were screams of pain and shouts of confusion. Jimmy kept a tight grip on the rail and just kept going.

'Jimmy – please . . .' cried Ronni. 'We'll kill ourselves!'

He said nothing. He pressed ahead. Ronni kept a

tight hold of his T-shirt and allowed herself to be dragged along. Then – dead ahead, a flashlight beam. He focused in on that.

Down another two sets of stairs and along a corridor, the air thick with dust.

A metallic clank – and then the flash beam disappeared.

'Hey!' Jimmy called. 'Hey!'

But another shell had struck, an alarm had finally gone off, and there was too much noise for him to be heard. They hurried blindly forward. They tripped and fell and righted themselves. They came to what was their best estimation of where the light had suddenly disappeared. Jimmy began to feel his way forward, his foot out in front, his arms stretched left and right, anxious not to miss the avenue of escape. It was the stench that made him stop, then the choking, fetid air. Somewhere below . . .

He foot-skimmed the floor until it came to a hole, then felt around with his hands to detect the circumference. Yes, wide enough. And there, a ladder.

'Jimmy . . . ?'

'Down here.'

He lowered himself into the hole, then began a rapid descent, no thought for what might be below.

'Jimmy – wait for me!'

'Come on!'

As they disappeared below ground level the *whump* and *crump* of the explosions faded, to be replaced by the sound of gushing water. The stink of sewage and rats. They came suddenly to the dank, slippery floor and stood in the complete and utter darkness. For the first time, Jimmy was actually lost – there were only two ways to go, but it was impossible to be sure which way was right. He was almost overwhelmed with the despair of realising that he had come so close, but was now on the brink of failure.

There was nothing for it but to yell.

'*Claire!*'

'Shhhh!' cried Ronni. 'What if—'

'Claire! Claire!'

They heard it echo along the sewage tunnel.

'*Jimmy . . .*'

'Shhhhh listen . . .'

Then there was nothing.

Nothing.

Nothing.

Until, from a distance of not more than a metre, a torch blinked on and they were blinded. As they shielded their faces and prepared for the worst a familiar voice said, '*What?*'

Encounter

It was not exactly as Jimmy had imagined it, this reunion, deep in the sewers beneath a theatre which was being reduced to rubble by a man who had deluded himself into thinking he was the President of the United States. Claire stood in the back-glow from the torch, bedraggled, thin, pale, angry. Jimmy didn't have the faintest clue what to say. He wanted to hug her, but could not bring himself to. He wanted to apologise for what he'd done, for letting her down, for allowing her to be shot, for betraying the *Titanic*.

But all he could manage was: 'Bad hair day, is it?'

The torch flashed from Jimmy to Ronni. 'Who's *she*?'

'Ronni,' said Ronni.

'She's my friend,' said Jimmy.

'Bad luck you,' said Claire to Ronni.

From away along the tunnel Dr Hill yelled: 'Claire! Come on!'

Claire looked at them. 'Well if you're coming, let's go.'

She spun away. They didn't see her wipe a tear from her eye.

Jimmy, obviously, didn't wipe a tear of his own away. That would have been ridiculous. Absolutely not. No way.

Ronni said, 'Are you OK?' as they quickly followed after Claire.

'Yes, of course I'm OK. Why wouldn't I be OK?'

'I thought she was your best friend?'

'I never said that,' said Jimmy.

After a while they stopped, gathering in a wider section of the sewer tunnel where it branched out in several directions. Jimmy was surprised to see how many of them there were – not just Claire and Jeffers and Dr Hill, but various crew and passengers he recognised, plus an odd assortment of men and women in animal masks which they were only now beginning to discard – wolf heads and cheetah heads tossed into the river of sewage and drifting away.

While Jeffers and Dr Hill conferred at the crossroads, Jimmy sat on the damp floor. He said nothing, he asked no questions. Ty had given him a big hug and tried to engage him in conversation, but as soon as he established the extent of the frostiness between Jimmy and Claire he decided to leave them to it. He winked at Ronni, then drifted off. Claire sat with her back against the wall, looking wherever Jimmy didn't.

Ronni crouched beside her. 'Aren't they cannibals?' she whispered, nodding towards the group still partially attired in animal costumes.

'No,' said Claire, 'they're actors.'

'But they're cannibals as well! They all are!'

'No,' said Claire, 'it was a trick. Everyone thought they were eating human flesh, but it was rats. Rat stew, mostly.'

'That's . . . not possible – I saw them . . .'

'You *thought* you did. You didn't. Is he your boyfriend?'

'Who, Jimmy? No. I thought he was yours.'

Claire snorted. 'I *don't think* so. So how come you two hooked up?'

'We were both at Fort Hope.' Claire's brow furrowed in the torchlight. 'Fort Hope – it's like the President's . . . where he keeps his army . . .'

'The President? The *President* President?'

'No,' said Jimmy, finally approaching, talking to Claire but not looking at her. 'He just thinks he is. He used to be a senator or something. That's his army up there, attacking New York, saving it from cannibals.'

'Well, what are we doing down here, then?' Claire asked Jimmy, although she was looking at at Ronni. 'Shouldn't we be up there supporting him? Telling him they're not cannibals?'

'No,' said Jimmy, 'we shouldn't, for the simple reason that the second part of his master plan is to sieze the *Titanic*.'

Without looking at him she asked if Jeffers was aware of this piece of information.

'No,' said Jimmy.

'Well don't you think you should tell him?'

Jimmy grunted, and passed on up the line.

Although the rat-catching actors had explored some of the sewage system, their escape from the theatre had taken them beyond those limits, and without any kind of map or guidance system, Jeffers decided it was time to take everyone back up into the city in order to establish their bearings. Then they would make their way back to Grand Central to hook up with the other groups – if any of them had made it back. Hopefully from there they would also be able to re-establish radio contact with the ship and warn Captain Smith of the coming Presidential attack.

Jeffers sent out a scout into each one of the tunnels in order to locate an access ladder to the surface. Within a few minutes a shout went up that one had been discovered. The other scouts were called back and the entire group set off into a right-hand tunnel. When they found the ladder Jeffers was the first on to it, climbing rapidly, followed by Dr Hill; the rest bunched around the bottom, pushing and shoving for their turn. They were all desperate for fresh air, and without the natural discipline Jeffers' presence encouraged, it all became a bit chaotic. Jimmy and Claire found themselves squeezed towards the back, while Ty grabbed Ronni by the hand and forced her forward. They were amongst the first to pull themselves up out of the scrum to begin their climb towards the world above.

Jimmy and Claire looked at each other. They looked away. There were a thousand things they wanted to say, they each wanted to know every detail of what the other had experienced. But still neither of them was ready to make the first move.

Jimmy took an elbow to the ribs as one of the former wolf men shoved in front of him. He cursed and stepped back out of the crowd. Claire pretended not to notice. She stepped into his space and pushed forward.

He was happy *and* angry. He wanted to hug her *and* slap her stupid head.

One by one they hauled themselves up until finally there was only Jimmy left. He looked up at the feet and bums disappearing upwards, moving towards a faint dot of light, like astronauts returning to their planet, mission accomplished. As he put his hands on the bottom rung and was about to pull himself up he was distracted by a noise off to his left – *there*, along the sewer, another prick of light.

Someone was coming.

City of Night

Tracer bullets lit the night sky. The thump of explosions continued to shake the earth. The group of fugitives snaked along the debris-littered sidewalks towards Grand Central, ordered to silence, torches off, terrified that at any moment their presence might be revealed and they would be captured or shot by the President's men. The cannibals themselves no longer seemed such a threat. When they had first emerged from the sewer they had spotted small, ragged bands of them fleeing west, away from the advancing troops. They saw others carrying white flags going in the opposite direction. Those that were still resisting would surely soon be overwhelmed, and then there would be nothing to stop the soldiers racing across the city towards the *Titanic*. They might not be able to lure it into harbour, the way King Slash had planned, but there was no shortage of abandoned boats the soldiers could use to get them close enough to use their undoubted firepower to force Captain Smith to surrender the ship.

It seemed to Jimmy that the past few days had all been about dread, followed by dread, with a little bit of dread thrown in for good measure. When would it ever end? Yes, sure, Claire was back, but he had managed to forget in her absence that she was mean and sullen and now he wasn't really sure why he'd bothered to search for her in the first place. He was cold. And hungry. They were entering Grand Central Station – he'd heard of it, seen it in films, but Jimmy wasn't one to be overly impressed by architecture or reputation. It was just a big building with trains. To make matters worse he stepped right into a huge pile of crap as soon as they entered.

Jimmy slid off his trainer and wiped it on an upended bench seat. *It* had risen right up over the knot and soaked into his admittedly already rancid sock. He peeled it off and tossed it angrily away.

'*What sort of a bloody animal makes that much crap?*' he was demanding when he was immediately *shhhh*ed by everyone around him.

First Officer Jeffers led them towards the rendezvous point. He stopped them a short distance from it and called out the names of the crewmen he had sent to accompany the other passengers. They were still six hours short of the agreed time, but there were already a large group of returnees waiting. They rushed out of the shadows as if the cavalry had arrived and immediately began shaking hands and patting backs.

Claire said to Jimmy: 'Shouldn't you be talking to them, getting their stories?'

'Shouldn't you be taking their photos? Oh yeah, you

let some little fella steal your camera.'

Without thinking, Claire snapped back: 'I got another one, smart arse.'

'Oh yeah? Where is it?'

'The cannibals took it off me.'

'You mean the rattibals?'

'That isn't even a word, you thick—'

Ty sighed out loud. 'Could you two just . . . give each other a hug or something and stop this bickering?'

'Huh,' said Claire.

'That'll be the day,' said Jimmy.

Ty wasn't prepared to give up so easily. 'Look, all you have to do is . . .' He turned and grabbed hold of Ronni. He crushed her to him. He kissed the top of her head and in a high-pitched voice cried, 'Oh Jimmy, I missed you!' He released Ronni and smiled at the two of them. 'See – easy as that!'

Ronni stood in shock.

'Get a life,' rasped Claire, turning away.

'Wise up, would you?' griped Jimmy.

Without acknowledging it, of course, Jimmy had to concede that Claire had a point about the interviews. Despite his adventures over the past few days, he was still a reporter, and he was determined if they got through this to make sure he got his old job back. So he set about interviewing the returnees, though he made it look as if he was just having a casual chat, so that if Claire looked over it wouldn't seem like he was working. Claire, meanwhile, salvaged a disposable camera from a shattered gift shop and began surreptitiously taking pictures whenever she thought Jimmy wasn't watching her.

The stories were all similar, and predictable. Few had made it as far as their original destinations. There had been encounters with cannibals and bandits and giant rats and escaped zoo animals. Those who had made it home had found either skeletons or no trace of their loved ones; they had landed with unrealistically high hopes. Now all they wanted was to return to the safety of *Titanic*.

Once they were settled at the rendezvous point, Jeffers and Dr Hill tried unsuccessfully to raise the ship using the radios of the returning crewmen; then ventured outside again in pursuit of a signal. They returned, grim-faced, less than ten minutes later.

'I don't know – some kind of jamming device,' was all the first officer said.

They sat about in small groups in the food court, most of them wishing that they could just move out *now* without waiting for the rendezvous deadline, but nobody was prepared to actually say it. Jimmy, Claire, Ty and Ronni occupied one booth. Ty got Jimmy to tell his story – everything that had happened since he'd lost Claire in the woods. Claire feigned disinterest. Ronni asked Claire what had happened to her since she'd gotten lost in the woods, and made sympathetic noises when Claire showed her her bullet wound.

Jimmy yawned and looked elsewhere.

'What I don't understand,' Ty said, 'is that guy, Cleaver, the minister, suddenly pulling a knife like that and killing Slash . . .'

'I always knew he was a killer,' said Claire.

'But why attack Slash when we were about to be released?'

'Because he wasn't a minister,' said Jimmy. They all looked at him. He nodded around them. 'You heard what he shouted? *Long live the President!* I saw his picture back at Fort Hope in an army uniform but until now I couldn't work out what he was doing pretending he was a minister. He was an assassin, sent out in advance of the attack on the city to kill Slash. What is it they say? Cut off the head and the body will die? Something like that.'

'And he heard about the *Titanic*,' said Claire. 'Maybe that guy in the woods told him, maybe that's why he killed him – maybe—'

'Too many maybes,' said Jimmy.

Claire glared at him. She was about to snap something back when Ty said: 'What about some peace and quiet for a while? I'm tired.' He rested his head on Ronni's shoulder and closed his eyes. Ronni looked up at Jimmy, mildly panicked. Jimmy smiled. Claire, despite her anger, couldn't help smiling either.

They slept as best they could in the hours leading up to the rendezvous time, curled awkwardly in the booths or stretched out on the cold marble floor. Jimmy tossed and turned; he kept imagining he was hearing a dull metal dragging sound, like a ghost dragging its chains. But when his eyes scanned the darkness there was nothing.

Although a bright day had dawned outside, little dispelled the gloom so deep in the heart of Grand Central. They had expected a steady trickle of returnees, but as they shook themselves and began to gather in preparation for their journey, it was becoming clear that nobody else was coming.

Jeffers formed the remaining passengers and actors into a column, two abreast with armed crewmen on either side. He checked his watch, gave one final look in the direction of the railway tunnels, then gave the signal for them to move out. Jimmy, Claire, Ty and Ronni were round about the middle of the column, excited but anxious. They all knew the chances of them making it back to *Titanic* were slim. Gunfire had largely died out during the night, which could only mean that the city was now in control of the President. Slipping through undetected was going to be very difficult. And there was no way to contact the ship to organise an alternative pick-up point. All Jeffers could do was take them to the harbour and hope that the ship's inflatables were waiting for them, as previously arranged.

But it seemed as if their journey was over almost before it had even started.

As Jeffers was directing scouts out of the front door to check for soldiers, they became aware of a clattering sound. It was somewhat masked by the height of the buildings surrounding them, but then the source of the noise suddenly burst into view: a huge military helicopter, descending on to the broad avenue before them, its massive rotor blades throwing up dust and debris, drowning out all other noises.

Jeffers was desperately using hand signals to get the forward scouts back into the station and pushing the column back behind him as the helicopter landed and its doors burst open. He had his pistol out and was about to fire at the first soldier who jumped out … when a familiar face appeared and began frantically signalling towards him.

Benson!

And now that he looked closer – behind the controls of the helicopter, Jonas Jones! Giving him the thumbs-up!

It was incredible.

Impossible.

But there they were!

Jeffers reversed his signals to now urge everyone forward. Jimmy had last seen Jonas close to the airport in New Jersey – that's where he must have found the helicopter and decided it would make for a much faster and safer return journey. And now he'd risked it all by coming to rescue the rest of them. As for Benson – he didn't know or particularly care how he came to be on board! He was there, he was safe, and he was going to take them home.

'Get on, now!' Benson yelled, his hands cupped around his mouth. 'There's soldiers everywhere – come on!'

They clambered on board, pulling each other up, rolling across the floor, crawling into any space they could find. Jimmy got one leg up, and Ty grabbed his hand and hauled him in. Jimmy turned to help Claire, but she wasn't there. There was only half a dozen of them left to board – she must have slipped past him in the scrum. Jimmy leaned forward to bellow in Jonas Jones' ear – 'Did you get it? Did you get the part?' He got a thumbs-up in response. Jimmy turned back, smiling, and tried to pick Claire out of the throng again, but he still couldn't spot her.

'Ty!' he shouted above the roar of the blades, 'Where's Claire?'

Ty had a protective arm around Ronni, even though she didn't need it. He nodded down the body of the helicopter. 'Didn't she . . .'

They still couldn't see her.

The last of the passengers was dragged up and deposited on the floor.

'All aboard!' Jeffers shouted.

'Ready for take-off!' yelled Benson, beginning to close the doors.

It was then that Jimmy saw her – just a momentary glimpse as she was dragged backwards into Grand

Central. He couldn't see who by, and he didn't care.

'No!' Jimmy shouted, and threw himself forward through the almost shut door. He landed in a heap on the road.

Benson's panicked face looked out after him. 'Jimmy!'

'Claire!' Jimmy pointed towards the terminal. At that very moment a bullet pinged into the ground beside him. Jimmy looked to his left. Soldiers! Still a considerable distance away, but crouched down, shooting towards the helicopter. Another bullet cracked off one of the blades.

'Jimmy!' Benson yelled. 'We have to go!'

Jimmy just shook his head and darted towards the terminal.

He charged through the entrance and there, not more than fifteen metres in front of him, was Claire – and the minister.

A beaten, blood–encrusted, swollen version of Calvin Cleaver with a knife to her throat, forcing her back.

'Stop!' Jimmy yelled.

Cleaver looked towards him – and laughed.

Jimmy had no weapon, he had no *anything*.

But he kept coming.

'Let her go, you monster!'

Cleaver kept moving backwards. He stepped into the exact same gargantuan pile of crap that Jimmy had tramped into the night before.

The gunfire from outside grew more intense.

There was an immense cacophony as the helicopter began to lift off – but the sound did not diminish as it should. It was hovering, waiting, putting everyone at risk.

'Let her go!'

Jimmy was right up close now.

'Jimmy! No!' Claire screamed. 'Go!'

'Yes, go, little boy!' Cleaver laughed. 'She's mine . . . and the ship is mine . . . and there's nothing you can do!'

Cleaver was mad. There was no doubt about it. It was in his eyes and mouth. But he was also right. There was nothing Jimmy could do but follow; there was nothing Claire could do – not even struggle; blood was already dripping from where the point of the blade had pierced the skin on her neck. Cleaver was obviously convinced that if he possessed Claire, then the *Titanic* would never sail away and leave her.

'Just let her go,' Jimmy begged. 'Please – take me instead . . .'

Cleaver cackled. 'You? You're worthless . . .'

Then Jimmy heard it, even above the noise of the battle outside.

A sound he had first heard in the night, and dismissed as a nightmare.

Claire heard it too and recognised it.

The dry metallic drag.

But Cleaver heard nothing. He was too busy

screaming at Jimmy: 'Get out of here or I'll rip the throat out of you!'

From out of the gloom behind him a huge, grey elephant stomped into view. It was almost upon them before it let out a deafening trumpet call, so close that Cleaver's head involuntarily twisted towards it. His surprise was so great that he momentarily relaxed the pressure of the blade against Claire's neck. Sensing it, she immediately elbowed him in his bony ribs. As he doubled over she tore herself from his grasp and dived to one side, just as the elephant's massive bulk ploughed into Cleaver, impaling him on one of its tusks. Cleaver screamed as the ivory spear erupted through his chest and blood sprayed out of him. The elephant roared again, throwing back its head and raising Cleaver off his feet, forcing the thickest part of the tusk into his torso. As Cleaver continued to scream, Jimmy dived to one side to avoid the advancing creature and Claire pushed herself back against the wall. The elephant rumbled past them and in a matter of moments it disappeared back into the gloom on the other side of the station, taking Cleaver with it.

Jimmy and Claire ran towards each other.

They stopped.

'I planned that,' said Jimmy.

Then he grabbed her hand and they ran for the doors.

Epilogue:
The Titanic Times

Every newspaper needs an editor, someone to make the decisions. It is not something that is easily done by committee. A newspaper needs a *voice*. The *Titanic Times* had two voices, and for several hours now they'd been locked in the office, shouting at each other.

The reporters and the rest of the team remained outside in the corridor, but they could hear it all. That's where Ronni found Ty, leaning against a wall, lazily chewing a sandwich. She was in *awe* of the *Titanic*. She had spent the twenty-four hours since they'd landed exploring as much of it as she possibly could, forgetting about sleep, just letting out little whoops of delight at every new, incredible thing she discovered. She bubbled excitedly to Ty about how fantastic the ship was.

Ty shrugged. 'You should have seen it before the President of the United States blew holes in it.'

'The holes aren't that big,' said Ronni.

'That's what they said about the iceberg,' observed Ty.

'We escaped, didn't we? And he was never really the

President. He was just power-crazy, wasn't he?'

'Aren't they all?' asked Ty.

More shouting erupted from within.

'What are they fighting about?' Ronni asked.

Ty swallowed another mouthful. 'Well,' he said. 'On the surface, it's about who edits the paper. So much has happened in the past few days that there's isn't space to fit it all into just one edition, so we're going to do it over several days. They're arguing about what stories go into tomorrow's edition. But I think, deep down, they're fighting about something else.'

'Like what?'

Ty shrugged again.

'I saw some of Claire's photos earlier,' said Ronni. 'They're really cool. The President's ships attacking the *Titanic*! It looks like a real war!'

'It *was* a real war.'

'And I saw her picture of that Mr Rodriguez being reunited with his wife after everyone thought she'd been eaten.'

'Have you *seen* her?' Ty asked. 'Who would want to eat *her*? Anyway, the photos take up too much space. Espeically if they want to run Jimmy's story about Fort Hope, and the elephant, and Cleaver, and then there's all the stuff about what the passengers found when they went to look for their families, and the cannibals, and King Slash and . . . Well, you know what I mean. There's just too much *stuff*.'

'Were you not looking for your family as well, Ty?'

Ty nodded, and was silent for a bit. 'Yeah, but once I saw what the city was like, I changed my mind. My parents are dead. I'm not particularly interested in finding a second cousin twice removed I never knew in the first place. This is my home. This is my family. Besides, I've met a girl now.'

'Have you?' Ronni asked. 'Who?'

Ty shrugged. 'She'll find out. In due course.'

Ronni decided to change the subject. 'It's gone very quiet in there. What do you think is . . . ?'

Ty nodded at the door. 'Well, I think they're either kissing, or they've killed each other.'

Ronni stood beside him. 'Which do you think it is?'

'I don't know,' said Ty.

Eddie's new in town, hanging out
on his own while he waits for
school to begin. Drawn in by a
gang of boys infamous for their
elaborate scams around town – the
Reservoir Pups – Eddie finds his
initiation involves breaking into the
very hospital his mother works at.
That's bad enough, but then he
overhears a plan to kidnap babies
from one of the wards. Soon Eddie
and the Pups are on the trail of a
gang of baby-snatchers...

Eddie's got great plans for
world domination. The trouble is
that none of them look likely
to come off. How is his gang of One
ever going to rival the
Reservoir Pups?

Then a dark, wizened, shrunken
object in a glass case is stolen.
The thief sparks a chase and
the chase sparks a battle
for what is right. Eddie Malone and
his cronies are back in business
— so Captain Black, watch out!

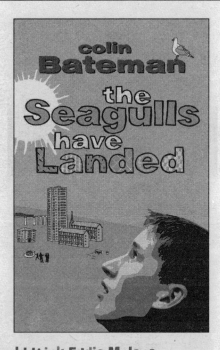

You would think Eddie Malone –
hero, warrior, gang leader and
intent on world domination –
would have had enough of babies.
And you would be right...
But losing a baby is not good.
And if it belongs to your mum, well –
it's a disaster.
Eddie is at his lowest ebb. Until
Mo, Gary, Ivan Cutler and
the others all appear.
Maybe Eddie will have his Gang after all.
But what should he call it?

TITANIC 2020

COLIN
Bateman

Everyone said the original Titanic was unsinkable.
We all know how that story ended. The new Titanic is
also supposedly unsinkable. But there are worse things
than drowning as Jimmy Armstrong quickly finds out.
Stowing away wasn't one of his better ideas but having
to work his passage and put up with spoilt girl Claire is
enough to make anyone want to jump overboard...
That is until he finds out about a mysterious, incurable
disease rapidly infecting the population, Suddenly
being at sea seems the safest place to be...